RQ26

Armageddon Was Just The Beginning

JUSTIN CONBOY

DEDICATION

I'd like to dedicate this book to my wife Barbara.

I can never thank you enough for changing my life.

You saved me, and brought our two boys into this world.

You're an amazing mother, so dedicated and loving.

You're the most beautiful wife and my best friend.

You have the business acumen of your father,
and the work ethic of your mother.

x

ACKNOWLEDGMENTS

I'd like to thank everyone who helped me in the production of this novel.
Especially Barb, Aoife, Laura, Anne and Clément.

Technical Acknowledgment:
Martin O'Reilly, Dublin.

Love to my family and friends, who have always supported me throughout my life and my writing.

1

THE VOICE WITHIN

Aaron stood at the head of the three-hundred-and-fifty-seat lecture hall at the California Institute of Technology, Caltech—his alma mater.

The hall was dimly lit, with numerous laptops irradiating the room.

He pressed a button on the wall; the whirl of a motor retracting the projector screen up sounded.

He pressed another button, and the lights brightened, much to the obvious annoyance of his students. Illumination always annoyed his vampiresque students.

"All right. Picture this scenario," he said, as he tried to grasp the attention of his waning crowd. Aaron grabbed a green marker in his left hand and a blue marker in his right.

He drew a huge rough sketch of Earth and added in some land mass.

It was basically a big blue circle with a few parts colored-in green.

He got a different marker from his leather satchel, which sat on his desk. He fumbled around the bag until a few markers made themselves available.

While facing the whiteboard, he tried his best not to lose the interest of the room, turning back to them occasionally and then adding another small, obscure object beside the sketch—a black elongated rock.

Aaron changed the color again, drawing a large red arrow pointing from the black object to Earth. He paused, looked at his rough sketch, and faced his class.

He stretched his hands in front of him, palms to his students, motioning them to answer the question on the tip of his tongue. The knowledge almost shone out of his hands. He addressed the twenty or thirty students who'd decided to grace him with their presence that morning. Sparse lecture mornings were all too common. He was used to the lack of numbers.

His evening classes usually doubled in size. It was probably because too many students were out socializing the night before, or maybe they were just too lazy to attend—or worse again, hadn't arrived home yet from their nights out.

Aaron rolled up his shirt sleeves and wrote, '20 × C' on the whiteboard. As he stretched high to write, he exposed a number of old scars on his forearms. He quickly pulled his arms back and rolled his sleeves down.

He took a deep breath. He nearly forgot about the scars.

The chance would be a fine thing.

"Now. Let's just say this is a space rock, the

object here in black, and it's hurtling toward earth at about twenty times the speed of sound." He made a few more strokes with his red marker. He drew what seemed to be an impact crater on the planet. "What kind of an impact would a fifty-meter space rock have on our planet?" He looked at the class again then drew a large '50m' beside the crater.

He remembered his college days. His students were keeping their heads down, no one dared put up their hand for fear of being ridiculed if the answer was incorrect. A stupid answer from a stupid student.

No such thing as stupid questions, just stupid students.

Aaron kept his chuckle to himself, barely.

"No such thing as a stupid answer. Anyone? Give me something to work with here?" he stopped, leaving time for a response again.

The dreary lecture hall gave him nothing.

"Anyone? Let's just say; would it destroy New York or London or Tokyo for example?" he asked his terminally tired students.

Did they not want to answer him, or were they just fed up?

He shook his head.

Sure, it's just my life's work I'm talking about!

He whirled back to the whiteboard to illustrate, for a second time, what he was trying to ask. Aaron peered back at his students.

Had someone said something?

"The world is going to end." The whisper hit his ears, but he couldn't tell where it had come from.

He scanned the vast room again, frowning. A quick flash of heated sweat crossed his back and shoulders.

Aaron addressed the whispered statement. "Okay, the world is going to end, or the world would end, due to the impact, yes? What do you mean by that? Let's flesh this out a little bit." He put his marker down.

"The world is going to end," the whisper reiterated.

"Okay, who said that? Raise your hand please, now." He wouldn't tolerate this type of joking around in his lecture hall. He was an ex-military man, after all.

He was a lot less strict than he used to be, but could easily snap back into military-mode, if pushed.

No one said a word.

He heard it again, the whisper.

"The world is going to end." This time, Aaron recognized the female voice.

He wiped his forehead. "Who said that? Where are you?"

A number of the students started to raise their semi-slumberous heads.

His head started to swim and his vision went hazy. His knees wobbled, and he had to lock them to stay on his feet. He was going to pass out.

Aaron snatched his briefcase and flung his markers into it. His papers followed the markers, just as fast. He glanced at the clock. He still had fifteen minutes left of class. He couldn't just leave.

His mind raced. Which was worse; storming out of the room or passing out in front of all his students?

One was as bad as the other. The humiliation of fainting or the 'weirdo freak' tag he'd pick up from the students for appearing to flee.

He'd been working at the California Institute of Technology for a few years. He was very well

4

respected by his colleagues and was also very well-liked by his students.

As an ex-Army engineer, he'd gone back to college and completed his doctorate in Astrophysics; a relatively young man to have had two distinguished careers.

"The world is going to end, and it's going to be your fault, Aaron. You're going to get us all killed," the voice whispered again.

It was in his head, not someone heckling from the class.

He recognized her. A voice he hadn't heard in a long time.

A voice he should *not* be able to hear.

He closed his eyes and leaned on his desk for support.

"You're going to kill us all," he heard, as a vivid image of a dead woman's face flashed before his eyes.

The sight of her dark, hollow eyes, scraggly hair, and prematurely wrinkled face made him gasp for air.

That split-second was enough to act as a smelling salt; he came to his senses.

"You okay, sir?" asked one of his dedicated female students from the front row.

Aaron cleared his throat, coughing into his closed fist. "Yes, I'm fine Jane, Thanks." He looked over at her and wiped his brow. "Yeah, I'm good. I think it's just something I ate. Sorry."

The class had all awoken from their drowsy inattention, along with their camera phones, as the excitement of a professor having a possible breakdown was too much to ignore.

"Can I get you a glass of water, Dr. Jacobs?" Jane

asked.

"No, no. I'm fine. We'll leave it at that," Aaron addressed the whole class. "I'll see you later. Thanks. I think it was something I ate for breakfast. I'm sorry. See you guys later, okay? We'll definitely have a second class after lunch. I'll be fine."

The class got up from their seats without being told a second time. The noise from them stampeding from the hall drowned out his voice. They ran out as quickly as any other day.

He took a seat and pretended to read over a manuscript, trying to compose himself and reassess what'd just happened.

The class was empty now, but Jane was last to leave. She looked back, just as the door was about to close.

He gave her a little reassuring wave and smiled.

"Are you sure you're okay?" she asked.

The girl was a good student. She was always on time, never missed a class.

Some might even have misconstrued that she had a crush on him.

"Are you sure you're okay, Aaron?" she repeated.

"Thanks. I'm fine now. See you at basketball practice." He watched her leave before returning to the manuscript. Aaron continued to peer at it with unfocused eyes. He was gobsmacked by what'd just happened.

He had no explanation; just stared until his cell phone beeped to indicate end-of-class. He needed a moment to compose himself before he left the room.

He picked out a picture of his little son, Ben. He studied it.

I can't wait for this day to be over already. I just wanna see my boy.

Jane let the door swing shut behind her. She walked down the hall alone.

She loved everything about astrophysics. She'd been a stargazer from a young age, and still so at twenty-two. She was a good Catholic girl from Westridge School, Pasadena in South California.

She'd been on the honor roll at high school, but not so much in college. She hated that she didn't have many friends, and didn't feel like she fitted in.

Jane didn't see her father much, he was a workaholic, and spent most of his time abroad. Her mother was too busy with her with her spiritual work in the country. They fobbed her off to private school a long time ago.

Her only true passion was her love for astrophysics and basketball.

Dr. Jacobs—or Aaron as he'd told them to call him—was also the coach of the basketball team. It was just a coincidence.

Or, at least Jane had convinced herself it was. She thought about him a lot. She didn't want to consider why; she just liked his company.

She liked that he was tall, with thick brown hair and was a favorite of both the female and male students, albeit for different reasons. Looking around at all the other girls, she knew they found him very attractive, strong and masculine. And some of the guys for that matter. The males found him to be a great role model.

He was smart and athletic. It inspired his students.
Work hard on the turf and harder on the books.

2

THE MEETING

It was very warm outside, and more so inside. Astronomer Dr. Eva Monnier sat in her observatory in Nice, France.

The dark room had two fans, on full blast, working hard in an attempt to cool her down, as she worked on her computer.

She allowed the fans to blow her hair horizontally in the breeze, anything to be cooler.

She was strong, single and independent. Astronomy was her true love; it fascinated her, and she was infatuated by it. She craved to know the secrets of the universe and made it her goal to find them.

The stuffy old Nice Observatory, or the *Côte d'Azur Observatory*, as it was known, was built in 1879. The beautiful, but old, building wasn't equipped with modern air conditioning but did once boast the world's largest, longest and highest refracting telescope.

The edifice was beautifully crafted using cut stone, designed by Charles Garnier, and its massive dome and metal latus structure were designed by the one and only, Mr. Gustave Eiffel.

It was an obsolete observatory, but still had a function for Ph.D. students and amateur astronomers. Its main function was as a museum piece.

The main thirty-inch telescope had been retrofitted with a high definition camera and stepper motors to allow for remote movement of the telescope.

It was Eva's job, as chief operator, to monitor and track observations from the telescope. She loved her job, loved the building, even though it was nearly one and a half centuries old. It gave her pride to keep a bit of French astronomical history alive.

She didn't like the heat, but with the building being protected; there was no chance of that changing. She just had to stay at her desk with the random pieces of note paper stuck to her personal computer, flapping in the cool fan air.

It was nearing the end of her night shift; nine pm was quitting time.

She locked the location of the telescope into her computer and set the recorder to two hundred frames per second. She did that every night. She liked to make sure she had a very good frame resolution set, and she didn't mind burning up a bit of the hard drive capacity in order to get clear images for the next day.

Eva set the recorder to 'proximity'. That meant the recorder would come on when something changed from one frame to the next. If the last frame was exactly the same as the previous one, it would not record that frame. It was a way of saving hard drive space.

She packed up her stuff but took a look back at the computer screen. Was it worth staying for a little bit longer?

Just in case the two asteroids she'd been following for the past few days collided in her absence. It would bug her if it happened and someone else got credit.

Whoever recorded the incident would get the praise for discovering the new asteroid if one of them split. They'd even get the privilege of naming it if they wanted.

A butterfly flitted in her tummy as she stared at the monitor. "Screw it. I'll stay for a bit. They're very close." Eva left her office and went upstairs to find the curator of the observatory, Professor Louis Marchione.

She always spoke English to her professor. He demanded it. He always said he wanted to make sure she had a good grasp of the language.

"The asteroids are so close to hitting each other, Louis."

"My lovely Eva, there's a one in a million chance those asteroids will make contact. One little pixel on that ancient telescope is about a thousand miles apart. You're not even sure if they're on the same plane, not to mention the same intersection trajectory. You don't have any triangulation data from other places around the world."

"Oh, you're such an ass." She poopooed his synopsis.

"Now, now, my dear, don't forget your English,"

the Professor said in his fatherly, condescending way.

Louis was an endearing character, an older gentleman, a great confidant for Eva.

He always took care of her, educated her, taught her the ways of the world; but he was always patronizing towards her. Maybe he got enjoyment from it, just for the fun of it. He knew how to push her buttons, again, probably just for the fun of it.

He brought her a croissant with an obligatory coffee every morning; caring for her while chastising her for the messiness of her observatory workstation.

Eva respected him immeasurably. Held him in such high regard. It was mainly due to his enormous mine of information, his love of the world, culture and his gentle soul.

Louis had a few years left in him to impart some of his knowledge, but as the years passed by, he'd told her it was imperative to impart it fast, and as much as possible.

His mind, in relation to astrophysics, was second to none, and she knew this only too well.

She shook her head and pranced back to her personal computer. "Okay, I'll watch it myself," she said in a huff.

Louis was correct; the two asteroids were only a couple of pixels apart. The resolution on her computer couldn't pick up anymore.

Eva watched and waited impatiently for the two asteroids to collide. Whether or not they'd actually do so was a mystery; her confidence had been yanked away by her professor.

Of course, Louis hadn't meant to diminish that confidence, he wanted to make sure she brought more accuracy and involvement into her data. Sourcing from different parts of the world, sharing with other people, other academics.

Contrary to that politeness, she didn't *want* to share a shred of information. She was too paranoid they'd try to steal her discoveries. She wasn't fond of open source. It was a concept she couldn't wrap her head around.

Eva stood, ready to go.

A few minutes passed, and the two asteroids finally met.

The two tiny white dots on her computer screen merged.

She'd been waiting for *this* all week.

Not that it was a big deal, it was *her* first deal, her first glimpse at the universe in real time, on her time, on her clock.

She put her hand to her mouth, hiding a smile of anticipation. She really wanted to be the first to see these asteroids collide.

Eva waited and waited. Then, she couldn't stand anymore. Her bag was large and heavy, weighing her down. She plopped into her chair. Continued to stare at the screen in contemplation and with hope.

The two white dots appeared again.

She examined their trajectories on the monitor and compared them to the original.
"*Merde!*" She figured the two asteroids missed each other. She turned and faced in the general direction of Louis. "*Merde!*" she shouted up to her professor.

"It's too early to tell yet, you'll need more telemetry. You'll know better tomorrow. It's not over yet."

"*Merde,*" she whispered again, as she picked up her bag and prepared to leave for real this time. She set the high-resolution camera again. "Now I'm glad I didn't share anything with anyone," she said to herself and gained one position for the two negative asteroids.

Eva was about to don her headphones and head for home when the computer bleeped twice.

The program had started tracking *two* asteroids.

She looked back at the screen and saw a telescopic image of three small specs. One of the dots was stationary in the middle. The other two were slowly moving off at the same angle that they'd approached each other.

Eva frowned. They'd appeared as though they'd passed each other, but... Maybe they'd hit? The trajectories seemed the same.

She noted the single nonmoving asteroid in the middle and clicked on it to have it tracked.

When she glanced out the window, it was dark.

"*Au revoir, monsieur tout savoir,*" she shouted up to Louis, as she left the observatory.

3

TIME OUT

It was lunchtime, and Jane listened to the rhythmic bouncing of the basketball, as well as the sharp squeak of sneakers as players turned quickly on the varnished basketball court.

Caltech's finest were playing against each other; the entire women's basketball team filled the court.

They were distinguished only by the yellow and red training bibs.

The court had raised wooden bleachers to one side. Not one supporter or groupie or mascot or hangers-on watched them. Not a single person showed up for this motley crew playing a trial game, *mano-a-mano*.

No one, except for their coach, Aaron. He sat half-way up, trying to see things from a different point of view, he'd professed when they'd started. Dressed in his coach's garb, he had anguish written all over his face.

He made his way down to the sidelines, mingling between a number of substitutes, throwing in a few roars of encouragement to a few players as he prepared to remove them from their duties.

Jane played small guard on the red team. Someone tossed the ball to her. She stopped just outside the three-point line.

There were four minutes left in this half-hour scrimmage. Her team was trailing by a single point.

"You have to make this basket, take the two points no matter what," Aaron shouted at her, just as she received the ball.

She took half a step back from the three-point line, took aim and threw a rainbow-arc at the net.

The basketball made its way in a perfect parabolic, looping toward the hoop.

Both teams were stunned into silence as they listened to the ball bounce off the hoop a couple of times.

They all watched in awe, then disappointment settled, as the ball fell toward the court, falling into one of the opposing teams' hands.

"Damn it! Come over here, Jane," Aaron shouted.

He pointed to one of the girls on the bench. "Swap in for her."

"Sorry, coach. I didn't hear you!" she said when she reached his side.

He wasn't extremely tall. Not *'basketball tall'*. He was six-foot at a stretch, but he still had to lean down to make eye contact with her.

"Didn't hear *what*? You obviously did, if you know why you're being subbed off!"

Jane sat quietly on the edge of the bench, biting her fingernails as she shook her leg. She didn't like when Aaron was mad at her. Sweat poured from her forehead as she blocked out everything, even common sense.

Aaron sounded the final whistle and made his way to the girls as they gathered together for congratulatory handshakes.

She couldn't help but track his movements as he applauded them all for their efforts, telling them there was a place on the different teams for everyone, and for them to hit the showers.

The yellow team high-fived each other as they left the court for the locker room.

Jane got off the bench and belatedly followed the red team into their dressing rooms.

One of the red team girls waited for her and shouldered her.

The discomfort in her upper arm was nothing compared to the sound of the laughter from the rest of the team.

All the girls, both teams, conjugated in the locker room, seeming to be waiting for her to enter.

She strolled in; adding fuel to the flames. Jane passed everyone, avoiding eye contact, studying the white and red tiled floors.

One of the girls on her team mumbled under her breath, "You're the worst basketball player in the world."

Pain seared through her heart but she stayed strong and showed no emotion as she sat beside her locker, and got dressed as slowly as possible.

She had two choices; change really fast and get the

hell out of there or change really slowly, and hope everyone left before her.

Either way, the object was to spend as little time as possible with these people, some of whom she felt actually hated her.

She definitely didn't feel like showering with any of the girls, especially her, 'number one fan'.

Ronna, the team captain, was obviously angry. The six-foot-two, 180 pounds specimen of a basketball machine was making her way toward Jane, flanked by two of her henchwomen.

The angry woman was pre-shower, still sweating and topless with her double Ds on display for everyone.

The fifteen to twenty girls in the changing room stopped what they were doing; scurrying over to see what was going to go down. They jostled for position, watching and waiting to see the fireworks which were about to unfold.

Jane was petrified but hypnotized by Ronna's bare double Ds eyeing her up and down as they approached.

"*You!*" the girl roared, pointing into Jane's face. "Are so fucking full of shit, Jane Stanley." The captain looked at each of her henchwomen and smiled unhappily. "Or should I say, Man-ley."

Everyone laughed.

Jane hung her head.

The posse was encroaching ominously.

"With your no tits, your stupid fucking jet black hair, you're so fucking weird, with your white translucent skin, and your stupid god damn, stupid *inability* to play basketball." Ronna continued pointing.

She leaned over her and snapped her fingers right in front of her face as if she didn't already have her undivided attention.

Jane was trying to grin and bear it, but she was just waiting for the pain, *physical* pain.

"You can't play fucking basketball because you're too goddamn small." The captain hammered home some truths.

She stared at the red and white tiles again.

Why red and white. Why not blue and white?

Ronna stooped down to her again, with her arms outstretched wide. Showing off her wingspan of what had to be seven feet. She towered over her, making Jane feel helpless.

Not one person as a protector, not in the lionesses' den.

Her five-foot-six frame was no match for Ronna. Jane kept her mouth shut and took the verbal abuse.

The captain's head henchwoman, second-in-command, Paula, stepped closer. "You're only here because Aaron has a fucking hard-on for you." She grabbed Jane's hair and pulled, forcing her to look straight up at the ceiling lights.

Her breath caught, but she bit her bottom lip as the agony washed over her head and pinched the back of her neck.

She would *not* cry out in front of these girls. It would give them too much satisfaction.

Is a woman with a handful of another woman's hair in her hand the personification of an absolute bitch?

"It's Dr. Jacobs to you," she mumbled, but it'd been meant mostly for her ears, not theirs.

"What did you say?" Ronna barked as Paula

released her hair.

Jane was fully expecting a slap in the mouth would follow her smart-assed comment. However, she declined to answer the captain's demand. It was smarter.

"Spit it out, before I hurt you bad, bitch!" the girl roared.

A female cleaner entered the locker room.

Everyone dispersed, like nothing was happening; '*nothing to see here*'.

Ronna glanced to see who'd come in. She was distracted, so Jane grabbed her bag and ran out. The hasty exit made before the captain could say or *do* anything else.

She exited into the hallway and sped away. There was no way a *topless* Ronna could be hot on her heels.

Just then, Aaron exited the male locker room, almost bumping into her, and they both skidded to a halt.

"Hey, how are you? You okay?" he asked.

"I'm good." Jane stared at the ground. Her sweaty hair covered her still overheated cheeks, from exertion as well as embarrassment. She fixed her hair, trying to go from just terrible to slightly-less terrible.

"You sure? I didn't mean to shout at you today. I don't know what came over me." He laughed, and the nervous edge had her looking up.

"Yeah, it has been one of those days, all right," she said. She glanced back toward the women's locker rooms. She needed a swift subject change. "Hey, you know how you were talking about those asteroids today?"

"Yeah," Aaron said, as they walked down the hall

back toward his office.

She threw another glance over her shoulder, as she continued, thinking on her feet. *Ask a question.* "Well, you know you said before, both velocity and mass were the determining factors in the energy dissipated on impact, and that's proportionate to the velocity."

"Yeah, the kinetic energy equation, half the mass times the velocity squared. It's proportionate to the square of the velocity." His words were as confident as his delighted expression, confirming what Jane had always suspected; Aaron loved talking about his class' subject matter.

"Okay, but what if the earth was moving away in the same direction as the asteroid; how would you work out the kinetic energy?"

"Well, you can't just measure the speed of the asteroid in relation to itself; it needs to be measured in relation to something else. Or relative to something else. That's kind-of where Einstein's Theory of Relativity comes from… kind-of!"

Should she play dumb or be 'clever Jane'? Which did *he* prefer?

Maybe a mixture of both.

Jane's comfort rose as they turned the corner, ever closer to his office. "Oh, so it's the same on Earth, we have a speed relative to the ground we're traveling on! Sort of!"

Aaron nodded. "Yeah, exactly. If two cars are traveling on a highway, at sixty miles per hour relative to the ground, but they're moving at zero miles per hour relative to themselves."

She bit her lip. "So, what I need to do, is figure

out the speed of the Earth relative to the asteroid and take them away from each other."

He shared office space with four other professors. Two were out of the room.

A man was at his desk, glaring in their direction as if they'd interrupted him.

Aaron paused at the door.

Jane waited for his answer, ignoring his office-mate.

"Well yeah. That's a start. But you need to think about everything, really. You need to open your mind to what's really going on. Is the asteroid spinning? Is it going to impact on the side of the earth spinning away from the asteroid, or the side spinning toward the asteroid? You'll need to either add those velocities into the relative velocity of the asteroid or take it away. Then there's gravitational pull; this will need to be added, acceleration due to gravity, it'll increase as the asteroid approaches the earth."

She frowned. "Oh, okay." She might've delved too much into the question.

"The earth's surface is spinning at a thousand miles per hour at the equator, but up toward the North or South Pole, the surface is spinning at nearly zero."

"Okay, well I gotta get back to class," Jane said and flashed a wry smile.

Get the hell out of here!

He frowned. "You have my class next! Second period. It's not for another fifteen minutes."

"Yeah, uh, I have to take a shower." She whirled away before he could answer.

Aaron went into his office and slid into his seat. "I thought she'd just showered," he said to himself.

His colleague, David Deen, shot him a look that said he'd been overheard. The man was sitting at his computer, opposite him.

He was a few years older than Aaron, late thirties, but thought he had decades more experience than him. It was annoying.

"You'd wanna watch that one! Dangerous. Keep an eye on her; *not* a wandering eye. If you know what I mean," he said without peering up from his computer.

Aaron didn't take his comment too seriously. "Thanks, David, but what're you talking about?"

The man finally peered up from his screen. "She's trouble. I think she likes you."

"No way. She's just a good student."

His colleague returned to typing. He laughed. "A good little student. I've seen those type of 'good students' before. Next thing you know you're getting a call from the dean."

"Which Dean is this? 'David Deen' or the Head of School? Bad pun David."

David laughed again. "Oh, nice one, I see what you did there. Anyway, I nearly did it myself a few years ago. It's tempting, trust me. Hot, twenty-year-old, twenty-one-year-old or whatever, showing attention to the midlife crisis professor. Just be careful, that's all I'm saying. I know you wouldn't cross a line." He shot him a serious look. "I'm just protecting myself here. I don't want some geeky nerd astrology teacher taking your place when you get fired. Christ, that would be awful. I can just about stand *you*." Sarcasm dripped from his last sentence.

"You're a funny little fellow, aren't you?" Aaron retorted, equally sarcastic, as he left the office and made his way back to the lecture hall. He walked down the corridor that connected his office to the vast room where he held his classes.

The hall was flanked by a wall on his left and windows on his right. He glanced outside as he walked, appreciating how pleasant the day was. The sun shone in on him, the trees were swaying gently in the wind.

He stilled. Shock washed over him, making his limbs tremor, as he peered at one particular area past a few trees, toward the bushes behind them.

A funny feeling passed over his stomach. He spotted a homeless-looking man outside the boundary wall of the college.

Aaron approached the window to have a proper look at the vagabond.

The man was wearing dirty jeans and a ragged jacket. His long hair protruded from his Caltech baseball cap. He had a dark tan and an unkempt beard.

The vagrant stared straight back. Locked onto his eyes with a laser beam stare that lasted for seconds that felt like hours.

Aaron broke the eye contact with the familiar face and focused on the floor. He took a deep breath and shook his head, then resumed his trek to class. He couldn't be late.

What the hell's going on today? He placed his briefcase on the table in the hall, still distracted by the man peering into his place of work.

He composed himself and peered up at his class, who'd already assembled. "Sorry about the split class this week. We'll be running a triple class from next week on. Anyway, so where were we this morning?" Aaron bellowed and clapped his hands.

"For example, a 'space rock'." He used air quotes. "Fifty meters across, or one hundred and fifty feet for those of you who were born in the seventies." He smiled at his own sense of humor. "Could destroy Greater London, or completely wipe out New York, Tokyo, Hong Kong; any major city really. It would devastate the surrounding suburbs, etc. Hands up if anyone has heard of the Cretaceous–Paleogene extinction event?" He scanned his mentally vacant class. "Anyone? I know it's orientation week, but surely one of you are not hungover." He paused with bated breath. "It was also known as the Cretaceous-Tertiary extinction? Nobody? Anybody? It was the sudden near mass extinction of all the animals and plants on Earth." Aaron zoned in on where Jane usually sat.

She was nowhere to be seen.

He sighed and shook his head. "It happened approximately sixty-six million years ago."

Just then, Jane entered the lecture hall, a few minutes late.

Why had she been late? She'd left before he had.

Students never ceased to amaze him. Women, of course, were ever amazing, and not wholly in a good way.

Everyone watched his star student as she climbed the five or six steps to get to her usual seat. Not too close to the front. Not too far back. A good seat to avoid the difficult questions. As if, she was ensuring she didn't give the impression that she didn't want any questions at all.

"Did it really happen? I hear you ask!" Aaron said sarcastically. "In geological records, the Cretaceous–Paleogene extinction event, or the K-Pg event, as it's commonly known, is marked by a thin layer of sediment called the K-Pg layer, or boundary. It can be found all around the world. In our rocks and soil, and even underwater in the sediment layers." He watched Jane finally take her seat and pull her book out of her bag. "Asteroids are extremely high in iridium. The earth is not. But, this particular layer, contains huge amounts of iridium in it."

He took his seat, at the head of the lecture hall. "It's believed the extinction was caused by an asteroid. One stretching maybe eight miles wide. As I said, sixty-six million years ago."

Jane piped up, "The extinction of the dinosaurs."

He ignored her, still annoyed that she'd come late to his class. "So, a fifty-meter asteroid."

She raised her hand halfway up. "Is there an asteroid predicted to hit Earth, ever? If so, what are the chances of it hitting us?" She'd always been good at rectifying situations.

"Well, there was a discovery of an asteroid in 2013. It was a few Crimean/Estonian scientists, who discovered this large asteroid, and realized it could possibly hit Earth. After a bit of calculating, they worked out that it could actually collide with us on August, twenty-sixth, fourteen years from now. They worked out it'd strike with a force sixty times greater than the largest atomic bomb known to man." He stood and got into a stride, walking along the plinth, gesturing with his hands, as if he'd prepared for this question his whole life.

This was his life's work, his passion.

"The object, technically named 'TV135', is one thousand, three hundred feet, or nearly a quarter of a mile wide, four hundred meters. The impact of such an object would cause damage over an area of one hundred thousand square miles. The comet which wiped out..."

Jane raised her hand again, much to the obvious annoyance of the rest of the bored students. Moans and groans floated around the room. Her interjections just prolonged the monologue.

"Yes, Jane?"

"Comet. I thought it was an asteroid? Could you explain what the technical difference between the two are?" she asked.

"Good question, Jane. I'll get to that shortly, but the quick answer would be, if an asteroid was the equivalent of a solid piece of stone, then a comet would be the equivalent of taking a ball of wet sand and freezing it solid. They're quite similar but completely different in so many ways. We'll touch on that a little more, later on." He continued. "Anyway, as I was saying, the comet which wiped out the dinosaurs was ten thousand meters across; that's twenty-five times the size of TV135." He pointed at his star student. "However, to answer your initial question, Janey, the actual chance of TV135 striking Earth is only estimated at sixty-three thousand to one. I think we might be safe from impact. There're a number of ways to calculate the chances of a collision of an asteroid or meteorite with the planet; the Torino Scale for instance. What's the Torino Scale? The Torino

Scale's used to categorize the 'impact hazard' of near-Earth objects. The closest one to Earth, TV135, rates a one out of ten, which means a very small risk. Basically, zero, but just slightly above zero."

"So, no, is the actual answer to my initial question. Zero chances of hitting the earth," Jane said.

He puffed breath from his lungs. "Correct, that would be a no. Not yet anyway. But the universe is as predictable as it is unpredictable. There are over fifteen thousand near-Earth asteroids or NEAs as they are known, for short. We find, on average, four new ones each day. We've discovered nearly half of all those NEAs within the past decade. It's a fluid subject. Maybe tomorrow, we'll find one heading straight for us."

He didn't take his students' reaction to his classes too personally. He remembered all the days he'd had to attend boring lectures and that mindless numbing of his youth.

Cooped up in class after class, when there was beer to be drank and women to be chased. Especially during the first week of term.

Youth is wasted on youth, he always said to himself. He smiled.

Aaron tried to capture a bit of his students' imagination, and interesting facts and figures were always a good way. "Did you know, each day, around two or three hundred *tons* of cosmic dust, meteorites and other types of objects fall to earth? All those little shooting stars, the size of a grain of sand entering the earth's atmosphere. All of them added up, all over the world, every day is equal to one hundred and fifty cars falling from the sky. But obviously, a meteorite the size of a car only falls occasionally. It's mostly meteors or dust, basically."

He checked his watch. Ending time was getting close. It was a relief he hadn't had a repeat of this morning's episode. He felt good again and tried to invigorate his students once more before the end of the class.

"The meteor that fell in Russia a few years back, the one we've all seen the dashcam footage of; the meteor flying across the sky faster than the speed of sound; that was about twenty meters wide and represented over a month's worth of cosmic dust, about twelve thousand metric tons of debris."

Jane raised her hand again.

Aaron pre-empted her question. "Yes, I'll explain the technical differences between an asteroid, comet, meteoroid, meteor, and meteorite are." He checked his watch again. Sometimes he liked to let the class go five minutes early but figured it was best to answer her in the classroom, as opposed to her door-stepping him when he got outside.

Maybe David had shared some wisdom after all. He placed his two index fingers to his temple and readied for his performance, or so it seemed to the lecture room. "Okay, an Asteroid is a small, inactive or dead, rocky body. Really, it's like a boulder you'd see down at the beach or in a field, but the main thing is, it's actually orbiting the sun." He drew a large rock on the whiteboard and labeled it 'asteroid'. He then drew a rock and speckled it with dots, labeling it 'comet'. "Comets can be dead, a bit like an asteroid, but they can become active at times. As I said before, they're like frozen balls of sand, any size really. The ices can vaporize, due to heat from the sun, and can form an atmosphere or *coma* of dust and gas around it, and may even leave a trail of that behind it. Again, they usually orbit the sun. Halley's Comet, for instance, a really good example of a comet with a large trail behind it, orbiting every seventy-five years." He still had a few minutes to appease the one student who wanted to know all this information.

Aaron drew a small piece of a rock beside the asteroid, with an arrow indicating the small rock had come from the asteroid, and labeled it, 'meteoroid'. "This little piece here is a meteoroid, and it is, for all intents and purposes, a piece of an asteroid or comet broken off, this is again, orbiting the Sun. A meteor is when the meteoroid enters the earth's atmosphere and vaporizes, the light from it is known as a meteor or a shooting star. If that meteoroid doesn't completely vaporize in the earth's atmosphere, and lands on Earth, what's left on the ground is called a meteorite. So, to recap, you have an asteroid or comet, a small piece breaks off, that becomes a meteoroid, that enters earth's atmosphere and starts to vaporize, you can see that as a meteor or shooting star if it lands on earth, the remaining rock is a meteorite. Simple as that," Aaron said. He capped his marker. "Class dismissed!" His shout was before anyone—Jane—could ask him any more questions.

The lecture hall emptied; he put his belongings back into this bag.

What a day. Such a strange day.

First the voice, the panic attack, the homeless guy staring, as if stalking him.

Time to get the hell out of here.

30

4

NO WAY, JOSÉ

When Aaron got home, the memory of that homeless man was still running around his head.

How do I know that guy? He looks familiar.

He opened the door to his apartment with a sigh.

"Daddy!" Ben said, throwing his little arms around his waist.

Katie was Aaron's sister-in-law and was also Ben's babysitter. She was a young lady in her late twenties. She was in a rush. "I've got to get to work now, they want me in for a few extra hours."

He gave her a quick kiss on the cheek.

"Ben's all set for bed, he's fed and I helped him brush his teeth." She flung her bag around, nearly hitting him on her way out the door.

"Okay, thanks, I'll see you tomorrow." He closed the door behind her. Aaron picked up a children's book. "Time for bed, buddy. I'll read you a story."

"Aww, Daddy. Please, can I watch one more cartoon? Just one." He ran back into the television room and jumped on the couch.

"No way, José." Aaron chased him down.

"Yes way, José," his son replied hopefully as he leaned backward over the arm of the sofa, gazing from upside down.

He blinked.

"You're upside down, Daddy."

"No, you're upside down, Ben."

"No. I'm the right way up, you're the one who's upside down."

Aaron laughed. "Fair enough. You're actually correct. From your point of view, I'm upside down. Relative to you, I'm one hundred percent upside down, even though I'm standing on my feet." He picked Ben up and took him to his bedroom.

His son laughing all the way down the hall, when he tickled his tummy.

"Do you want a story now, or for us to do double books tomorrow night?" he asked, hoping his son would go with the double books option the following day. Aaron was mentally exhausted and just wanted to put his feet up for the evening.

"Umm. Double books tomorrow."

He smiled. He'd won, even if Ben would never know it. He tucked him in and gave him a big kiss goodnight. He headed to his computer, in the corner of the TV room. He needed to see how many asteroids were found today. "Just two. Interesting. Well done, France, a double. Two thousand, four hundred and fifty meters, and a second at two thousand and six hundred meters, wow, they're big. Excellent."

It was getting dark. He sat on the couch, flipping through channels. Not finding anything of interest. Up; watched the channel for a second, went up again, watched the channel, and so on.

His eyes were heavy, taking over his body. His mind and great strength were no match for the all-conquering gravitational force of his eyelids.

The remote fell out of his hand and onto the carpet with a plastic *thud*. His tall long figure slumped into slumber along the length of the couch.

His head fell back onto the armrest of the couch. His eyelids began to flutter.

Aaron started to shake, all over his body. His eyelids began to release their force on him and slowly opened.

His body shuddered, as if he was in a demonic state, almost as if he was possessed.

"You're going to kill us all," he whispered.

Aaron's mind was black but clear. Clouds wavered in. The blackness was diluted in a haze.

A figure appeared from this unclear vision, slowly revealing to him, somewhat like the Sacred Heart of Jesus.

A tall form with long black wavy hair, Caucasian in appearance, donned in a long, rough-hewn cloth robe, full length to their sandals, with hands raised in an accepting and loving way.

There was a red stain darkening the fabric, around the area of its heart.

The fogginess of the dream, back-lit by a bright light, began to clear as the person mysteriously floated toward him.

The person smiled. "You're going to kill us all,

Aaron. But I forgive you. I will always forgive you. Will you forgive me? You've never forgiven me for what I did to our boy. I was trying to protect him. I didn't mean to leave the two of you behind. I tried to take you with me. But you stopped me."

The figure floated closer, coming through the darkness and bright fog. It came close enough for him to be able to make out it was a woman.

A beautiful young woman, in her prime. Blood soaked through the large hole in her robe, on her chest.

Aaron was almost relieved; he'd been expecting her. He hadn't talked to her in well over a year now. The words came out thick and fast; he didn't know when he was going to be cut off again. "I loved you. I love you. I don't blame you. You didn't know what you were doing. You'd lost your mind, lost your senses. Trust me, no one blames you. I'm sad that you're not with us anymore. He misses you so much. *I* miss you so much. We loved you so much. We still do."

She came close to his face. So close, he could smell her perfume.

The scent brought back years of emotion. A tear rolled down his cheek. His heart broke again, for the thousandth time.

He could nearly kiss her, his wife, his love, if she just leaned in.

Just lean in Debora.

She was so close, but so far.

Just a distant figment in his longings.

She touched his face; he relaxed and let his guard down. "You're going to kill us all." Her voice was a gentle whisper that tickled his ear.

An unmerciful scream deafened Aaron as the figure floated back into the fogginess and went into the light behind her.

He woke from the screams, frantically scanning the room.

He could still hear screaming.

Panic threatened. Wasn't it just a dream?

Why am I still hearing the screaming? Where's it coming from?

Aaron shook his head to clear it and ran to Ben's room. He scooped up a distraught little boy and held him tight. "You're okay, you're okay. Daddy's here now."

He rocked his son until Ben stopped screaming. "Daddy."

"You're okay, son. You're okay. It's just a bad dream."

Ben gazed up at him. "I saw my mommy."

His heart broke as he studied the distress on his son's face. He wiped the sweat from his forehead; his blond hair matted to it. "I know, buddy. You're okay. She didn't mean to scare you. She loves you."

Ben frowned. "She didn't scare me. She was trying to save me."

"What scared you? What made you scream?"

The little boy's eyes were wide, as he explained his nightmare. "Everyone was fighting. Like a big war. There were soldiers shooting each other. I was in the middle of it. There were millions and millions of them. Mommy grabbed me and saved me. They were going to hurt me."

Shock washed over him at his young son's mental

capacity for that kind of nightmare. "Mommy loves you. She won't let anything happen to you." Aaron stared directly into Ben's bright blue eyes. "I won't let anyone hurt you. I promise."

"Promise?" Ben asked, tears streaming down his little face.

His sorrow and distress made his gut tighten. He wanted to take all the child's pain away.

Aaron grabbed the boy's thin shoulders and made him look at him. Gave him a reassuring squeeze. "I love you so much. You're a strong little man. I can't believe you're nearly six already. I promise you, one million percent I'll always look after you."

"What do you mean, one million percent? I thought you said there was only one hundred in percent? There's no such thing as anything more than a hundred percent!"

Aaron laughed at how clever his son was.

Nothing gets past this boy.

"This is the only thing that can be over a hundred percent; my love for you and how much I'll protect you."

"You'll protect Katie, too?"

"Yes. Your mom would want us both to protect your auntie."

Ben picked up his little bunny rabbit, displaying it. "And Taxed?" he asked. Despite the odd name, Taxed was important.

"Yes. As much as it's difficult to say, I will protect Taxed, one hundred percent too." He smiled. "Now get some sleep, we have a big day tomorrow."

Ben lay in his bed again, with Taxed snuggled in close to his chest.

Aaron switched off the light and stood at the door.

"Dad!"

"Yes, my love?"

The little boy tilted his head back. "I love you, Daddy."

"Night, night, Ben. I love you, too." He quietly closed the door.

Aaron made his way to the living room and sat on the couch near the electric fire. He picked up a framed picture of Ben; one of him as a newborn in the hospital, his beautiful mother cradling him, a beaming smile on her face.

He shook his head. What a waste of such beauty, both personally and physically. He sniffled and swiped at a rebel tear under one eye. "Why, Debbie? What the hell happened?"

5

OBSERVE

Eva arrived early to work the next morning, at nine. It was blessedly quiet. She'd left the sixty-inch observatory telescope in the same position as the day before.

She scrolled through the footage she'd saved overnight, and pressed play, watching the monitor, studying the two asteroids.

They were just about to move off her screen and out of view.

She waited, staring for a moment, then they did indeed, disappear.

Eva put her briefcase on her desk and sorted her stuff for the day. She glanced over at her computer, just to confirm the visibility of the asteroids.

They were still gone.

Something caught her eye, and snagged her distracted attention. It was odd; the small speck in the middle of the screen.

Eva squinted. She reached for the monitor and scratched the glass surface to see if there was a clinging piece of dust or dirt.

The tiny single pixel image on her TV doubled in size.

She blinked, not moving her eyes off it. There was something out there, but no alarm had been raised by the tracking computers.

Eva picked up the phone and called Louis.

Her mentor was upstairs in his office. He had to come down to have a look. A portly man, fond of a drink, good food, and game for a laugh. Always dressed smartly, usually in a suit and cravat. "This is footage from last night. How come the computer didn't track it?"

"Because the difference between the frames was too small to cause an alarm. It only started recording when the pixel got bigger, plus the one minute it buffers, before any activation on the image difference."

He arched a bushy eyebrow, and his lips parted, "So are you thinking what I'm thinking?"

She nodded. "Yes, I think so. It's an asteroid, and the reason it doesn't appear to be moving is that it's coming straight for us?"

Louis smirked, but it had an obviously nervous edge. "This is very serious! Okay, so obviously it's not moving up or down, it could be coming toward us, or away from us!"

"Yes, but it would've gotten smaller if it was moving away from us, not bigger."

"So, to go over this again, why didn't we get the

first alarm on the asteroid?"

"We simply had the telescope pointing straight up. Our position was directly under the original asteroid before it broke up."

"Do we have the size and speed of it?"

Eva shook her head. "No, we'll have to get in touch with a few other observatories to give us a better angle, so we can get a two or three-dimensional aspect on the asteroid." She clicked on the asteroid and programmed the computer to track it.

Her boss shook his head. "The next few hours are going to be crazy."

"*Crazy* is an interesting choice of word for what's going to actually happen. Or what we think is going to happen," she said. "Let's hope it's not our worst fears."

Louis stuck out his hands as if looking for forgiveness. "Crazy, Eva! Detrimental. Unbelievable. The end of the world. Whatever word you want to use."

"Armageddon."

Louis sat in her seat. "It's imperative, Eva, that we get our facts and figures right here. There are a number of permutations that can come out of this situation. Everywhere from a direct hit, to Earth moving out of the way due to its natural orbit around the sun or the asteroid burning up on entry."

"I agree. Not to mention the mass hysteria this could cause. I'm not putting my name to this if it's all going to backfire." Eva placed her hand on her trusted mentor's shoulder. "Let's get advice, get help, double check everything and then disclose."

He nodded. "I think you're right. Yes, I think you're right. It's time to share our information. A problem shared is a problem halved."

She leaned into her computer. "I've tracked the asteroid myself, but I'll broadcast the findings and ask for some more telemetry from other observatories around the world. NASA and all the other relevant authorities can get involved as soon as they find out about it. As you said, a problem shared is a problem halved."

"Just track the asteroid publicly. Don't say too much about it. We'll give it a few hours and see what comes of it." Louis said, no doubt trying his wisdom at convincing her to wait.

It was just like Louis to try to protect her, but their planet needed the protection right now. "Okay, I'll hold off for a short while and publish it later today."

6

IT'S COMING

Aaron flipped through some old photos, reminiscing of his family's past.

The computer beeped.

A new asteroid had been provisionally registered. There was a note attached, asking for some other observatories to track the asteroid so they could get a proper size and vector of it.

"Hmmm." He sat in front of the computer and tapped away at the keyboard, logging onto the college off-campus observatory. He had remote access to it and all its functionality.

Luckily, none of his students had been using it.

The chance would be a fine thing. He typed in the provisional number for the asteroid.

The computer accessed the coordinates from central records in Paris. The telescope panned, tilted and zoomed automatically to the correct location.

Aaron studied the monitor. He could make out a blurry image of the asteroid as he opened a trajectory predictor on his PC.

A window popped up. The application started tracking the asteroid while retrieving the coordinates from the central location.

He watched the calculations being processed, waiting for the computer to do its thing.

The simulation of Earth and the asteroid popped up on another window.

He pressed *play*. The video showed the asteroid moving directly toward the planet. "Jesus Christ. Is this thing coming straight for us?"

He opened a three-dimensional sizing program and told it to scan the asteroid. It digitally wrapped the asteroid in a three-dimensional mesh. Then it would roughly calculate the size.

Again, the computer took only a few minutes for the results to come in.

It reported that the asteroid was approximately thirteen hundred meters wide, or nearly a mile wide in Aaron's conversion from meters to miles. Meters were the international standard in metrics, but he still liked to convert between the two.

Its approximate shape was that of an elongated sphere.

It was traveling at about twenty-five kilometers per second and was about one hundred and ten million kilometers away.

He did a few calculations on the back of an envelope. "One hundred and ten million divided by four hundred thousand equals five hundred. Okay. So that's about the distance from here to the sun. Eight minutes if it's traveling at the speed of light. But it's traveling at twenty-five kilometers per second. Hmmm." He took a breath to compose himself. "Okay, calm down. That was a pointless piece of math."

He returned to his scribbles.

"What's the impact going to be like? One thousand, three hundred meters wide is the equivalent of the Estonian asteroid multiplied by about three. So, sixty nuclear bombs now turn into about one hundred and eighty nuclear bombs, which will devastate about; let's up it a little, maybe half a million square kilometers. Okay."

What size is the planet's surface?

"Two hundred million square miles. What's that in kilometers? This fricking metric versus imperial conversion is the bane of my life."

Aaron Googled the earth's surface area, just to be sure and so he could keep his figures in the same form. "Five hundred and ten million square kilometers. Okay, the asteroid will devastate five hundred thousand square kilometers as a worst-case scenario."

He wiped his face with the back of his hand, and the sound of his stubble scratching through his fingers was reassuring, a positive habit. "Okay, okay. That's not the end of the world, literally!"

He Googled the observatory in Nice and got the phone number.

Aaron waited for the phone to connect, typing the "area of Texas" into the search bar.

'Six hundred and ninety-five thousand, six hundred and sixty-two, kilometers squared.' came up on the screen.

"Okay, so this asteroid would take out nearly all

of Texas."

Hmmm, okay.

The phone rang again before he heard a French accent on the other end.

"*Bonjour,*" a female said.

"*Bonjour,*" Aaron replied.

"*Oui, monsieur. Qui puis-je dire appelle?*"

He looked at the name attributed to the asteroid. "*Bonjour, puis-je parler à* Eva Monnier, *s'il vous plaît,*" he said in slow broken French. He stumbled over his words; his limited French. "Umm. May I speak to Eva Monnier, please."

"*Oui, monsieur.* What is your name? *S'il vous plaît.*"

English, thank God!

"Aaron Jacobs," he replied to whom he assumed was the receptionist, connecting his and Eva's phones.

"*Bonjour.* Eva *parlant. Comment puis-je vous aider?*"

He spoke slowly, praying she was fluent in English, too. "*Bonjour.* My name is Aaron Jacobs, from the California Institute of Technology, in the United States of America." He glanced at his numerical scribblings and a mistake in his calculations glared back.

He sucked back a gasp and hung up the phone. Heat kissed his cheeks and the back of his neck. He swallowed hard. "You, stupid fool, Aaron," he whispered. "The asteroid's practically a sphere. Its mass is a multiple of its width, for crying-out-loud. Doctor Jacobs, my ass!" He snatched the envelope up and threw it back on his desk. "The volume of a sphere is four over three times pi, times radius cubed." He typed in '*volume of a sphere calculator*' into Google.

The formula appeared in his results. There was a

box to enter the radius, and the computer would calculate the volume of the asteroid.

Aaron typed in the radius of the Estonian asteroid and awaited the results.

'Two-hundred-meter radius is three point three five million meters cubed.'

He then typed in the radius of the new asteroid.

'Six hundred and fifty is one point one five billion meters cubed.'

He divided the volume of this asteroid by the volume of the Estonian asteroid, TV135.

Thirty-four, approximately.

"So, the volume of this asteroid verses TV135 asteroid is thirty-four times bigger. Presuming they're made out of the same material, and hence same density, it will have a mass of thirty-four times TV135, which was one third the width!"

His phone rang. There was an obvious foreign number on the caller ID.

Aaron rushed to finish his math. "Oh, fuck. Thirty-four times bigger than TV135. That's nearly twelve times the size of Texas!" His breath stalled as he went on automatic pilot and reached for the phone. His shoulders shook and a shudder worked its way down his spine.

Oh my God, that's nearly four million square kilometers.

Aaron put the phone to his ear before he lost the chance to answer. "Hello."

"Hello, Eva Monnier speaking, you called this number."

He tried to compose himself. Her voice seemed calming to him. Like she knew what she was doing. As opposed to him. "Oh, hi, Eva. My name's Aaron

Jacobs. Sorry, my phone must've cut off a moment ago!"

"It's okay. What can I do for you?" she asked.

"I've been tracking your asteroid." Aaron wiped his forehead as he conjured up the courage of his calculation.

I can't get this wrong.

He needed to tell her the dreadful news. "It's not good. I've just done some quick calculations. Forgive me, if I'm wrong. But this is a massive asteroid and it's heading straight for earth."

"Yes, we know. We have some estimates here, but from our angle, it's very difficult to predict the size. It appears a few hundred meters in width."

"Eva, sorry, it's thirteen hundred meters in diameter, from my angle. You were looking at it head-on, like looking at a train head-on. You can only see the front of it. This is a massive asteroid. It's potentially devastating!"

"Devastating; what do you mean? *S'il vous plaît.*"

She had a soft gentle voice, he was trying to picture her in his head. He liked her French accent with the English spoken word. Her tone was soothing, considering the topic of conversation. "Well, it would basically wipe out most of the US, or all of Europe and surrounding areas." Aaron was worried he wasn't getting across just how serious this situation was. "You need to record this on the Torino Scale. The nearest asteroid to us is a fraction of the size and is only twenty-five thousand miles away. It's categorized as a one out of ten on the Torino Scale. *This* is going to be a ten out of ten. If you record it, it'll be known internationally, and we can start to address the situation immediately."

"*Oui, immédiatement.* I was going to do that anyway. I just needed some other observers to verify the numbers to me. This is bad, yes. Do you know how long we have until impact? I cannot calculate the speed from this angle."

"I think we have about fifty days until impact. But I haven't added the earth's vector yet. I'm going to run some simulations to try and figure out *where* it will hit. Hopefully, it won't be on land. But it looks like it's between the forty to fifty latitudinal lines. France, Germany, Russia, California, Washington, New York, Japan. You name it, we're all targets."

He heard her clear her throat, as if she needed a moment.

"Would we not be out of the way in thirty days?"

"No. It looks like we are on the arc tangent to it. We'll come out of direct target, but come back into direct target at the other end of the arc!"

"Thank you, Aaron. I need to talk to my boss. I'll call you back soon."

He opened his work computer remotely from home. Then the asteroid simulation program. He added the information he'd gathered. He typed in coordinates; sky position, solar elongation, magnitude and status of the object.

He pressed *run* and held his breath. He didn't have a lot of information but needed to look for an approximate impact zone to start with.

Eva hung up on Aaron Jacobs and called Louis to

tell him the horrible news. She blurted incoherent gibberish right as he picked up. "Louis, this is bad, worse than bad. I'm coming up to you."

She didn't give him time to answer. Just set the receiver in the cradle and grabbed a few documents, making her way down the corridor connecting the observatory to his office.

Eva ran up the staircase, brushing past anyone in her way. Obnoxious? Yes. Justified? Definitely.

She didn't bother knocking.

"We have a massive asteroid heading straight for Earth. It's over a kilometer wide. One point three to be precise"

Her mentor's mouth dropped open. He took off his glasses. "It's not April Fool's Day."

"No, Louis. I'm serious."

"Show me the evidence. The corroboration."

Eva frowned. He was dismissing her as if she was a child. She took a breath so she wouldn't give in to her immediate rage. She had the information, but it was irritating that he was demanding it, instead of taking her word. She went to the side of his office desk, and placed her documents on his table, spreading them out to show the asteroid.

The one they'd thought was two, but had actually been *three.*

She pointed to the mark representing the hidden problem. "I didn't see the third asteroid, because it was too far away for the pixel on the computer screen to pick up. We didn't see it until today because it wasn't moving relative to our view, not until another scientist from the United States spotted it."

Her delight at the idea of finding and naming the

asteroids had been replaced by dread and terror.

"*Sacré bleu*, we must report this immediately. Let me have a look at the asteroid from the telescope, and we'll call it in from your phone. *Oui?*" Louis said.

They rushed down to the observatory.

The place housing the telescope was a square stone room, with a large dome roof. The telescope sat in the middle. It was mechanically fixed into place with a pan and tilt mechanism.

Louis climbed the small metal stairs to the viewing piece.

Eva had pointed it at the third asteroid.

"Give me your phone," he called.

She obliged and watched him type '*International Astronomical Union*' into a search engine.

The phone number appeared.

"Register the asteroid on the computer, click on it and it'll give it a name," her boss told her as he put the device to his ear.

She dashed to her computer and clicked on the asteroid.

Eva confirmed the thing was a new discovery.

The program automatically registered a new name. RQ26.

"*J'aimerais signaler une catastrophe!*" Louis exclaimed, his voice betraying his fear with his shaking words.

7

THAT GUY

The smell of bacon filled the kitchen as Aaron finished making breakfast for Ben. "Get in here and eat up; Katie will be here soon."

His son came bounding into the kitchen and sat at the breakfast bar. "Why can't she live with us? It would save her calling over here every day!"

"Because she can't, she has her own life. This is just temporary, anyway. You'll be back in school soon."

Just then, Katie opened the front door with her key. "Hey Ben, good morning to my little man." She messed up Ben's already morning disheveled hair.

"Hi, Katie," Aaron and Ben said simultaneously.

He kissed his son's head and gave his sister-in-law a hug and a quick kiss on the cheek as he rushed out the door. "Gotta run, I have extra work today. I have to get in early." He didn't want to mention the asteroid. He wasn't sure if it was public knowledge yet and definitely didn't want to upset his family.

Katie isn't the type of person who watches the news, anyway.

"I love you, Daddy," Ben shouted.

"I love you too, kiddo." Aaron made his way down from his third-floor apartment and into the underground garage.

He slid into his Suburban and drove up from basement level onto the main street. Aaron stalled. Had he just spotted the homeless-looking guy again?

He glanced back, and the guy started running away.

Aaron jolted as he accidentally confused his gears; drive and park. He slammed the car into drive and turned right instead of his intended left.

He chased after the running man, screeching past a pedestrian and a dog.

The man yanked hard on the leash and collar, obviously fearing the worst for his pet.

A squeal from the dog followed the matching one from Aaron's tires.

How did the homeless guy know where he lived? He saw red. How *dare* this person come to his work, let alone his home?

The mystery man turned down a small narrow alleyway.

Too small for his car.

He hopped up on the dead-end fence, flicked his legs over and fled as fast as he could into the distance.

Aaron was too far behind to catch up. He sat in his car, fixated at the point where he'd last seen the homeless guy.

He bashed the steering wheel. "Fuck!" His hand smarted; he grasped it with the other. His fingers throbbed as if accusing him of an unnecessary injury.

He waited for the traffic to clear before performing a U-turn and making his way to the university.

Aaron strode down the hallway to his office. There weren't many people around. Maybe it was just a bit early. Too early for professors, and definitely too early for students.

He got to his desk and put his briefcase down before logging onto his computer.

He looked out his window, scanning the bushes and trees. Paranoia edged over him. Was someone out there?

Aaron opened the simulator program he'd started the night before. It was a three-dimensional graphic user interface. It generated a video in time-lapse.

He watched the Earth on the video graphics begin to spin, along with the moon revolving around it. The asteroid moved slowly toward Earth as the planet spun.

By now NASA, Oxford, Cambridge, MIT and hundreds of other authorities around the world would be working on similar programs, trying to get an accurate assessment of the situation at hand.

He was another cog in the wheel in what would fast become an international incident. He wanted his own data because impact information wouldn't be released for a few more days. Until all the agencies agreed.

The simulation was working away, calculating millions of pieces of information, and presenting it as a pretty three-dimensional video.

Aaron was impressed with how quickly it worked. The earth, spinning and spinning as the asteroid edged closer and closer.

Like a game of roulette.

Where she stops, nobody knows.

David Dean entered the office with a smile. He looked flustered and excited. "Morning, Aaron. Did you see the news? It's something to do with your field of work." He logged onto one of the news networks on his computer. His colleague rotated the screen toward him. "It's a meteorite. It's going to hit Earth sometime this year. It's going to crash into the Nevada Desert, they're saying. It could even hit Las Vegas."

Aaron glanced at the monitor and glared. "Fake news, if ever there was fake news. It's unresearched and unfounded. And why would that be a *good* thing? How did *that* brighten up your morning?"

David shook his head. "These things never happen. They're always blown out of proportion, exaggerated. When have these things *ever* hit the earth?" He smirked.

He didn't bother to answer; his colleague's ignorance knew no bounds.

The female reporter announced, *"And now some more on our breaking story. A massive meteorite is on its way to Earth. It's predicted to crash into the Mojave Desert, near Las Vegas. Up to one million people inhabit Sin City, at any one time, depending on the season. The City of Light's may be lit up for all the wrong reasons this year."*

A graphic, a little bit similar to that on Aaron's

computer, played behind the reporter's head. A crude graphic of an impact hitting Las Vegas finished the clip off.

"Hopefully, most of the meteorite will burn upon entry to the atmosphere," Aaron said while fobbing off the news flashes.

David moved his screen away and started typing again. "I know it's your field, but they're reporting it. It's a pretty big story. I doubt they would've run it if it wasn't real. Here's a second source." He showed his monitor again.

He peered at his own computer. The program was almost finished. The graphic of the asteroid was close to striking the planet. He spared a glance at David's screen, and the male reporter was exuberantly breaking the news.

"A massive space rock is hurtling toward Earth and it is going to hit us. Reports from the International Astronomical Union based in Paris, France, have recorded a meteor, of some description, with a flight or impact trajectory for the planet. Not much has been released yet, but experts predict it could even hit New York or London."

Aaron frowned. "Turn that fake news bullshit off, please. They haven't a clue where or when it'll hit. Two completely different reports."

"Well, the first one was more accurate. At least they said a place where it would hit." David leaned back in his chair. Confident in his rebuttal.

He threw his hands up and shook his head. "One report's saying it could hit London, the other is saying it could hit a place the size of Britain! Come on, gimme a break."

"Yeah, okay." David made a face and pulled his

screen back towards himself.

The results were in on Aaron's machine. He zoomed in on the area, then clicked over Europe and zoomed in further. He readjusted with his mouse and scrolled over Switzerland, clicking one more time over Zurich.

He Googled the city's population. One million, eight hundred thousand came up for the metropolitan area, from the last census. "Christ," he said under his breath.

David looked over. "What did you say?"

"Nothing."

"How do you know these reports are all fake news anyway?" His expression was a mix of curiosity, and maybe a tinge of embarrassment?

"Let's just say, I know. It's my job to know. But, it's my job to get the facts and figures correct first. We don't deal in fake news here, David," Aaron said. He'd hold his cards close to his chest.

His work phone blared.

"Hi," he barked, trying to give the impression he was too busy to talk to whoever it was.

"*Bonjour*, Aaron," Eva said.

He sat upright, to attention. "*Bonjour,* Eva."

"Did you get any more info on the asteroid?" the French astrophysicist asked.

"Yes. It's heading for Zurich. I'm working on the date. The computer says, one million, nine hundred and ninety-nine thousand, nine hundred and eighty-seven point two seconds."

Eva did some verbal arithmetic. "That's nearly two million seconds. Divide that by twenty-four hours. Let's say twenty-five for the sake of argument. That means, multiply the two million by four and divide by one hundred. That leaves eighty thousand. Divide that by three thousand, six hundred seconds in a day. "That's around twenty days, plus about fifteen percent for what I left out; let's say three days. So, a total of twenty-three days, give or take a few hours."

"Hang on, let me change the units of measurement in the program." He clicked on the 'seconds' unit and changed it to 'days'. "Twenty-three, point one four eight days until impact," he said, seconds later.

"I was fairly close," she said, sounding a tad smug.

"That doesn't give us much time. They were based on last night's numbers too. We've even less time now."

"Time for what? Even if we had twenty-three years, what could we do?" Eva asked. Panic threatened to climb up her throat from her gut, and she swallowed to stave it off.

"Well. What's the best course of action? What did your boss say?"

"Hold on." She ignored the American's question, putting the phone to her chest as Louis passed by. "Less than twenty-three days until impact. Aaron from Caltech has done the calculations."

"Where's the impact zone?"

"Zurich. But basically, most of Europe, when you include fallout."

"Oh my God." The older man made the sign of the cross.

"What'll we do? What's the next course of action?

Aaron wants to know," Eva asked. A shudder crawled down her spine, like spiders. She fought it, fidgeting in her chair. "Twenty-three days. Jesus."

"Get Aaron over here, we'll go to Paris with our findings. He's probably half a day ahead of everyone else. He's the guy with the most relevant information. They want him there immediately. Send on whatever data he has, we'll double, triple check everything."

She put the phone to her ear again. "How long will it take you to get to Paris? Louis thinks this is the real thing. We need to get a move on with it."

"I don't know, maybe twelve hours, but probably fourteen, including getting to the airport."

"Okay, get here straight away. Send any data you have before you come, we'll go through it again. We need you in Paris." Her voice was just the edge of a demand, but she didn't care.

"I can't just pack up and go to Paris. I have a son. I can't just leave him here."

"Oh. Okay." Eva searched her brain for an answer. "Do you have anyone who can look after him?"

"Yes, probably."

"Okay, can you get it taken care of quickly?"

"Leave it to me."

"Dépêche-toi s'il te plait"

Louis grabbed the phone. "That means *'hurry'*, Aaron. We need you. I'll re-run the impact and fallout from your data." Her boss put the receiver in its cradle.

Aaron could see that David was listening intently

to his conversation.

"Twenty-three days. What's that in reference to? Was it the meteorite from the news? Paris, is that the impact zone?" he questioned.

"Can you tell the dean I need someone to cover my classes today? I have to go, immediately. Family emergency. I can't explain now." Aaron's voice and expressions were urgent; worried.

His head spun as he tried to figure out what exactly he'd overheard. Was it worse than the news his colleague had claimed was fake?

"David. Are you listening to me?"

Aaron watched his friend's mind in a spin; he looked like he was contemplating too many scenarios. *Was Aaron rushing off to Paris? Why?*

"You wouldn't just rush off and leave your son if it wasn't of the utmost importance. This must be serious, very serious. What's going on, Aaron? Are we in danger? Who was that you were talking to?"

"No one. It's a work thing. We're not in any danger. Calm down."

David shook his head and stood up. He didn't seem convinced. "Tell me what the fuck is going on!" he commanded.

Aaron sat in his chair directly opposite David's chair. He pulled in close and looked at him, he put his hand on his shoulder. "I can't tell you right now. Hysteria is exactly what we need to avoid. People giving and receiving wrong information only causes panic. Chaos and fake-news are a recipe for disaster."

He gasped. Stared his colleague down. "Disaster!"

"Can you please just calm down? I'll tell you what I know. I won't tell you what I'm not sure about." His voice was even, which helped David take a breath.

"That's fine; just don't leave me in the dark, for fuck's sake. I'm your friend, I'll help you. I've been your friend for years now Aaron. I don't know how many classes I've covered for you in the past couple of years. Just tell me what the hell's going on." He was still demanding, but he didn't care.

Aaron nodded his head, acknowledging that David had been there for him in his time of desperate need. "There's an asteroid, *not* a meteorite, heading toward Earth."

"What's the difference?"

"Let's just say, one would basically burn up in the atmosphere, and the other won't."

"Is it a big asteroid?" David asked.

"Yea, it's nearly a mile wide."

David put his clenched fist to his mouth. He looked worried, but confused. "Is that a big asteroid?"

"Yeah, it's massive." Now the man's tone was concerned, with a touch of helpless. "But the size is only one thing, it's the velocity which is also very important."

"Is it going very fast?"

"Yes. Very fast. Multiple times the speed of sound."

"What scale of devastation are we talking?"

"I can't answer that until I run proper simulations. I only have provisional data. We need to find out what the asteroid is made of, first. That's another important piece of information. The density will be a huge factor. We know the velocity, we know the volume, to a degree." Aaron packed up a few things from his desk.

David ran his hands through his hair. "So, what's

the story with Paris? Is the asteroid going to hit there?"

"No, I don't think it'll hit Paris. The head of the International Astronomical Union is based in Paris."

David grabbed at his stomach. "So, if it's not going to hit Paris, does it have a chance of hitting us?"

"As I've said, I don't know; I've only run one simple prediction model. We need the IAU or NASA or someone in authority to run the proper model. Will you ask the dean to get someone to cover my classes, or not? I don't want to talk to him myself. I have enough going on." He went to their shared office door, with his bag slung over his shoulder.

David threw his hands up. "Will it hit us or not? What's your simple model prediction? Please."

"It'll hit Europe."

He watched as his coworker slumped back into his chair. Not hitting the US was definitely a relief to him.

"The Alps maybe. Hopefully just the Alps, that would be better, by a massive multiple, instead of hitting Zurich. Europe, I'm sure it'll hit somewhere in Europe." Aaron seemed to be muttering, but then he pinned him with serious eyes. "That's all I know, for now, David. I'm not being a dick. I just can't tell you stuff that's uncorroborated. These are just early predictions. I don't want a mass evacuation of Paris, just because someone gives out some bogus information."

"How do you know this anyway?"

"I discovered the asteroid with a French astrophysicist, Eva Monnier, last night. We've been working on it since then. The International Astronomical Union asked me to go to Paris with our information immediately."

"Okay. I'll cover your classes for you. I'll just put on some video or something. Keep them entertained. What about Ben?"

"I'm going to get Katie to take him."

"Katie, the hot little number," David said with a smile. "Do you want me to call and make sure she's okay?"

His colleague glared. "She'll be fine without you calling."

"She's fine, all right." He laughed.

"How can you make jokes at a time like this?" Aaron threw his hands up.

"Aaron," David shouted after him as he disappeared into the hallway. "For once in our lives, the asteroid *isn't* going to hit the USA. There's a first time for everything." He laughed again.

Aaron rounded a few corners and corridors. He called Katie from his cell phone.

"Aaron. Hi, what do you need? You'll get me fired here," Katie said, her voice edged with some urgency.

"Sorry to call you at work; I need you to get Ben. I have an emergency, and it'll likely be a few days until I'm home. I know I only have you down for the school run, but I'll need you full time for a while."

"Why, what's going on? Is it that meteorite that everyone's talking about?"

Ugh, she already watched the news.

He didn't want to take time to explain. "It's not a meteorite." He didn't want to be abrupt, it just seemed absurd that people didn't know the difference between a meteorite and an asteroid. It wasn't Katie's fault, she'd been bombarded by unqualified, unfounded news from the mainstream media. "Yeah, it's about the 'meteorite'."

"Let me go outside, the boss is making me take an official break. Ben's not a problem, Aaron. I can do it, but I'm going to need to be paid a bit more. Especially if it's three or four overnights."

"I completely understand. That's no problem at all. Whatever you want."

"I can't stand this fucking job anymore," his sister-in-law confided.

"Well, quit," he encouraged, not something he'd do in normal circumstances.

"I can't. I need the money for my rent," she said, and he could hear the sigh in her voice.

She didn't know a huge asteroid was hurtling toward their planet and might ruin her long-term plans.

"Screw it, Katie, you're a great woman. You shouldn't be working in that shit-hole. I'll pay you what he'd pay you, and you can sleep in the spare room. You shouldn't be there, wasting your time; you should be out living your life, meeting people, making the most of everything. You're amazing with Ben. He loves his Auntie Katie. I'd be delighted to have you there all the time, like an official nanny. The money doesn't mean anything to me. Take this opportunity and run with it. The world is your oyster."

Katie's silence stretched a few seconds, as if she thought he'd lost his mind. "Are you, all right?" she asked finally.

"Yes, I'm fine." Aaron was almost out of breath

from his inspirational monologue.

"Seriously, you want me to move in as a nanny or something, and you'll pay me a full salary?"

He'd always adored his wife's younger sister. He could trust her; she loved Ben and they were amazing together.

If Katie had Ben, he'd worry less about both of them; they'd look after each other. Maybe give him some security in this horrible situation.

Would money even be relevant by the end of the year, anyway? They all had to survive this asteroid.

"Listen, I have a new rule; what Katie wants, Katie gets."

She laughed. "Are you sure you're okay?"

"I am. Just pick Ben up after school please, as normal. I'll call you later. Love you, and kiss Ben for me. I'll be home soon."

"Okay. Love you, too. But hang on here a second. She put her cell on video mode, and pointed it through the cafe window. Her boss was standing there in his off-white shirt, eyeballing her.

The man raised both hands into the air, as if it would get her to hurry up and return to work.

Katie outstretched her hand in front of her and raised her middle finger directly in the firing line of her boss.

His mouth opened slowly with disbelief. He looked as if he was just about to go out after her when she took off her work hat and threw it at the window.

Aaron laughed as she hung up on him.

8

LONG DRIVE UP

Louis and Eva used his old yellow Citroën 2CV to drive to Paris. They made their way through the beautiful French countryside.

She drove, reasonably fast, while he sat in the passenger seat, holding onto the roof of the 2CV for stability.

"Eva, *ralentissez, s'il vous plaît*," her boss demanded as his laptop fell to the floor.

She slowed as she turned onto the motorway.

A road sign passed them by, nine-hundred and ninety kilometers written under *Paris*. The sat-nav had six hundred and twenty miles written on it.

"Sorry! We're on the motorway now. It's plain sailing from here all the way," she said as Louis picked up the laptop from the floor.

The machine was ringing.

Her mood switched immediately from calm to agitated and impatient. "Open it quickly? Someone is trying to video chat."

"Oh, my Lord, will you calm down? I'll open it. If you weren't driving like a *lunitique*, I'd have it open already," Louis said.

When the laptop was open, the screen activated and she could see someone trying to open a chat in her peripheral vision. "Click the green phone symbol there," Eva demanded, as the noise of the cars whizzed by them at one hundred and twenty kilometers per hour, making the scene all that more erratic.

He clicked the phone symbol. "There, I clicked it, you concentrate on the road and I'll concentrate on the 'Minitel'."

She gasped a laugh. "It's not a Minitel, it's a laptop, you buffoon."

"I should've driven, and you should've run the Minitel here from the passenger seat," he continued, sounding annoyed now, like a father would be with their petulant daughter.

Eva spotted a handsome looking man whom she assumed was Aaron on the screen, she noticed that Louis didn't realize their new American friend had answered and could see and hear his rantings.

She wasn't in the office now; the things going on in the real world had a way of leveling people. No one was anyone's boss anymore. She *was* acting like the petulant daughter. "If you were driving, it'd take us two days to get to Paris. Now answer the call please." She tried to hide her exasperation, but her voice betrayed it.

"I did answer it," Louis retorted and faced the laptop toward her.

Aaron was sitting in a business class seat, thirty thousand feet in the air.

"Hi," Eva muttered, distracted from paying attention to the road. "Aaron?"

"Um, yeah. Is this Eva? Hi. How are you?"

She was impressed by Aaron's rugged American good looks. She was trying to put a face to the voice for the past day. She was happy with what she had thought; judging by his voice over the phone. Blue eyes, square chin.

Very handsome. Mid-thirties? Still, age appropriate.

"Yes, this is Eva," she said as Louis ripped the screen from her view.

"Concentrate on the road, Eva. Hi, Aaron, this is Louis here, I spoke with you on the phone. How are you? It looks like you're on the plane."

"Hi, Louis. Yes. I had to book a business class seat, as it was such short notice. Besides there are free drinks."

Eva could see Aaron showing Louis a gin and tonic in a nice large fish bowl glass; containing lots of ice and a slice of cucumber. She'd looked away from the road again.

"We have free WIFI too. I never even knew you could get WIFI on a plane!"

"Me neither, Aaron. But you can't beat a good hip flask of cognac," her boss said as he took out his small hip flask and took a swig. "Hennessy XO. Only the best."

She shook her head. They didn't have time for niceties. The hip flask said it all. That was why *she* was the one driving.

"Very nice, make sure and keep me a small glass of that," Aaron said.

Eva was trying to keep her eyes on the road, but glanced over in jealousy as he sipped his drink. She had her foot completely to the floor, and was going at a top speed of one hundred and fifteen kilometers per hour—just over seventy miles per hour. "Are you two serious? How can you be so *blasé* at a time like this?"

Louis swiveled the laptop camera toward her whenever she spoke. "My dear, Eva, there's nothing we can do right now, *this* second. I think it's wise for us to at least live in the moment and put our emotions to the side."

She was flabbergasted, and not for the first time that day. "Louis, am I the only one taking this seriously? There are millions of people's lives at stake here. The whole continent could be no more. I'm actually really worried."

"Eva." The older man paused. He pushed the flask toward her and laughed. "Here, have a drink."

Aaron laughed as well.

The two men were as boisterous as each other.

"For fuck's sake. The two of you!" she said as she shoved the alcohol away. "I'm driving!"

"Eva, if you can't find humor in the face of adversity, you'll never know true humor." His tone was light, which made her roll her eyes.

She ignored him.

"I'm doing some better analysis on the university computer at Caltech. I'm running an impact assessment, too. We'll know exactly where and when it will occur. We'll need to figure out what the asteroid is made of. We need your help with that." Evidently, the American was trying to get her back on his side.

He does have a really nice American accent!

She couldn't help but tune back in. At least Aaron was speaking business. "Asteroid mitigation. If we work out what the asteroid's made of, we can figure out density and surface hardness."

"Wouldn't it be lovely if it was made out of water! It'd probably evaporate on entry," Louis said.

"Water, no. I seriously doubt that, but it could be a porous rock consisting of nickel," Aaron said.

"If it's iron, we're in trouble," Eva said. It was a reality check full of doom and gloom, but they needed to consider the possibility.

Louis took another swig from his hip flask. "Big trouble." He took yet another swig, as if he couldn't help himself. "Did you guys know there's geological evidence of devastating asteroids hitting Earth on six occasions?"

"Yes," she and the American spoke simultaneously.

She peered at Louis with slight disbelief. Eva wanted to roll her eyes at the juvenile question, and Aaron's tone told her he was on the same page.

Maybe the booze was getting to her boss' brain.

"I'll put that down to your training, by such great teachers, as myself," Louis said contently.

Aaron flashed his cell to the camera on the laptop. "My Twitter feed is going crazy; the news has broken, big-time. They're attaching mine and your name, Eva, to the reports."

"How the hell are they reporting on something we haven't even qualified?" she demanded.

"Even though our names are attached to the story, we know only too well what sort of news era we now live in. It's all about who's first to the story, no one gives a crap if it's true or not. Get it out there and we'll just ignore the errors later."

"Never let the truth get in the way of a good story," Louis said. He'd told Eva that saying before; his friend was a reporter.

"Okay, my battery's running low here, I'll see you guys in Paris in a few hours. *Au revoir*," Aaron said.

Just then a sharp *'bing'* sounded over their connection, but it was the American's computer, not hers.

"Wait!" he shouted. "I have an email here from an aide at the White House."

Louis cursed lowly, and Eva gasped.

"What does it say?" she barked, she couldn't help but demand. Panic threatened to take her over, and she split her concentration; half on the road, and half on the American's smooth baritone, so she could stave off the terror.

If the White House was contacting him, it confirmed her worse fears.

Aaron read aloud, *"Dear Doctor Aaron Jacobs, you have been cordially invited to Hong Kong for an emergency Global 8 Summit. This invitation is in respect of your discovery of the RQ26 asteroid, and your current work to date. We understand you are an expert in the field of astrophysics as well as being an Ex-Marine…'* You're great, you're great, et-cetera. *We understand you are traveling to Paris at the moment. There will be a ticket to Hong Kong waiting for you at Charles de Gaulle Airport upon your arrival. You have been added to the manifesto. Your fellow discoverers, Doctor Eva*

Monnier, and her colleague Professor Louis Marchonie have also been invited.' Yadda, yadda, yadda. They even know where I am and who I'm meeting!"

"Wow! This is big," her boss said.

"Very big," Eva said, caught between the devastation approaching, the worry that brought and the accolade of being invited to the G8 Summit. Her life's work was paying off, but the outcome was causing a sickly feeling in her stomach.

"Guys, my laptop is about to die. I'll meet you in Paris, and we'll travel to Hong Kong together. Talk soon." Aaron hung up.

"*Au revoir*," Eva and Louis replied, as he closed the computer.

"G8 Summit?" Louis asked, then his expression became sly, and he arched an eyebrow. "Yes, he's definitely your type."

"Shut up. I'm a professional woman, don't be so stupid," she said, slapping his shoulder while rolling her eyes.

He laughed. "You're a beautiful woman, he's a good-looking man. Besides, the world's probably going to end in a few weeks, what have you got to lose?"

"You're not funny," she grumbled, refusing to look at him; for once, concentrating completely on the road.

9

PRESS CONFERENCE

The US Press Secretary stood at a presidential podium. Her large frame was in a navy suit, and outlined the lectern. Her long black hair framed her stern face.

Her expression demanded silence, without her having to verbalize a word.

The press conference room at the White House was twice as packed as usual, crammed and imitating a sweat box.

Olivia Hargreaves glanced at her notes and looked at the crowd again; the cameras flashed. She scanned the photographers, camera operators, and journalists. "Today, we wake up to the news that an asteroid is heading toward Earth." She paused so that the public acknowledgment could sink in. "This is true, but it's early, and we're working hard to figure out the exact impact zone, date and time of impact."

The camera snaps intensified every time she looked up.

"Reports that the impact will be in Las Vegas are unfounded. There have also been reports that the impact will result in complete devastation of the planet, and this is also unfounded." She glanced at her notes for a second again, and the flashes died down. "We've been in touch with governments of countries and mayors of cities whose hometowns have been mentioned as 'disaster zones'." She made air quotes. "Namely, New York, London, Paris, Hong Kong; they have also examined preliminary data, and believe the reports of these places being hit by the asteroid are also unfounded, and actually not in line with the asteroid's trajectory."

"What about Paris?" one female journalist asked.

"We'll take questions after. Thanks, Rebecca," Olivia said.

Rebecca Crawford, a small pretty blond firecracker, raised her hand, persisting. "Who *are* Aaron Jacobs and Eva Monnier?"

Ignoring the question, she continued, "I'd like to introduce, Dr. Timothy Carlton, the NEO strategist for NASA."

The overbearing reporter raised her hand again, proving she was bordering on petulance today. As if she assumed Olivia didn't feel this situation was serious.

"Near Earth Objects!" Dr. Carlton said, revealing an English accent, as if assuming what the reporter's question would be.

The whole room seemed to still, and Rebecca slowly lowered her hand.

"I hope that answers your first question," the scientist finished. He took out a few notes, fumbling with them, as if he was nervous. He fixed his floppy hair a few times. His skinny frame disappeared behind the podium as Olivia vacated the area. "So, anything that's within two hundred million kilometers of Earth, one hundred and twenty-five million miles to my fellow imperialists here, or about five hundred times the distance from our planet to the moon." He rubbed the sweat from the right side of his face. "Oh, and they are also over one hundred and forty meters across."

Olivia handed Dr. Carlton a tissue to wipe his forehead, noticing he was extremely nervous.

"Timothy… Sorry, Dr. Carlton," Rebecca hollered.

"Oh, you can call me Tim," he said without making eye contact. "Rebecca."

"Tim, you can call me Becky. Is this a big asteroid?" the reporter asked. She held her arms wide to illustrate.

"Yes, it's one of the biggest on record. There are only a handful of asteroids in the Near-Earth Object realm this size."

"Is it devastating to Earth?" she continued.

All the other journalists appeared to be leaving Rebecca to her own devices. She seemed to have established an instant, comfortable rapport with Dr. Carlton, and the other journalists seemed to know it, but so did Olivia.

"We're not sure yet, we're working on more accurate calculations. This asteroid was caused by a collision of two other larger asteroids. It splintered off on its own direction; out of any previously traced orbit. A rogue asteroid, if you will."

The reporter crossed her long slender legs.

The doctor must've noticed because he looked down.

Rebecca bit her pencil. "And is this, in your knowledgeable opinion, a doomsday scenario?" She smiled, before she started giggling. "How many days do I have left to find myself a fella and settle down?"

Giggling had turned into outright laughter from the full cohort of journalists.

She was a smart journalist, obviously not afraid to use her feminine wiles to help get any story, or an extra sound-bite.

Olivia wanted to roll her eyes.

"Umm." Timothy shot her a look.

She shook her head. He couldn't admit the worst, and cause uncontrollable hysteria. There was enough hysteria and fake-news doing the rounds, she didn't want him to compound the situation. The truth would have to be for later, when they knew more.

"No, it's not a doomsday situation. But it's difficult to answer that right now, until we get our numbers crunched, and as soon as we do, we'll let you know what they mean and..."

Olivia went back to the podium. "That's all for now. As Dr. Carlton said, we'll run the numbers again, along with London, Paris, Hong Kong, Tokyo, and numerous other cities and countries around the world. An exact answer will be announced as soon as we know. There is a G8 emergency meeting in China tomorrow. We'll know more then. The best of the best will be in attendance. Russia, Canada, USA, UK, France, Italy, et-cetera, et-cetera will be there. Thank you."

"Olivia, what's the situation with getting good reportable information?" Rebecca asked, despite Olivia's closure and dismissal of the press conference.

She wasn't shocked, the reporter was undeterred. They'd had plenty of run-ins over the years.

The journalist didn't take any prisoners, but neither did Olivia.

"Rebecca, there are two types of people in the world; stupid people and smart people. Smart people can extrapolate answers from incomplete data." She left it at that, gesturing for Timothy to leave the stage and exit through the back door.

Olivia was delighted to see that Rebecca was extremely confused, wondering why she didn't finish what she was saying.

The reporter rushed the stage, obviously still irritatingly undeterred. She approached the scientist.

Olivia had to interject. "Rebecca, we're done for now." The woman could be manipulative, and she didn't want Timothy to be distracted from the job at hand. Definitely didn't want the truth to get out at this stage.

Dr. Carlton had a bit of a social awkwardness, a vulnerability to a degree.

Rebecca was the opposite. She was brash, confident and treated *everyone* as a headline.

"Sorry Olivia, no problem, you're right, sorry," she conceded.

Olivia narrowed her eyes. What was Rebecca up to?

The constant irritant waved her hand and backed up.

She stood at the door, frowning in the reporter's direction. Why would Rebecca change tactics so soon? She shook her head and herded Timothy out the back door.

"Hey Olivia, just one-more quick thing here," Rebecca called.

She headed back to the pain-in-the-ass journalist, hopefully out of Dr. Carlton's earshot. "What?" she said, just short of a demand.

"Speaking of the asteroid and all that. What's a horoscope?"

"What're you talking about?"

The reporter smiled, but it had a sinister edge. "A horoscope is a telescope that can only see *your* face!" She sauntered off, leaving Olivia to glare in her direction.

She fumed, but she had no more time for all this tit for tat carry on. She grabbed her cell and checked if Dr. Jacob's flight had landed. "Give me a second Timothy; I have to call one of our colleagues in Paris. You're going to China right away. You'll be traveling with the President, and will meet the rest of the team over there."

Dr. Carlton nodded and headed off with an intern.

His cell phone rang.

"Hi, Dr. Jacobs, this is Olivia Hargreaves, from the press office of the president."

"Hi, Ms. Hargreaves. I got your email. Thanks a million for that."

"Did you get your tickets? Did you meet up with your two counterparts?"

"Yes. We had a meeting with the International

Astronomical Union, and handed over copies of our files. We're waiting here for our flight. It shouldn't be long now."

"That's great. What do you make of the French team?"

"They're very smart, very knowledgeable, excellent to work with. We already have a great working relationship."

"That's perfect. I won't be there myself, but there will be a car to pick you up when you guys arrive."

"Okay, great. Thanks."

Olivia looked at her cell go black. She turned on her heels. "I need a drink. I'm not too sure how stiff, but I definitely need one."

10

G8 SUMMIT

Aaron rode in one of the four black Mercedes S-Class sedans, as they approached the front door of *The Four Seasons* hotel in Hong Kong.

The two miniature American flags attached to the front of the car fluttered in the wind.

A valet bellhop, dressed in a pristine black and olive suit, opened the door of the car for President Jameson of the United States.

He stepped out of the first car and was followed by a number of advisors and dignitaries.

Major John Russell among them, was behind the president, in uniform.

Paparazzi cameras strobed in the evening's twilight.

The president moved on as another black Mercedes pulled up.

Dr. Timothy Carlton, along with two more

assistants, left the car and headed into the lavish hotel.

Aaron's hands were clammy, a sign he was slightly overwhelmed by the whole experience. "I don't usually go to the *Four Seasons*, but when I do, it's for all the wrong reasons!"

Eva stepped out of the car door, one long leg after another. "You're not the only one."

Louis pushed himself out after her. "No. We mustn't be defeatists. We have a job to do here. Important input. I believe in us." The older man shut the door himself, much to the obvious displeasure of the valet, who made a disgruntled noise in his throat.

The high-pitched sound of some screaming burned Aaron's ears, as if he'd been hit by something. He cupped his face and winced.

"You're gonna kill us all!" was like a mantra he couldn't get away from.

He blinked a few times, then he shook his head.

"Are you okay?" Eva asked, her pretty face highlighting her concern.

"Yeah, sorry. Just a little sharp headache. It's gone now."

Louis put his hand on Aaron's shoulder. "*Ça va?*"

"*Oui,*" he said, nodding. "*Ça va.*"

Both his companions looked worried now.

They'd only known each other for a few days, yet the bond between them seemed like it'd been forged over many years.

They proceeded into the main lobby. The beautiful white marble was polished to a perfect sheen. A fabulous crystal chandelier hung deep from the high ceiling.

They met many of the other delegates, along with

the president himself.

Aaron was a bit shell-shocked, meeting the U.S. President.

President Jameson smiled as he shook their hands in turn. A tall man, gray-haired, with a beautiful tailored blue suit. He was surrounded by assistants and aides.

Eva appeared thrilled; regressing into a little girl for a minute or two.

Pleasantries were exchanged all around with the president leading the way. "Dr. Jacobs, so you're the guy who discovered the asteroid."

"No, actually, it was my colleague, Dr. Eva Monnier, who spotted it first," he said, pushing some limelight toward Eva.

The major broke up the proverbial pleasantries. "Okay, let's get a move on. Time is of the essence. We need to have a multi-international cooperative plan in place by the end of today. Whatever it takes, whatever's needed, everything, that is, except time."

"Indeed," the president said. "Let us proceed."

They all made their way to the United States strategy room. Each country had their own room, decked out with high-speed computers, data assistants, large screen emulators, and video conference facilities.

Aaron looked at the eight large strategy rooms; one for each country. Each one had a flag on the door.

"Do we have any basic plan as of yet? Besides nuking the bloody thing," President Jameson asked when they were all settled.

"As of yet, sir, that's our actual only option at the moment," Major Russell the fit looking gray-haired military man said.

Dr. Timothy Carlton raised a hand. "Well, technically, we wouldn't have the power to blow it up. The asteroid's too dense. We'd have to drill into it; we'd need millions of megatons of explosive power. It's just not feasible. It's impossible."

The president's expression betrayed his obvious confusion.

Aaron acknowledged that the two statements seemed contradictory.

The leader of the free world frowned. "So, we can nuke it or not? Which is it?"

The major started to speak, but Dr. Carlton interrupted. "Well, it's actually a bit of both. We won't nuke it to try and blow it up, but we'll nuke it to cause a deflection."

"We can trigger an explosion, which would cause huge forces on one side of the asteroid, and this would cause equal and opposite forces toward the opposite side. In turn, it could cause the asteroid to deflect away from the earth," Aaron presented his two cents.

The president looked even more confused.

"Like a cue ball hitting the eight ball. They would fly apart from each other," Eva added, her French accent making her analogy as appealing as she was.

President Jameson nodded. "Okay, I get it now."

"But don't pot the cue ball. This is very important. The closer the asteroid gets to the earth, the bigger the angle of deflection that is needed, therefore the more nuclear explosives we need," Louis said.

The president shot a look at Major Russell. "So, what do I do now?"

"I think we all agree; this is the only course of action. I think you'll find all the other countries have come up with a similar idea. But, no *one* county will be able to pull this off by themselves, not even us," the major replied, dipping his eyes to make his statement something like a suggestion, the man in power could decide upon.

"We'll need to know how many spaceships can be deployed within the next week or two. We also need to know who has the largest nuclear armaments, how many megatons explosive power they have, what weight they are. We need logistics; where they are, whether or not we need to transport them to the US, and where the closest space shuttle is," Dr. Carlton said.

President Jameson took a seat and started laughing. "You want me to ask the Russians all this, *and* you want me to tell them the equivalent from our side?"

"Yes, you have to. We can't do it without them; as the major said." Eva gestured to the military leader.

The president looked around the room. "It's very technical. Why don't you guys ask for this info, Dr. Jacobs? Dr. Carlton?"

"Mr. President, with all due respect, and I'll use an American baseball analogy here; it's time to stand up to the plate. They won't listen to Aaron, Dr. Carlton, Eva, or even the major; they'll only listen to you." Louis leaned forward in his chair, his voice urgent; his words clear despite his accent.

The president reclined in his black leather seat, his expression contemplative. "Okay, everyone please take a seat. We'll need a bit of give-and-take here. Drs. Jacob and Monnier, explain to them what we want to do. Major Russell, you tell them we need to work together. Dr. Carlton, you cover what we need, and I'll ask for support by entering a unilateral worldwide agreement to share all space and nuclear information for the next month."

"How do they know you're serious about the urgency?" Louis asked, as if he needed to play devil's advocate.

Aaron studied the president's expression as they waited for an answer. His new French friend wasn't wrong for voicing what they all were probably thinking.

"We'll tell them about our largest nuclear bomb, and our newest space shuttle. Both classified." He held his hands out, as if he had nothing more to offer.

Eva's mentor shook his finger as if he was scolding a child. "No, no, no."

The president jolted up, his eyes narrowed as if he couldn't believe what the Frenchman had dared to say to him.

"This is good. This is very good," Louis finished.

The room breathed a sigh of relief.

Louis was the oldest person present. He was probably the most knowledgeable. If he was happy, everyone should be happy.

"If I know the Russians, and I think I do, I think they'll go with that," he concluded.

The president clapped his hands once, which seemed to grab the whole room's attention. "Right, that's it. We all agree. Let's get a move on and get this done. Major Russell, I'll need a briefing on our top bomb and space shuttle." He rose from his seat.

They exited their individual strategy room and went to the ninth room, the main conference room.

This was a large mission control for all the eight countries to jointly talk. There was a big round table with room for the heads of state, and two other delegates from each country to sit beside them.

It was equipped with large screens and numerous computers. The place was a larger version of where they'd just come from.

All the delegates took their seats.

Behind the roundtable, was a second circle of seats and tables, for each country's staff and experts.

President Jameson took his position, flanked by the major and Aaron.

Eva and Louis went to the French seats and Dr. Carlton made his way to the UK area.

"Why're they going over there? Why are they not with us?" the president demanded.

"The UK Prime Minister and French Premier requested that they sit with them," Major Russell said.

"No, I want them over here on our team. *We're* the leaders here. We have the plan. We have the expertise. We need to keep the best people together. They need to be on our team."

"I'm sorry, sir, but I can't overrule these heads of state."

The president tapped his microphone, causing a dull *thud* through the speaker system.

All eyes landed on him.

"Excuse me, there're a number of French and British members of our team who've been requested to go to their relevant country tables. This is a joint effort, so we'd like to have our team members back."

The Russian president let an audible scoff. He was half slouched in his chair. He was a bald man, small and stocky. He looked like an ex-Russian mafia member. Not to be messed with.

The French Premier cleared his throat. His perfect suit, pocket square, and matching tie was the nicest attire in the room. He was a small slim man, sixty-five years of age, but looked much younger. "Sorry, this is just not possible. We need them on our team. *We* discovered the asteroid. They are an important part of our team and our ideas."

The British Prime minister nodded. Her nasally high-pitched English accent was piercing. "I do apologize, but I'm in firm agreement with my colleague. Dr. Timothy Carlton is an important member of our team. He has extensive knowledge of this subject."

The German chancellor lifted a hand. His over pronunciation of his English words, slow and calculated. "Can we please not start off this meeting with unbelievable disagreement and arguing already? Honestly, we *all* will need to put everything behind us today. Everything, no squabbling as to who found the asteroid or who is going to fix the problem."

The Russian spokesperson to the right of his president made a face. His thick deep accent was like a baritone compared to the other sopranos. "It's very, very important that the Americans do not hijack the proceedings here. We're a team; we're all in this together."

President Jameson sighed, and the microphone caught his obvious exasperation. "I'm not trying to ruffle feathers already. I'm just trying to keep our original team together."

The Russian president laughed. "Oh, теперь вы

хотите, чтобы иностранные люди в вашей стране,"

His countrymen started laughing, as well.

President Jameson pointed at the Russian president and glared. "What did you say? English, so everyone can hear you. Why do you always speak Russian at these meetings? Bloody waste of money on all these translators, just because you won't speak English."

Aaron asked Louis what the Russian President had said.

"Something to do with wanting foreigners in his country all of a sudden!" Eva's mentor whispered.

The Japanese Prime Minister bowed as he stood. "I propose we stop arguing and get down to business. The sensible thing to do would be to have the French and UK delegation placed either side of the US delegation. Hands up if you agree!"

The USA, UK, French and Japanese heads of state all raised their hands.

The Japanese Prime Minister smiled. "Great, what about those who object?"

The Russian and German heads of state raised their hands. Italy and Spain both chosen to abstain.

"Thank you for being the voice of reason here," President Jameson told Japan. "I propose the Japanese Prime Minister be made the Chair of the Meeting today. Will someone second that? And if anyone else wants to propose a different chair, please do, along with a seconder."

The UK Prime Minister quickly shot her hand up. "We'll second you on that, President Jameson."

"We'd like to propose the German chancellor, and we'd like someone to second our proposal," the

Russian president said. He gazed around the room, but it remained quiet.

President Jameson only gave him about five seconds before moving on. "Without any other nomination, the room would formally like to offer the Japanese Prime Minister as our Chair for the meeting, if you'd kindly like to accept."

"Thank you so much, President Jameson. We would love to accept this honor."

11

SPECULATION

Olivia sat in an Irish bar, watching the rolling newsfeed; relaxed in an oak chair and leaning on the mahogany bar, drinking a coffee. The pub was very convenient for her, and she liked the character of the place.

The weary-looking bartender was leaning on the bar also, slouched over, also watching the news.

No words were exchanged, as they were engrossed in the current asteroid dilemma.

Don Rutherford, the anchor, conducted an interview with a number of high-profile experts from the UK.

Peter Ainsworth was an Iraq War I & II expert, a brash bright clothed eccentric man.

Paul Southend was a financial trader on the FTSE, a clean-cut 'City' boy.

Don initiated a debate about the impending

asteroid. "So, the G8, which includes Russia, meetings are being held; but, is this unfair on the other one hundred and eighty-seven countries around the world? Why are the richest most powerful countries leading this initiative?"

"To be honest, this is a power struggle; all about land," Peter Ainsworth answered, his tone and manner as if he was feeling bashful. Waving his hands already, he glanced to the right as Paul Southend interjected, pointing his finger to the sky.

"Hmm. I don't think so; this is about money right now. The big countries want to be the ones who solve this problem, so they can forever hold the rest of the countries in debt. I agree, to a degree, that it's a show of power and strength, but it's really all about money. It's to say, 'We can prevent this mess, but you owe *us*'."

Peter Ainsworth waved his hands again. "No! Sorry, I disagree, this is definitely about land. I don't personally think this asteroid incident is going to pass off without a hitch. This is a near earth incident, there will be consequences. We don't know right now if it's going to hit the USA or Europe. It could hit anywhere, for all we know. If it hits us, money will be the last thing on our minds!"

"Yes, okay. Points well made," the news anchor cut in.

"The computers say India, by the way. But, this is serious high-end mathematics we are talking about. Anything could happen." Paul Southend's expression was smug.

"It's always about the land!" Peter Ainsworth insisted. "And if it is going to hit India. It'll cause devastation to that whole region. You can draw a small circle stretching from India to Japan and over China. You'll have more people in that circle than outside it. Half the world's population live there."

Don Rutherford laughed sarcastically. "Well, let's go live to the G8 summit in Hong Kong, where our US correspondent, Rebecca Crawford, is on standby."

Olivia nearly choked on her coffee when she saw her nemesis on the television. She'd been overlooked by the president for the G8 trip, which was why she was drinking coffee back in Washington.

Hold the fort back home.

She shook her head; a slight pause ensued, before the satellite time delay passed.

Rebecca stood in front of the camera, in a trench coat, holding a brightly colored umbrella. "Hi, Don, it's a wet evening here in Hong Kong. The rain is bucketing down. The traffic is still as busy as usual."

The camera panned past her shoulder and showed the evening gridlock traffic at a standstill.

"This former British city has been an innovator and inventor of many of today's amazing technologies. I'm sure the technologies for saving the earth are already created; it's just time now to see if the leaders of the free world can work together and use every invention known to man… For Earth's sake."

Don Rutherford addressed his guests again while he read from his notes. "Right now, we don't have an exact location for where the asteroid will hit. We know it'll be in about a month or so. Europe was the first quick math, back of the envelope, in relation to where the asteroid could hit. Some people think we should evacuate Europe and move to Africa right now.

Others think that the Africans shouldn't allow the Europeans into Africa, 'build a wall' if-you-will! Others think Russia should let the Europeans in. Some ex-Russian countries are trying to rejoin the Russians, so they'll have freedom to travel out of their areas. The Americans are proposing to take in the UK citizens, but no other country has. They're planning on creating settlements across the US. The French and Germans are not happy with this, as they feel the world is leaving them behind."

"I don't think there's any real reason to start getting hyped up about this, until the computer data can pinpoint *where* the asteroid will strike. We don't know what's being said behind closed doors. This is all made-up tabloid BS. What's the point in moving to Africa if the asteroid's going to hit there? It's just nonsense. This is why the G8 need to get the answer out to the public as soon as possible!" Peter Ainsworth said.

"I've heard they're not releasing the final impact zone because they can't blow up the asteroid, it's too big. But they can deflect away from Europe and into the path of Africa or India." Paul Southend only seemed to add more toward conspiracy.

"Or the Pacific Ocean! You don't have to be such an outlandish conspiracy theorist all the time, Paul. Maybe modesty in this situation would be much better," Peter Ainsworth retorted.

Paul Southend's expression screamed his offense and outrage. "Well, maybe you should open your mind a little and explain why eight countries, who have the greatest computer power in the world, can't seem to do a little bit of applied math and find out where the impact zone it going to be!"

"Peter. Do you think Paul has a point? It's been a few days now." Don Rutherford spoke, his tone belying he wanted to diffuse tension, so he sounded more like a moderator than a news anchor.

Peter Ainsworth's smile had a reluctant edge and he leaned forward, with open hands, on display. "This is what I'm saying; you're sensationalizing the situation without any concrete evidence. You'll cause mass hysteria and people will die because of it."

"So, you're accusing me of causing civil unrest, resulting in death and destruction. Bloody ridiculous statement." Paul Southend's Scottish tone revealed his anger, and his face reddened.

"No, but it's one media station adding one percent to the problem. Do this another hundred times across all media, and you'll have a problem." Peter Ainsworth nodded to illustrate his point.

Don Rutherford cleared his throat. "That's all we have time for now. We'll have our two guests, Peter and Paul, back at the same time tomorrow."

Olivia watched a young man in the pub take a swig from his pint. "Turn this shit off. We're all fucked. Why do we have to have these wankstains tell us what we already know?"

The pub owner chuckled as he surfed channels. "I'll have a look for you. We'll see what else is on." He flicked to the popular European news channel, France 24, where an equivalent interview was taking place in English.

A furious panelist was thumping his fist on the host's table, "Sorry to sound cliché but, *sacré bleu*, this is a joke, *c'est ridicule*, why have we not had any more information on the situation? They're hiding something."

The host intervened. "Well, if they are, it's in France's best interests, after all, the first indications were, France would be the place hit by the asteroid."

The furious panelist compounded his point. "*C'est la vie, c'est la vie*, the information has no foundation. We should know. They should tell us. We are the people. *Le peuple de France La République.*"

"Is there any sport on, mate?" The young man asked in what Oliva could only describe as a faint English accent.

An English man in an Irish pub in the US!

"No, all the football's canceled for the foreseeable future. The cricket, the golf, everything. I think all the rich people have gone into hiding. It'll just be poor numpties like me and you who'll be toast when the asteroid hits. We're all fucked, *mate.*"

The young man laughed, another sign of defiance in the face of adversity. "Sure, I better start a tab, so," he chuckled again.

Olivia smiled, remembering why she liked to come to this pub for her coffee.

The pub owner joined in on the end-of-Earth humor. "The chance would be a fine thing." He asked if the guy wanted one for the road.

"I do, kind sir. One for the long and winding road. The road to nowhere."

The sound of important breaking news went on-air on the TV, catching their collective attention.

"This just in. Russia has said they would take back former Soviet states, as long as they return to the Soviet Union. A return to the old USSR, or CCCP, as it was known in Russia. The strict communist system would be re-established and would welcome all members back unconditionally, this would include free movement between states," said the reporter.

"Fucking hell," the pub owner spat. "You'd love that," addressing the young man. "England versus the USSR, that'd be a good bit of footy. I'd like to see that again."

12

G8 PLUS 187

A dreary evening engulfed the summit conference room. Eva watched the walls darken as the glass-domed ceiling shut out the sun with clouds. The rain was coming down hard.

"What're the ramifications if we were to shoot down this asteroid? Excuse my ignorance. I'm engaged with doctors in their field here," the Japanese Prime Minister said.

Eva stood to address the room. "It's all about timing. The sooner we get to the asteroid, the sooner we can deviate it." She sat back down, but continued speaking. "The asteroid is traveling at twenty-five kilometers per second. Or, as you would you say… sixteen miles per second."

"So, the ramifications?" the Japanese Prime Minister echoed.

"I don't know right now. But I do know the

ramifications increase negatively the longer we wait. Earth has a two-dimensional surface area relative to the asteroids vector."

"I know English isn't your first language, my dear, but we have a saying over here, and it dictates that difficult issues should be discussed in plain English," The concierge to the United Kingdom asked, in his deep baritone, almost Churchill-like.

"Excuse me, I was under the impression everyone in here had brushed up on the word 'vector' before we started taking the planet's future into our hands."

Aaron stood beside her. "Thank you, so much for your insight, Eva." His urgent tone made her frown, as if he felt he needed to quell tension.

Major Russell stood to address the room. "Major John Russell here, US Marine Corp. We all agree if we're going to send a mission to the asteroid, then we'd better move fast."

Murmurs and nods of agreement swept through the room.

"So, we're setting up a special task force. It's called Project 'G195'. This is to represent the one hundred and ninety-five countries, officially or unofficially, on our Earth. This isn't a 'G8' thing anymore. This is all of us working as a team."

The room repeated agreement with another all-encompassing hum.

"If it's all right with the Chair, may we ask Dr. Timothy Carlton, from the UK and NASA to put some numbers on the board so we can all agree that our calculations are accurate." Major Russell retook his seat.

Dr. Carlton took to the floor; he looked down at

the lush red carpet as if preparing himself.

A hush surrounded him as he moved to the front of the room, stopping under the main big screen behind the podium.

"I think from the feedback we're getting from everyone..." he paused. "the only real option is to try and deflect the asteroid, and not actually blow it up. Is that fair to say?" He looked around, as if for a morsel of support.

Eva had never heard so many different accents in one place at the same time, it was comforting.

A united front.

A pin drop could've been heard.

She raised her hand. "Fair enough, but could you explain, in layman's terms," she shot a look over at the British delegate who'd questioned her terminology. "Why can we *not* blow up the asteroid, and why deflection is our only real choice?"

"Thanks, Dr. Monnier, that's a great question. This will kind of be an exercise in what we can't do; which will be good, because it will lead us onto a much more focused exercise on what we actually *can* do," President Jameson said.

Satisfaction rolled over Eva since the US president had backed her up so quickly. She sat taller.

"Is everyone still in agreement with this process? Everyone, not just the heads of state. Please, everyone be equal in here. We have the smartest people in the world in this room. We have video links with all the major research centers in the world. Please, if anyone finds an issue or a miscalculation, please let us know." The Japanese prime minister was magnanimous, as always.

A positive response rippled through all attendees, with a number of delegates giving the Chair a small hand of appreciation.

"Thank you, all. Please proceed, Mr. Timothy." He bowed and gestured for the scientist to carry on.

"The main issues we have are time, mass and velocity." The English scientist sounded more comfortable now that he had the backing of the room, it seemed. "This is not just the math and physics; there are logistics and tangible needs, as well. Do we have the tangible utensils to blow up an asteroid hurtling through the air at twenty-five thousand meters per second?" He stalled. "While we're on that, could we get an exact velocity of the asteroid relative to the sun, please? Do we have the tangible utensils? Do we have the nuclear power? Do we know how much nuclear power is needed to deflect the asteroid?" Dr. Carlton took an audible breath. "Every day the asteroid gets closer, and hence the angle needed to deflect it past the earth increases. So, the nuclear explosive power needed increases every second of every day." The man seemed to be in his element now; he was pacing under the big screen TV. He looked at his feet as he spoke.

It was almost as if he was speaking to himself inside his own head. She didn't envy him for having the spotlight.

He looked out at the crowd, the double row of seats and tables, pens and notepads everywhere, laptops open, everyone paying attention. "The more nuclear explosives we need, the more weight or mass we'll need to push the asteroid into outer space. This means we will need more shuttles." Dr. Carlton whirled toward the whiteboard, and started scribbling calculations. He was very quick, neurotic and seemed borderline nervous. "Four over three times Pi, times half the diameter cubed." He circled the 'half diameter cubed' part. "Which is half of one thousand three hundred meters, cubed."

"One billion and—" Aaron shouted.

"Stop!" the Brit returned, as he continued to scrawl. "Half of one thousand three hundred is six hundred and fifty, which is nearly two-thirds of one thousand. A thousand cubed is one billion. Two thirds by two thirds by two-thirds is eight over twenty-seven. Pi times four divided by three, is basically four. Four times eight over twenty-seven is thirty-two over twenty-seven, billion. Take off a little bit for my overcompensation." He faced them again, peering at his new American friend. "One billion, one hundred and fifty million meters cubed."

Eva smiled and fist-pumped. "I like your maths."

Aaron smirked, holding his calculator in the air. "Math! It's pronounced *math*."

"Yes, the Germans invented the first Mechanical calculator in the 1600's. Well done. Now, what about payload? What about nuclear power," the German Chancellor put in, his stern expression shouting how much he *wasn't* impressed by the show of intelligence.

The room fell quiet.

The nuclear power stalemate would have to be addressed eventually.

The German Chancellor looked over at the American president, then over at the Russian president. "To be honest, I'm kind of addressing this question to both of you." He smirked, but Eva felt his air of superiority from her seat.

The Russian president reclined in his chair and gestured to the US president with open hands, offering for him to go first. A simple gesture, like in a game of poker.

President Jameson paused as he appeared to contemplate his next move, which he'd agreed with Eva and the rest of the team. "The basics are, we have a power to weight ratio issue here. That being said, we need to know how to bring these two things together in a timely manner or fashion."

The Russian president leaned forward. "This is very true, President Jameson, we wholeheartedly agree. It's time to put the past behind us and think of our future," he said, as if in his own little way of encouragement.

"Thank you for the vote of confidence," the US president retorted to his Russian counterpart. "We have a nuclear warhead, which is about one and a half times more powerful, with respect to weight, of that of your *Tsar Bomba*. The 'world's most powerful' bomb."

The Russian president laughed. "You're telling me you have a nuclear bomb of approximately seventy-five megaton equivalent with a weight of twenty-seven thousand kilograms."

Aaron handed his president a piece of paper, he smiled at Eva.

She was quite surprised at just how confident her Californian dreamboat was.

President Jameson had a quick scan of it. "I thought you guys originally reported the *Tsar Bomba* was one hundred megatons? Not fifty."

The man in question coughed, as he looked toward his assistant, to his left. Embarrassment was etched across the face of the Russian leader; slowly reddening to anger.

His right-hand man stood. "President Jameson, yes, we did report one hundred megatons, but we only exploded half of the *Bomba* that day. The plane which dropped the *Bomba* wouldn't have gotten out of the way in time. It would've been a suicide mission for them. Not to mention, the fall-out from the whole one hundred megaton *Bomba*. But it was only half that weight. To be precise." He retook his seat. "Trust me when I say, our *Tsar Bomba* is one hundred megaton equivalents at fifty-four thousand kilograms."

"Okay, we're getting somewhere. We have one hundred megatons at fifty-four thousand kilograms and we have a number of these." The UK Prime Minister looked over at the US president, her expression expectant.

He, in turn, pinned his gaze on the Russian president. "Do we have enough of them?"

The Russian President bit at President Jameson's goading. "We have a two hundred megatons equivalent nuclear *Bomba's* at a weight of forty thousand kilograms each. We have seven *Tsar II Bomba's*," he admitted, but his expression was one of rueful confession.

The US president stared at his major.

Major Russell shrugged and shook his head. If those two indicators weren't a sure sight they had nothing more to offer, his grimace said it all.

"So, we know who out trumps the other here in relation to nuclear power. Has any other country got anything to add to this?" The UK Prime Minister asked, but it was just short of being a demand.

The room went completely silent.

A definite show that the two superpowers present were Russia and the US.

The President of the United States stood and left the room.

His aides followed.

Major Russell also stood, and cleared his throat. "We'll take a short recess."

The US military man hurried away, and a shocked murmur traversed the attendees.

Eva glanced at Aaron, but her American friend just shrugged. She looked at the Russian president, and his expression was decidedly smug.

"C'est fini." She mouthed toward Aaron.

13

WHO'S WHO?

When Jane arrived at school, the place was abandoned. She only spotted two or three people on campus.

The doors and windows were all left open. The fate of the planet had hit home with every student, except her, apparently.

College was usually the last thing on their minds anyway, and now it seemed to be even further down their list of priorities, if that was even possible.

She made her way through the corridors. The silence was deafening as a piece of wadded paper fluttered past her.

A real 'Earth's going to end' feeling descended over her.

She headed past the main lecture hall and on past the sports complex.

As she rounded the corner, heading to Dr. Jacob's

office, Dr. Deen, the other professor who shared an office with Dr. Jacobs, nearly ran her down. "Oh, sorry Hi, Jane. How are you? Kind of strange being in here all by ourselves," the man said. He fidgeted, as if he was nervous.

How does he know my name? He's not one of my professors.

"Yeah, it's kind of strange. Why are you here today? Are we all off, or is it just the students?"

"I could ask you the same thing." Dr. Deen whipped his head around with a frantic edge. "I just came in for a minute to pick up some of my belongings."

"Are you okay?" Jane didn't know him, but it seemed he was acting…strange.

"I'm fine. You?"

"I'm good, yeah. Just hope we can find an answer to the asteroid problem."

"Yeah, those darn asteroids."

This guy is weird.

"Is Dr. Jacobs around?"

"Nope. He's in China with the G8 delegation. He's an advisor to the president. He was one of the first people to discover the asteroid."

"I saw his name on the asteroid tracker."

"There were loads of TV stations here earlier, but they've all gone now. They were all looking to talk to him." Dr. Deen continued to seem on edge. He peered down the hall, then checked out the window again.

"Is everything okay? I'm only here to see Dr. Jacobs. I'm not here to freak you out."

"No. No. It's fine. There was just a weirdo homeless-looking freak walking around the place earlier. I think he was trying to find Aaron, too. He was saying his name out loud."

"Oh. I'll keep an eye out for the 'weirdo homeless-looking freak'," Jane said, and she went over to Dr. Jacob's office.

"Are you searching for anything in particular, Jane?" Dr. Deen followed her back to the office.

"I want to get the key to the observatory control room. Just want to have a look at the asteroid myself, and see if I can help."

"Well, Aaron always said you were his brightest student, so if anyone is going to find anything, I'm sure it's going to be you."

"What?" She'd heard what he said, but maybe she wanted him to repeat it.

"If anyone is going to find something, it'll be you."

"No, the bit before that."

"You're his brightest student."

"He actually said that?"

"Oh, God! I gotta go. Yeah, he said that, but don't go falling in love with him. He's twice your age."

"Don't be silly, that's not what I was thinking," she replied, but her face became flush and betrayed her true feelings.

"Well, he's not here, but here's my keycard. It'll get you into all the places he can get into." He handed his lanyard to her. "You can keep it. I'm not coming back. This asteroid is gonna hit France. So, I'm off to New Zealand!"

"Why New Zealand?"

Hmmm! I thought he said you were his brightest student!"

It slowly dawned on her, but instead of a lightbulb moment, she let it sink in. "Other side of the world to France. I get it."

"Exactly. Well, give or take a few hundred miles. Okay. I'm gone," Dr. Deen said as he rushed out, then down the hall.

She examined the keycard in her hand. "Okay, thanks."

He shouted from the end of the hall, "And watch out for that freaky homeless-looking guy. Fucking weirdo. Sorry about the language. Not sorry."

"Okay. I will." Jane went over to Dr. Jacob's desk and had a peek around. She kept her hands to herself, at first. There was a picture of him, a woman and a little boy.

A set of rosary beads were draped over the picture frame with the cross hanging in front.

I didn't know he was the religious type, being a scientist and all.

The computer screen had a number of Post-it's stuck to it. A multitude of paperwork mountains were peaking all around his desk.

Even though it's a mess, it seems organized.

She looked back at the woman in the picture frame and stared. She wasn't fazed by her.

Jane had her next ten moves planned out, she just needed to focus and implement them.

She sat in the swivel chair and continued to stare at the picture; hypnotized almost. Looking at the woman, the little boy, and her professor.

Jane squinted and stretched her neck closer to the picture frame. Something flickered in it.

Something was *moving*.

A strange feeling came over her. Why was the picture flickering at her?

She gazed down at the keyboard. Ah, the flickering was caused by the reflection of the glass in the picture frame.

She froze in the chair.

There was someone behind her.

Jane dared not turn around, but she had to eventually. The courage to turn gently built up in her.

She swiveled around in the chair.

The person was looking straight back at her.

Her heart sank to the pit of her stomach, but she relaxed an iota.

The person was outside. Staring in from the wide window.

He was homeless-looking, as Dr. Deen had mentioned, and he was watching her.

Unmoving. Just staring.

She caught her breath and stood. Mouth open, she placed her hand on her heart and felt it beating beyond anything she had felt before.

The man dashed away.

Jane ran to the window just in time to see him bounding into the hedges and out of sight. "Fuck! That fucker scared the shit out of me."

She pressed her hand to her heart again and tried to calm herself. Then placed her other hand in front of her and watched it tremble.

Jane slowly made her way back to the window to see if the man was gone for good. She peered over at the last place he'd been.

A tree and bush twitched in the vicinity of where he'd been standing.

"Oh, shit, he's coming back." She ran to the utility door and used the keycard D1. Deen had given her. The reader beeped as she wrenched the door open.

She looked out the window and was still able to see the area where the man had been lurking. The angle was slightly better from the utility room.

Jane watched, confused at the sight and maneuvers of the man. She couldn't help but think he was in distress.

Why is he running away from me?

Was he really shouting Aaron's name earlier?

He seemed to be stuck in the overgrown shrubs, the thorny bushes or something.

She opened the window and leaned out for a clearer view. "Are you okay?" she shouted.

There was no answer.

"Shit, what will I do? I hope he's okay," she said to herself, to drown out the silence in the room.

Maybe he was in serious distress, and couldn't answer.

She pulled a spare chair over to the window and pushed it up until it was fully open.

She lifted her leg out to climb through but held the window so it didn't fall on her.

Jane wanted to help the man but didn't want to be left outside if he was dangerous.

Okay, just go a few feet closer and see what's going on, then run back to the window and into the utility room.

Her voice of reason reassured, mixed with curiosity and a sense of danger, as she jumped down to the ground. She crept closer, one foot at a time.

First, she spotted the man's feet, his legs, then his torso.

The bushes and shrubs obscured most of him. She couldn't see his face or hands yet. Her need to know drove her forward, and she approached the man's feet.

His body was shaking as if he was having a seizure. He lay in a small trail between the bushes and shrubs.

Jane knelt beside him. She had little regard for the jeans she was wearing as her knee became damp.

The man was mumbling, and she could make out the words, but it sounded as if he was repeating the same thing. "Pea boo, pea boo, sea sea sea, too too too." He lay in the shrubs, still trembling.

She leaned in to grab the end of the branch so she could see his face.

"Pea boo, pea boo, sea sea sea, too too too," he said again.

Her arm shook as much as he did, and her fingers twitched as fright threatened to take her over. "Okay, just grab the branch. Lift it and run." Jane gently moved the branch away from the man's face.

The whites of the man's eyes were the only thing visible, as if they were rolled back in his head.

She screamed and dashed away, stopping at about ten feet. "Fucking, fuck, fuck. Fuckiddy fuck."

Two deep breaths later, Jane had composed herself. She had to go back to the man.

She edged closer again.

The murmuring was lower now, but the same words. "Pea boo, pea boo, sea sea sea, too too too."

The eerie noise sounded like a sentence she'd heard before, but she couldn't make it out.

"Pea boo, sea sea, too too. Pea boo, sea sea, too

too." The man's voice grew louder as she lifted the branch again.

His eyes were still white, and his hands shook manically. White spittle gathered at the edges of his mouth. "Pea boo, see, too. pea boo, see, too."

"Are you okay, sir?" Jane shouted and grabbed one of the man's hands, trying her best to settle the demented figure. She shook him. "Are you okay, sir? Please wake up."

His voice grew louder as he tensed up into a catatonic state. "Peak boo. Peak boo."

"Please, sir. Wake up. Please," she begged and shook him one more time.

The man's convulsions stopped, and she released her hold on his wrist.

His eyes stayed rolled back and he jarred upright, in front of her face, with his arms outstretched.

"Holly mother of divine God," she shouted.

The zombie-like creature was going to kill her.

"Peek-a-boo, I see you," the man shouted, then he fell back into the bushes.

Jane screamed and pushed back from the man. She fell on the manicured lawn.

The sun shone down on her as she lay there, adrenaline coursing through her body. She trembled from head to foot, but couldn't make herself move. All her limbs felt paralyzed, frozen with fear. In a pins-and-needles state.

She closed her eyes when darkness encroached and she couldn't fight it.

14

SPECTRUM

The eight heads of state stood lined up outside the hotel in Hong Kong. Dress ranged from suits to smart-casual to rolled up sleeves.

The Russian and US presidents were in the middle of the group.

Everyone was putting on a brave face, one of unison and togetherness; masking the reality of the discussions.

A large gathering of paparazzi and TV crews were assembled behind a long barrier.

The whole world was watching them now.

Journalists were standing outside the cordon fence, backs to the action as they sent their live broadcast back to their respective studios. A number of reporters were trying to ask a few impromptu questions, trying to get a scoop.

"Rebecca Crawford here, from WDCTV. Do you

have an agreement on what the best course of action will be? Are we gonna nuke the thing?"

"Oh, you betcha. We're gonna knock that sucker out of the park," the US president said with a smile.

The personal assistants and delegates of the heads of state started ushering them back into the hotel, allowing their superiors to lead the way, and the delegates followed suit.

Rebecca scurried over to the end of the barrier beside the wall of the hotel. "Timmy, hey Timmy," she said waving her hands toward Dr. Carlton.

He smiled and looked around as he made his way over to her. "Hi, Becky, didn't think I'd see you out here so soon."

"Timmy. Here you are with all the big boys. You're some operator."

Dr. Carlton giggled like a teenager.

"You got any info for me, Tim? Please. They're feeding me scraps here."

"Umm! I'm sorry, Becky. I really don't. I'm not allowed give any info out anyway." He looked her up and down and fixed his hair.

Rebecca reached over the barrier and fixed his tie. "Look at you, Timmy. You need to look handsome when you're in the company of all these important guys in their suits. You gotta look your best, and you're so stiff. You need to loosen up and act like you belong here. You're the brains of the operation, Dr. Timothy Carlton. You're the hero. Not them." She put her hand on his bicep and squeezed. "You're the hero, Timmy, not these political airheads."

"Yeah, okay. I'll do that so. I'll try that so…" he said, with an obvious nervous edge.

She had him now. "You gonna help me out, Timmy?" Rebecca flashed him a seductive once-over. "I need some info, you gotta give me something."

"Becky, I really can't."

"Well. How's about we go for a drink tonight? Just me and you. We'll loosen up, and figure out what you can and can't say. It'll be all off the record, of course." She moved her focus from his bicep and started fixing his hair.

Seduce this simpleton, he's not the smartest one here. I am. Rebecca wasn't one for taking no for an answer.

"Umm. Okay. I'll call you about eight?"

"Yup. That's great, now you go get 'em, champ." She punched his shoulder playfully and winked.

Dr. Carlton rushed away, following the delegates. He waved back at her as he entered the hotel.

The UK Prime Minister addressed the attendees in the conference room. "Thanks for joining us, Dr. Carlton. We'll get cracking. Time is of the essence. So, can someone tell me how we get these nuclear explosives up onto the asteroid?"

Eva put her hand up.

The Japanese Prime Minister smiled. "Come on. You're not in school now. No need for the raised hand. We're all equal in this room. Speak up, my dear," he said, as if the condescendence was an encouragement.

The Russian and US presidents scoffed with sounds, likely at the sentiment. The in-stereo ridicule seemed to be duly noted by the other six heads of state.

She glanced at her notes and stood. "The European Space Agency, represented here by the UK, France, Germany, Italy, and Canada; along with seventeen other unrepresented countries have launched a space probe towards the asteroid. The device is equipped with an infrared sensor, which will give us a very accurate reading as to what the asteroid is made of. There is also LIDAR equipment on the probe—that's a Light Detection and Ranging device— which will create an accurate three-dimensional image of the asteroid, so we can figure out its volume. It basically scans the asteroid with a laser."

"Can you tell us what it might be made of and what the ramifications might be from this probe? How important is the probe?" the Italian president asked. He hadn't said much over the course of their numerous meetings, so it was as if he needed to put in his two cents.

"Yes, sir. The probe is extremely important. We can use the infrared light to detect what color spectrum the asteroid is in."

The deep baritone of Eva's Churchill-like adversary piped up again. "Spectrum comes from the Latin for Light, I'll have you know," he said knowingly.

She smiled, ignoring the interruption. "Yes, that's actually quite true. That's where we get the name Spectroscope from." Eva looked at Aaron, he smiled back to her.

All eyes were on her.

She felt the hush of the room listening to her as she educated them.

A rare thing for these people; to have an

intelligent beautiful young woman educate them, she joked to herself.

"The asteroid will give off certain light spectrums, which will also help determine the make-up. The infrared probe is a very modern way of accomplishing this in space. It has to be relatively close before we get some very good information back. The light will be examined and matched with different spectra of certain elements and compounds. For example, if you look at an amber street light, its composition is usually made from the sodium gas, which is in the bulb. The white lights you might get at home have mercury vapor in them. Different elements have a different color spectrum."

"A bit like a DNA profile of light, would you say?" the UK dignitary asked, as he looked down the length of his nose at her.

"Exactly." She smiled. "You were paying attention. I'm honored."

Laughter rolled throughout the room; even the grumpy old man cracked a smile.

Eva smirked and sat down.

President Jameson stood and cleared his throat. "I must say, the importance of the probe cannot be underestimated. The device will technically decide if we're going to blow up the asteroid or deflect it." He pinned her with a hard stare. "Do you have any idea when it'll be close enough for our first real analysis as to what we are dealing with?"

She stood again. "We sent it yesterday. It should be close enough to the asteroid to give us a ninety-nine percent indication later this evening. To answer the Italian Prime Minister's other question, if the asteroid is made of iron, we will not have enough time to drill into it. If it's a type of sandstone, we may be able to drill and detonate the nuclear bombs."

15

WAKE UP

Jane slowly opened her eyes and allowed the light enter them. She winced and crushed them shut as the intensity reached her pain threshold.

A dark contrasting figure stood above her, shouting inaudible instructions.

She could only make out a dull bass voice. She tried to open her eyes again and her vision started to focus on the dark blur.

Where was she?

The dull inquires floated in and out of her senses.

"Are you okay? Can you hear me?"

Jane focused on the person. She took a deep breath and regretted it immediately. The smell of the man nearly made her gag. She finally looked at the homeless man. Apprehension washed over her body.

He had bright blue eyes. They were kind eyes, not what she'd anticipated.

A breath of relief—at least a little bit—whooshed out.

"Are you, all right? You fainted. Passed out."

His voice was definitely not what she expected. It sounded normal to her. Familiar, friendly, articulate and pronounced. Educated.

"I'm fine." Jane dragged her palm across her face. She covered her mouth as the fear washed away.

An inquisitive acceptance had taken over. Almost like a light switch had been switched on inside her soul.

She felt calm and still, but had never felt so alive, like she could feel things in slow motion. The trauma had ended, but the adrenalin remained.

If he was going to hurt me, he would have done it by now. He doesn't' sound like a bum. He sounds educated.

She managed to sit up. "I'm fine. Are you going to hurt me?"

"Hurt you? Why the hell would I hurt you? I've never harmed one of God's creatures in my life."

"God's creatures. Am I one of them? Is that a good thing or a bad thing?"

"We're all God's creatures. Even the bad ones," he replied.

"And you're not a bad one?" Jane asked as he helped her to her feet.

"Just because I look like a bum, and come across as a mental case on the loose, doesn't mean I *am* a bum and, or, a real mental case on the loose. Don't judge a book by its cover!" He picked up his belongings from the ground. His hat, and his battered nickel-lined paper cup he likely used for begging.

"Are you okay after your seizure?"

"I am," he said.

"You look a bit young to be a homeless person."

"Again, book…cover."

Jane wanted to go back to Dr. Jacob's office. "Thanks for the help." An awkward pause filled the air between them. "Okay, well, I'd better be off." She started walking backward into the grass.

He gave a small wave from his hip.

She turned on her heel and walked slowly back to the window.

The homeless man stood there watching her; she could feel his eyes still on her.

After a few steps, her curiosity got the better of her. She whirled back to the man. "Do you have a name?"

"What do you think?"

"Umm. Yes."

"Correct."

"What is it?"

"Corey. My street name is Coco. You?"

"Me? Jane."

Corey laughed. "Me, Tarzan."

She smiled. "What was happening to you in the bush? Your eyes were in the back of your head. Then, your arms were outstretched in front of you."

He winced. "I could ask you the same thing. You were passed out on the ground. One could've figured you were a student who was high or drunk or something."

"Yes. I'm a student. You know, someone once told me not to judge a book by its cover!"

Corey closed the distance to her, one step at a time.

Jane wasn't bothered by the pace of his approach. It was slow enough for her to process the potential danger. She didn't have many friends, so even a bum was on her list of potentials.

His demeanor was completely different from his appearance. She could see a gentle soul behind the façade

The majority of homeless people had ended up in poverty or become homeless due to the lack of affordable housing, but there are a considerable number of people who choose to be homeless.

"If you must know, I passed out, because I saw you having some sort of seizure. Eyes rolled into the back of your head and white froth foaming at your mouth." She reenacted parts of her story. "Then your arms stretched out in front of you and you sat upright like a fucking zombie. That's why I passed out. I nearly pissed myself." She shook her head as the homeless fella looked towards his crotch area on the queue of, 'I nearly pissed myself'.

I'd say this guy has pissed himself a few times, going by the smell of him.

"And I challenge any twenty-two-year-old girl in the world to try and not pass out at the sight of, what they believed to be, a real-life zombie."

"Hmmm. It wouldn't be a real-life zombie, would it?" Corey teased. "Probably a dead-life zombie."

"No. It would be real-life from my perspective; dead-life, from the zombie's perspective."

"Sounds about right," he accepted. "By the way, I'm not old. It's just my outfit that makes me look old. Early forties!"

"Yeah. Your outfit, your unkempt hair, your

beard, your nails, the wino-tan."

"Ouch! You don't hold back, do you? You got any friends?" he asked sarcastically.

Jane digested the passive-aggressive insult. "I wouldn't have passed out if it wasn't for all this asteroid crap. I thought an alien had landed or something and was going to kill me."

"That's a fair point. I've seen aliens before."

"Really?"

"No." Corey laughed. "Aliens wouldn't invade earth and dress like me. Why would they circumnavigate the universe at over one hundred and eighty-six thousand miles per second, just to show up looking like a bum?"

Jane blinked as she thought of where she'd heard that number before. "Wait. The speed of light?"

"Yup. Well done."

She smiled. "Do you like space and stuff?" She immediately regretted using, 'stuff.' He was likely to think she was stupid.

"You mean astrophysics?" he asked, with a chuckle. "Don't judge a book by its cover!"

She whirled away again at his repetition. "Yes. Of course, I meant astrophysics." Jane didn't know this guy, and he had the nerve to make fun of her? She crossed him off the potential friend list.

Corey came after her. "Okay, okay. I'm sorry. I was just teasing. I was just getting you back for calling me a bum."

"But you *are* a bum."

"Umm. Technically yes. But I'm not, really. I just like the anonymity."

Jane headed slowly back toward the window.

"Why don't you stay in the university for a while? It's kind of abandoned; with all the asteroid stuff going on." She climbed in. "Come on. There's no one here at all."

He nimbly climbed in after her. "What were you doing in Aaron's office, anyway?"

"What were *you* doing peeping into his office anyway?" she retorted. "How do you know it's Dr. Jacob's office? Do you know him?"

Corey didn't answer.

They exited the utility room and went back into the office.

Her new 'friend' looked at the professor's chair, his desk, then cast his eyes over the cluttered computer area, no doubt noticing the Post-it's stuck to the side of the screen.

Jane went to the door to check if the keycard worked. In case Dr. Deen had given her the wrong key.

Always good to double check things. Especially when you wonder how on earth that particular person became a professor in the first place.

She listened for the beep as she passed the card across the sensor.

A sniffle sounded over her shoulder. When she glanced over, Corey was holding one hand to his mouth and a picture in his other hand. His eyes were filling up, as if he was overcome.

The photo was the one she'd peered at for so long.

His thumb obscured Dr. Jacobs, and half of the little boy's face.

Corey was obviously very upset; his stare seemed

to be focused on the woman. He sniffled again, as if trying to hold back tears.

Jane frowned. "Are you okay, Corey?"

"It's Coco, Jane; my street name."

She reared back a step. He'd barked at her, as if she was the cause of his distress. "You're not on the street now, Corey. Are you okay? Who's that person? That's Aaron's wife, yeah? Who is she to you?"

"His former wife. She's dead."

"How do you know her?" She could see the resemblance in his face even past the beard and the scruffy look. "She's your sister?"

"Yeah. Aaron was my brother-in-law."

"Oh. I'm so sorry." Jane put her arm awkwardly around him. She didn't have much experience in comforting someone, but she wanted to try. It was the best she could do.

Corey nodded. "It's okay. She's in a better place. She lost her mind. She did something horrible." He placed the picture down on the desk. "Okay, let's get out of here."

Jane was about to ask a pertinent question. He looked at her and gave the slightest shake of the head.

Hmm. I'll ask that question another time maybe!

"Yeah, okay. I was gonna go to the remote observatory. I have a keycard, which should get us in. Do you want to come with me? We can talk about it there."

"Hmmm. Let me check my calendar." He started flicking through an imaginary book. He licked his thumb as he turned one of the imaginary pages.

She shook her head, but couldn't help, but smile. "Come on. Let's go," she ordered.

Corey put his imaginary datebook in his pocket and followed.

Jane could appreciate the joke, a little icebreaker. He obviously liked to deflect with humor. Her own antidote to awkward situations was sarcasm.

They went past the sports' hall changing rooms.

She pointed to the men's room. "Do you want to take a shower? There're plenty of towels and toiletries in there. Everyone forgets shower gel and shampoo, so there is a basket full of stuff in the janitor's closet."

"No. I'm okay, thanks though. Where are you going by the way? You do know that the Caltech Observatory is in the middle of the Pacific Ocean, and has been closed for a number of years."

"Yes, I know that, thanks for the update," she said sarcastically.

He smiled.

"We're going to the remote observatory. It still uses the old decommissioned telescope in the Pacific Ocean, but it has a remote camera on it with pan, tilt and zoom motors to move it. Dr. Jacobs had them installed when the observatory was closed. His own little pet project before they decommissioned the whole thing." Jane opened a side door with the keycard; the lock beeped as it released.

They entered a dark stairwell, the automatic lights flickered on; they climbed three stories.

She used the keycard again to open another door at the top of the stairwell and they were able to enter the remote observatory.

Corey gazed around the room with wide eyes and his mouth agape.

She knew how he felt; she loved this place.

The beautiful, well lit, penthouse-style room had a stunning panoramic view over the entrance to the university.

The windows were tinted for comfort. There were three computers; one was hooked up to what had to be a one-hundred-inch flat screen monitor mounted on the wall.

The other computers were research desktops and personal computers. There were a few tables and chairs, a coffee machine and restroom facilities.

"This is amazing. It's like a tree house for an adult. Except it's not in a tree," he gushed.

Jane smiled. "Yes. I love it up here. It's quiet, yet has everything you need. You could almost live up here if you wanted to. It's like an oasis. Dr. Jacobs can remotely access the observatory from his house. Remote, remote, if you know what I mean."

His gaze went to the big screen. "Jesus. I think she was right!"

"Who was right?"

"My sister."

"Okay. I wasn't going to pry, but now I think I'm curious to know a little more about what happened to your sister."

"No, it's okay. I'll tell you. I have nothing to hide. Not anymore." He pointed to the live image of the asteroid on the hundred-inch monitor.

Jane toggled the joystick and pressed one of the buttons.

The telescope zoomed out to give a full view of the asteroid as it spun through space.

"Aaron must've set this up remotely. I won't mess with it too much," she said. She went to the coffee machine and started it up for the both of them,

"My sister started to become unsettled, unstable. She was hearing things; voices in her head." Corey went to a computer and sat down at the desk. "Aaron would tell me she thought the world was going to end."

Jane finished making coffee and handed him one. "Was it dementia, or something like that? The same thing happened to my aunty."

"I suppose it felt a little like that. In the end, she was diagnosed with paranoid schizophrenia. She had severe mental illness." He shook his head. "What she must've felt, going through all that…"

She poured some milk in her coffee. She wanted to hurry so all of her attention was on Corey's story. "And she already had their son, at this stage?"

"Yeah, Ben was about one, nearly two at the time. He was walking and starting to string a few words together. She loved him so much." The man was deeply upset. Corey's grave expression revealed his pain. "It was the love she had for Ben and Aaron that made everything worse."

"How bad did it get?"

"Well. You'd think suicide was as bad as it could get, but that was actually a better outcome than she intended."

What the heck does that mean?

"How could that have been a better outcome?" Jane couldn't imagine anything worse.

"She got worse and worse. She became extremely aggressive. Aaron was worried she'd injure Ben or him. I was worried sick she'd do something bad. She was my blood… So, I felt it was my problem to deal with."

"But how could her suicide be a better outcome?"

"This all went on for months. I started getting more and more anxious and worried, so I started camping outside their house, day-in, day-out. It was affecting *me* mentally now at this stage. It still is. I'm not a bum. I had a really good job, a fiancée. I had a wedding planned, a honeymoon, too. We'd even talked about having kids, the whole lot." He took a sip of coffee and stared at the floor for a few seconds. "He was fighting with her every night. The poor boy used to cry all night. I could hear them. I still do. It was like a living hell. She was on meds, but she felt they were suppressing her ideas. Her ideals. She thought the world was going to end."

"Fair enough, but why was she taking it out on Aaron so much?"

"Sorry. I shouldn't be burdening you with this story. I hardly know you."

"No. No. Go on. I know Aaron for a few years now. He has been very good to me. Anyone who is a friend of his is a friend of mine."

Corey looked up at her finally. "She blamed him. Said it would be him who would end the world. That he'd be involved in it. She was trying to warn him."

Jane clutched her coffee cup. Taking every tiny bit of comfort and warmth that it offered.

He put his hand over his mouth and rubbed his beard. "She stopped taking her meds. We didn't know she had. We couldn't watch her twenty-four/seven. She went into a sort of 'acceptance mode'. Debs— Debora was her real name, we always called her Debs or Debbie or whatever derivative of Debora we could come up with—was acting as though she was healed, like the meds were working one hundred percent. But she was *acting*. That was the point. She had us all fooled." He finished his coffee in one go. "She had one last plan." Corey went over to the sink beside the coffee machine.

Jane's eyes followed him across the room.

"She was going to kill Ben, Aaron and herself."

"Oh my God," she gasped.

"Honestly, I wouldn't be telling you this if I didn't trust you. Obviously, you have a great relationship with Aaron."

"No... I... thanks. I appreciate it." She nodded to him to continue.

"I overheard her talking to herself, explaining that she'd wait until they were both asleep and stab them to death, then do herself in after."

"Jesus Christ," Jane blurted.

"I know. Sorry, Jane. You don't need to hear this. You don't need to know any of this."

She shook her head. "No, I want to know."

He sat back down. "I approached Aaron that evening. He was with Ben. He took one look at me and told me to get away from him. I'd deteriorated into what you see now. He didn't want Ben to see me like that. I stayed outside their apartment again. Aaron put Ben to sleep and sat on the couch. He stayed there all night, trying to stay awake. But he couldn't. He fell asleep at about six in the morning. She got up and went to the kitchen. Got a knife. I screamed at the top of my lungs. I ran around to the front of the apartment and started hammering on the door."

"Oh my God. You poor thing, having to witness all this." She put her hand on his shoulder.

"A minute later, the front door opened. Aaron was standing there with blood all over him. He'd got to Debbie in time, but she turned the knife on herself. Slashed his arms. I thought she got him."

"She died." Jane swallowed another gasp.

"Yeah. Aaron had a few cuts, but he was all right. Ben wasn't touched." Corey shook his head again and smirked. "So that's why it could've been much worse."

Jane tried her best to change the subject. "So why do you still wear this outfit? Why not start over and move on with your life?"

He laughed and stood. "Because, low and behold, I started hearing voices in my head. I kept visualizing my sister's death. I became an insomniac over it all, and just roamed the streets at night. I felt anonymous; as if I belonged out there."

Sorrow washed over her. She wanted to say so much, but words wouldn't form. Finally, she pushed something out, figuring after what he'd told her, she could ask him anything. "What made you come back and look for Aaron?"

"I saw the report about the asteroid. I went to the library and used the computer. I got onto the public site where all the asteroids are tracked and was shocked when I saw the name of this one is RQ26."

"RQ26? What has that got to do with anything?"

16

STRAIGHT LINE

The US delegation reentered the conference room after a short recess.

Dr. Timothy Carlton was waiting for them. He watched everyone as they finally took their seats. "So, what do we need, and what do we have? Those are simple questions we all need to answer. Honesty is what will help us overcome the literal destruction of our family's and hometowns; of our allies, neighbors, and friends. Honesty."

A number of heads of state and delegates applauded.

Dr. Carlton smiled, but it held an obviously nervous edge, and he covered his mouth with his hand.

Aaron had stayed standing while the rest of the US delegates sat. He held a few papers. He gestured to the Brit, indicating he would like to interrupt, and Dr.

Carlton nodded. "Thank you so much, Dr. Carlton. Excellent stuff." He pinned the Japanese Prime Minister with a look. "Dear Chairperson, I have a few answers to a number of questions our esteemed colleagues were asking earlier."

The Japanese Prime Minister nodded.

"The velocities, times and masses are as follows; the Earth is traveling at approximately thirty kilometers per second around the Sun."

"Imperial please," the UK consulate bellowed.

"Well, in physics we use metric."

"Well, in here we will use both please," the grumpy British man declared.

"Thirty kilometers per second is about nineteen miles per second. With the asteroid moving at just over twenty-five kilometers per second, the distance between Earth and RQ26 is around ninety-five million kilometers. This is in a straight line, right now, as we speak. Well, as of a few moments ago, when this was handed to me from our NASA contingent."

It didn't miss his notice that the Russian president and German Chancellor were having a quiet discussion.

He had been trying not to let it distract him.

"What about the arch of the ellipse? The rotation of the earth around the sun is curved," the Russian president called without waiting for acknowledgment he could speak.

Aaron nodded. "Yes, for simplicity, we've just shown the math as-the-crow-flies. We have the trajectories calculated for the arch of the ellipse. Basically, we're just using the chord length from here to the impact zone. The asteroid will pass inside the trajectory of the planet while it's arching in its ellipse around the sun, but it'll come back into the trajectory of the asteroid in twenty days' time." He used his hands as examples of the asteroid and Earth. He raised them for all to see. "By then, the asteroid will have traveled nearly forty-three million kilometers, or twenty-seven million miles at twenty-five kilometers per second or fifteen and a half miles per second, and will intercept us."

The Russian president nodded. "Okay, okay, that's fine. I get it. We'll go as-the-crow-flies."

President Jameson cleared his throat. "Thank you, Aaron. Excellent job. I trust your guys at Caltech and NASA, who have run this simulation numerous times."

"Yes, sir," he acknowledged and took his seat.

The president extended his open palm toward the Russian president. "Congratulations to you, and your excellent use of the English language. Well done. You've come a long way."

The Russian president must've sensed sarcasm, "No, no, thank *you*, President Jameson." The US President's name was more like a slur than respectful thanks.

The Japanese Prime Minister stood up quickly. "Okay, thank you all. So, as of this second, do we know where the asteroid will hit?"

"We have Bern, Switzerland, at twelve zero one hours, local time, in twenty-days' time," the German Chancellor said.

"We have Geneva. Approximately the same. We've compensated for the gravitational pull of the planet. The asteroid will be pulled slightly lower and to the left, as you look at a normal map," one of the Russian scientists added.

Aaron felt his president's eyes on him. He scurried through a few papers and nodded. "Yeah, we have slightly lower than Zurich. Noon on that day. Local time." He sat in silence, but he was confident. The pressure to not make a mistake was presenting itself in the form of beads of sweat on his forehead.

The rest of the room held a collectively confident air, too.

Everyone seemed to be pondering the situation at hand.

The information had come from the finest minds and the fastest computers in the world. It was correct, and they all seemed to know it.

After what felt like an eternity passed, the French Premier raised his hand. "What's the situation with devastation?"

The Japanese Prime Minister read over some papers. "We're looking at an area of devastation the size of mainland Europe, with the fallout of debris and destruction protruding past Ireland, Norway, into Russia and down past the Sahara Desert, and into the lower half of Africa."

"We concur. We have an estimated kill zone of two hundred million people and, devastation to another two hundred million people," the Russian president said.

Aaron sat there motionless.

Ben should be okay. We're five thousand miles away. We should be fine.

He looked over at Eva and Louis.

Surely, they'll give Eva and Louis asylum in America for

the work they've done.

"Okay, this is all very bad, but what's the solution to the problem? Granted, we don't think we can blow it up or split it; we *can* do something, but what if everything goes wrong? Let's just say, the nukes don't work, the spaceships aren't prepared in time. What about an evacuation?" President Jameson asked, looking around the room.

No one answered.

"We can take the Brits in," the leader of the free world finished, breaking the renewed silence.

"*Oh là là.* What about the French?" the French Premiere asked.

"Sorry, we have twenty days to fly sixty million people from the UK to the US. That's three million people per day. I don't even know if we can manage that, it's a lot of people." He looked around the room again. "Right now, that's an Executive Order. We're going to show our allies we mean business, and we're going to bring them to the greatest country in the world. We have a duty to them. We're going to our private room now to organize our side of things; we'd like the UK contingent to join us."

Aaron stared over at Dr. Carlton as he gathered his things.

Eva turned to Louis and put her hand to her head. Louis comforted her.

The German Chancellor shot to his feet. "You are leaving all of us to suffer. You can't make this announcement now. It'll cause mayhem. It'll cause a stampede." His voice rose with each word, he was red-faced and shouting, pointing an accusing finger.

"Don't you dare talk to my president like that, and

don't you dare make demands of the US. We'll decide for ourselves what the best course of action is, and we'll report back to the Chair," Major Russell said. He was also standing now, and his tone mirrored the German's.

The United States and the United Kingdom delegates exited the room.

17

RQ26?

Corey took Jane's empty coffee cup and went to the sink. "RQ26. That's how they name the asteroids. When I saw the number, I got a really weird feeling about it."

She sat at one of the computers and pulled her hair back into a ponytail. "I thought the numbers were just randomly generated by the International Astronomical Union in Paris or NASA or someone. No?"

"No, there's a strict rule-set, laid out by the IAU. RQ26 for example; the first part will have the year it was discovered. It could be 2000RQ26 or 2020RQ26 or whatever. The important part is the second part. That's broken up into a few things." He paced.

"How do you mean?" Jane grabbed a piece of paper to take notes.

"You really like astronomy?" Corey asked.

"Yes."

"And you're paying attention?"

"Yes," she said, with a smile and a laugh. "I promise. I'm paying attention. You're building this up to be pretty big."

"Good. Because this isn't really all that complicated, I don't want to be wasting my time explaining if you're not going to pay attention."

She grabbed the back of her ears and grinned. "Okay, I'm all ears. Let's go."

He nodded. "Okay."

She put her index finger up. "Wait a sec. Is there any way you'd go shower? You do know how ridiculous this seems? I have a stranger dressed like a bum teaching me astrophysics."

He smirked "I'll shower if you can grasp this concept in one go. How's that?" He perched on the edge of her desk.

"Sounds great." Jane flashed a thumbs up. "Shoot."

"Twelve months in a year, so each month has a first and second half. That makes twenty-four halves. One letter from the alphabet is used for each half, but not *i* or *z*."

She quickly scribbled the alphabet with each month attached to it.

"Got it?" Corey asked when the pen stopped moving.

Jane tapped the paper. "Got it."

"So, what does *r* stand for?"

"The first half of September. Which we're in now."

"Excellent. Now here's the tricky bit!" He grinned

and stood up. He went to the window and looked out at the beautiful day.

"I'm ready," she replied, hovering her face over the page in that awkward way students always wrote in exams.

"So, each one of the second letters has a number associated to it, between one and twenty-five. We use z, but we don't use i."

She peered up from her notes, disgust written in her expression. "Are you kidding me? Who made up this formula?"

Corey put his hand to his forehead and started laughing. "I think it was the stupid French."

She scoffed.

He shushed her and continued looking out over the desolate university. "I'm only halfway through. It gets even more complicated."

She stopped laughing. "What? Okay, go on."

"Then we take the twenty-six and we multiply it by twenty-five."

Jane gestured with her pen. "You're joking, right?"

"No. I'm serious. Just bear with me, it'll work out now."

"But what do I do with the q?" She knitted her brows, staring at what she'd jotted. It didn't seem to make sense.

"That has a number associated with it, one to twenty-five, not including i."

She scanned her notes again. "Sixteen," she replied, but didn't sound confident it was actually correct.

"Yes," Corey said as he turned to her. "So that

sixteen needs to be added to the twenty-six; times twenty-five."

"Oh, for fuck's sake," she exclaimed. "Twenty-five times twenty-six." She stopped writing and turned on her computer.

"What're you doing?" he asked, tilting his head to one side.

Jane gestured to the monitor. "I'm going to use the computer to calculate the answer."

"Are you joking now? Can you not work that out on a piece of paper?"

She glared, but then arched an eyebrow. "Why should I when I have a calculator right here."

"Honestly!" He shook his head and laughed.

"You said you weren't old. Are you from that generation who told us we wouldn't always have a calculator in our pocket?" Jane pointed to her smartphone.

"Well. We have no deal if you use a calculator." This is a learning exercise."

"I suppose you make people learn formulas?"

"Of course, I do!"

"Aaron said his teacher used to tell him never to memorize something that he could look up."

"Aaron is it?"

Jane snagged a fresh piece of paper and drew two diagonal parallel lines up-the-way from left to right. Then moved down and across the page about half way and drew five more lines, parallel to the original two. "This represents my twenty-five. Two lines and five lines," she said, as she continued, adding two lines perpendicular and intersecting to the original two sets of lines.

She moved halfway up the page and drew six more intersecting lines. "These lines represent my twenty-six. The two lines and the six lines. They are intersecting my other lines."

The shape she'd sketched was like a diamond, with the number of lines representing the numbers she was trying to multiply.

She drew a circle around the left intersection and a circle round the right intersection; then an oval around the middle top and bottom intersections.

Jane muttered as she started counting the number of intersections that the five and six lines made. "Thirty," she announced. She looked up at Corey.

He offered a smile.

She drew a zero over the right intersection and carried the three as she started counting the top intersection, where the two lines crossed the six lines. "Twelve." She wrote '*twelve*' in the middle area and started counting the lines of intersection between the two and five bottom lines. "Ten," she said as she wrote the number ten beside the '*twelve*' and '*three*'. "Ten plus twelve plus three is twenty-five."

"You could hear a pin drop," he said jokingly.

"Shush," she said. Jane carried the two and started counting the intersections between the two by two lines. "Four plus two is six." She placed the pen on the table and made eye contact with him. "Six hundred and fifty."

Corey beamed. "It's brilliant. Absolutely love that way of multiplication. The Japanese Multiplication Method."

She smiled.

He patted her back. "It's easily one of my favorite

ways to teach first graders how to multiply. It's remedial."

Jane stopped smiling. "Look, I did the sum. I got the answer."

"It's not your fault. It's mine. Society's fault. We give you computers, smartphones, calculators. You never have an opportunity to actually calculate numbers in real life anymore." Corey wasn't trying to patronize her, but her expression shouted she thought he was.

"Maybe we don't need to. Maybe the curriculum is outdated." Jane didn't sound impressed with him.

He nodded. "Yes, and maybe you need to add the q to your answer."

"Six hundred and fifty plus q. Q is sixteen. Six hundred and sixty-six. Are you for real? Six, six, six."

"Yes. That's the answer. Well done. As promised, I'll take a shower and for completing the sum in the most elaborate way possible, I'll even have a shave."

She smirked. Was he joking? She cocked her head to one side and studied him. "So. You're telling me you're basing the whole 'end of the world theory' on a coincidence that this, ridiculous in my view, the numbering system is coming out as six, six, six? How do you know all this? How are you so smart? What the hell are you *not* telling me, Corey? Seriously." She was getting more annoyed as she questioned him.

"I might even cut my fingernails." He seemed to be ignoring her demands.

"Tell me, how do you know all this stuff?"

Corey sat beside her again. "I used to work here,

many years ago. I was a colleague of Aaron's, that's how he met my sister."

"Did you know him well?"

"He was my best friend. But after everything that's happened to us over the past number of years, it caused us to become estranged."

"So, you're not friends with him anymore?"

"Nope," he said as he pressed his lips together.

Jane returned to her pages and calculations. "Honestly, are you serious? Six, six, six!"

"Yes. Jane. Yes, I am. Forgive me if it freaks me out a little," he snapped.

She smacked her lips shut and stared. What the hell sort of trauma this man must've suffered; what trauma he was still going through.

"Oh, and Jane, maybe the fact that there *is* an 'end of the world' asteroid heading its way to Earth is another indication of the end of the planet. Not just the *six, six, six*." His last three words were a pretty good impression of him imitating her voice.

"Okay, Corey. Sorry. I was joking a little, too. I hardly know you. I'm trying to help you."

He seemed to take breath. "Okay. I know. Sorry. It's just a lot to fathom. That seizure I had today. They're getting more and more common. More and more vivid. I can see something happening. It's getting closer. I just can't make it out properly. I need more time to figure this out. It's something big, I mean bigger than the asteroid hitting the earth. That's just the tip of the iceberg."

Jane stood and hovered over him, looked him in the eye. "Corey. There's a lot going on here. I'm on your side. Why don't we just take a break? You get cleaned up and we'll start afresh." She kept her voice low, gentle.

"Okay. I'll go to the men's changing rooms. You said there was shampoo and stuff there?"

"Yeah. There's also a lost and found cabinet between both changing rooms. Students are constantly leaving shampoo and other toiletries along with sweatpants, and different items of clothing behind. You'd be surprised at what some people forget and never come back for."

"Okay. I'll be back in fifteen minutes." Corey held out his hand for the keycard.

She pulled a face. "Fifteen? Could you not make it thirty or forty minutes?"

His grin was slow and wide. "Thanks, Jane. You've taken a serious leap of faith with me today. You're a genuinely special woman."

Damn straight I have.

She stayed at the computer and logged on with her university credentials. She heard the door close, as her new friend left the observatory.

Jane checked to see if he was gone. Then opened her email and started addressing one to Dr. Aaron Jacobs.

18

STALEMATE

Aaron was in the United States' private room, along with the entire US contingent and most of the United Kingdom delegates.

Dr. Carlton was the last person to leave the main conference room. He waved his arms, and all eyes landed on him. "Guys, they're going ballistic out there. Excuse the pun!"

"Let them. We won't make any hasty decisions. We'll let them sweat for a while, and see how hostile they get. That'll determine how we will respond," President Jameson calmly interjected.

Major Russell cleared his throat. "That's the best option. We'll wait and see, but don't be fooled when these guys start turning on us."

The president waved off the military man's warnings. "The Russians will have to realize it's them who have to help the French and the Germans.

There's no way we can get them all into our country on such short notice."

Should I say something about Eva and Louis, or hold out for a while?

Eva was also at the table, since she'd been given special access to the US chambers. She shook her head, making her dark hair dance over her shoulders. "With respect, we have to do something, President Jameson. We can't just leave everyone to die."

"We will do something. I'll see to it that you and your immediate family are looked after in the US," he answered with a smile.

Aaron sighed with relief.

"I'm not concerned about me and my family. I'm concerned about my whole country, as well as the others in danger, President Jameson." Although she seemed calm, her accent thickened, conveying her anger. Her eyes flashed, and he was grateful she wasn't looking at him like that.

The president placed his hands out as if to calm her. "Dr. Monnier, I'm not in charge of this asteroid. I didn't plan it. There is no point in shouting."

Aaron put his hand on her shoulder and squeezed. "Eva, let's just all take a break. Everyone, actually, just get something to eat. Make a call to loved ones, and try and refocus our efforts. We have a lot riding on this. Let's not get side-tracked. We're all on the same team."

Major Russell nodded. "Everyone, please take thirty minutes, but if I hear of one single word being leaked from this office to the press, I'll have all non-US delegates removed from this office."

"Here, here. I'll second that. We don't like snitches!" The president smiled at his joke, but his voice and expression were deadly serious.

Aaron shook his head but wanted to focus on comforting Eva.

She knocked his hand off her shoulder. "Aaron, why do you keep talking over me every time I'm saying something?"

He pulled back immediately, a bit shocked. "I'm sorry. I'm just trying to protect you."

"I don't need you to protect me. Why can't you see that? It's not *your* job to protect me."

He scratched his head; he hadn't seen this side to Eva before. He hoped he hadn't screwed up permanently with her. "I'm sorry. I won't do it again. I just don't want you to get on the wrong side of these guys. They'll shut you out if you go against them all the time."

Her brows drew tight and a frown marred her pretty face. "They'll shut me out. How do you mean? Me personally?"

He put his hand on her forearm. "No, Eva. You, your family, your country. They don't *need* to help you." Aaron pleaded with her. "Listen, you've done a lot of great work here. You're an important part of this process. We need you. I really care about you, and want you on the team, but if you keep losing your temper with people, you're going to be out in the cold."

Eva slipped her arm out of his grip again, until their hands met. She grabbed his hand. "Okay, I'll try not to be so hotheaded. These bloody men are moving too slow for me."

He stood tall above her, too tall for his liking as he was bearing straight down over her cleavage. He looked away immediately. Aaron smiled, as he watched how she gestured twice as much with one hand since the other wasn't free. "I have to call my son. I'll be right back. Just take a break and get something to eat."

"I will. Thanks." She released him.

He went to a quiet part of the hotel to make his call. He could feel the blood coursing through his veins faster than usual.

The Eva effect!

Katie answered. "Hi, Aaron," she said, excitement in her voice.

"Hi, Katie, how are you?"

"I'm good, wait a sec, and I'll put you on video."

His sister-in-law and Ben both appeared on his screen.

"Hi, Daddy!" His son beamed.

"Hello, my little man. How are you? Are you being good for Katie?" Aaron choked back a tear as he watched his son. The stress was beginning to tip him over.

"I've been a really good boy." The child nodded, his smile never wavered.

"He couldn't have been better. He's the best little boy to look after," she confirmed, also wearing a broad grin.

Aaron was delighted that they were so happy together. Although, the sight of Debora's sister with Ben was confusing. She looked so much like his wife that he couldn't help but imagine Debs was alive and well and sitting there enjoying her time with their boy.

"When are you coming home, Daddy?" his son asked, ever inquisitive.

"I'll be home in a couple of days. We're nearly

done here. Just putting the plan into action. Once that plan is a 'go', it'll be out of our hands."

"Are you going to be going to the moon?" Ben asked. His innocent face was open with his curiosity.

Aaron laughed. "No, actually this will be an unmanned mission. Or an *un-astronauted* mission."

"Tell Daddy about your new song," Katie said.

"You have a song, really?"

Relief, pride and a little excitement washed over him. It'd been a stressful couple of days.

He might've discovered the asteroid with Eva, but neither of them had expected to be so involved with the advice and input to the heads of state.

It wasn't technically out of his comfort zone, but was definitely a hell of a lot more involved than he'd prepared for. He was a professor. Not a superhero.

Aaron sat on the edge of a pillar in the hotel lobby. The place was empty except for some security officers. "What's the song, buddy? Sing it for me."

"Okay, Daddy."

"Just to let you know, I had nothing to do with this. I don't know where he got it. Oh, and it has actions." Katie giggled.

Aaron grinned. "I don't care. I want to see it. I'm ready."

Ben was in full view of the camera as he started his performance. His little voice carried in song, high and melodic. "*There is a moon down my pants and it really likes to dance.*"

The little boy whirled as he watched.

"*Half-moon, full moon, it'll put you in a trance!*" Ben flashed his butt as he sang the ending.

He pulled his cell to his chest in case anyone

could see it. "What the hell was that?" He couldn't stop laughing. It might be inappropriate, but it was hilarious.

"Wait, wait, there's more," Katie said.

"I'm not sure I want to see anymore," he admitted.

Ben continued anyway. *"There's a sun on my bum and it really likes to drum."* Again, he turned around quickly and started drumming on his butt.

His sister-in-law was laughing as she returned the video back to herself. "I'm sorry, Aaron. But it was just too funny. We had to show it to you."

Aaron was half-mortified but was keeping in line with the juvenile tone of it, for his son's benefit. "Honestly, Katie. You've been watching that kid a couple of days, and look what you've done to him." He laughed again.

Katie obviously thought the whole thing was hilarious, and so did his son.

Their giggles certainly made him smile. He missed them both.

"I love you, Daddy!" Ben announced. "I miss you so much and can't wait for you to come home. You're the best dad ever."

His cell beeped, notifying of an incoming email.

"I love you too, buddy. I'll be home really soon. I can't wait to hang out with you."

"Aaron, be honest with me, are we in any danger? What's going to happen to Europe, and will it have a knock-on effect on us?" she asked seriously, no trace of her earlier laughter.

He didn't want to lie. "Listen, I can't say too much, but we're going to be fine. Right now, we're working on a plan. We have it finalized, sort of. We're just working on logistics."

"So, can you guarantee that nothing will happen to the United States?" Katie frowned.

Aaron took a quick look at his cell. There was a message from Jane Stanley, his student. "Yes, Katie," he said. He held the cell phone up again and read the subject line.

'Met your homeless brother-in-law.'

Confusion and a little shock rolled over him. "Katie, I'll have to call you back. I gotta go."

"Wait! Why, Aaron? What's going on? I need to know. Your son's here. I'm responsible for him. I need to know. I'm not going to tell anyone. I promise."

He sighed. Had no choice but to give her something. "It's about your brother," he confessed.

"Corey? What about him?"

"I think he may have shown up. I spotted him a few days ago at the university."

Katie was shaking so much her picture wobbled, as if she was jarring her cellphone, too. "Where is he?"

"He's at Caltech. I'll make a call and call you right back."

His sister-in-law started crying. "Okay, I'll put Ben to bed now. Just let me know if Corey's all right." The words were barely audible; tears were rolling down her cheeks now. She was becoming inconsolable.

He ended the call. He needed a breather. "Five years. Jesus Christ," he said. He was drained, and he hadn't even read the whole email.

Could this day get any more strenuous?

"Yes," he muttered as he opened the message from Jane.

Hi Dr. Jacobs,

I'm in the observatory. I got the key off Dr. Deen. I bumped into this homeless guy. He was having convulsions and nearly scared the life out of me. But it's all good now. He says he's your brother-in-law. He seems really nice. The university has basically been abandoned, so I told him he could come in here and crash for a bit. We've come up with a few hypotheses in relation to the asteroid. Corey thinks it's something really big. Something worse than the asteroid hitting Earth is going to happen. Actually, I think he believes you're going to make a mistake and cause something catastrophic to happen. Like you're going to make the world end. He's adamant about it! He was also discussing with me how RQ26 has something to do with Six, Six, Six, the number of the devil or something. Anyway...'

"Oh man! This is perfect, just perfect." Aaron shook his head as he searched through his contacts for the landline to the remote observatory.

Eva exited the US chambers and waved her arms to get Aaron's attention. "Are you coming? The UK and US heads want to start again."

"Can you just tell them I'm on my way? I have important information I'm waiting for. I have to call someone immediately." His words sounded rushed to his own ears, but he didn't stop to explain.

She arched one dark eyebrow, but didn't question. "Yeah. No problem, I'll do that." She turned on her heel and went back to the chambers.

He paced, but when he sensed Eva was still watching him, he smiled and gave her a thumbs up. "I'll be back in a second."

The landline rang at the remote observatory only once.

"Hi," a female said by way of answer.

"Jane, is that you?" he asked.

"Yes. Are you okay?"

"Yeah. I'm good. How has Corey been acting? Has he harmed you? Is he there with you now? Just say 'wonderful' if he's beside you." Aaron was worried she was being held against her will and his brother-in-law had finally had the same breakdown his wife had had.

"No. He's not here, but he'll be back soon. Don't worry about me. Are you sure you are okay?"

"Call me on video so. I want to see," he demanded. It was the only way to prove his student wasn't being coerced into doing something she didn't want to do.

"Yeah. Okay."

Aaron switched to Jane's video feed. He could see the room now; she panned the camera around the perimeter slowly. There was no sign of Corey.

"Did he do anything to you? Did he hurt you, Jane? Please, tell me he didn't!"

"Hey! No need to worry about me," she sounded a bit surprised, and if he wasn't off his mark, maybe pleased?

"Yes, I'm worried about you. Of course, I am. There's a homeless person with a family history of psychological issues in my observatory with one of my students. And he's telling you I'm going to end the world just like his sister was telling me," Aaron shouted. His anger was in his words, he couldn't help it; why was she questioning his seriousness about the situation?

"Oh wow, that's so sweet, Aaron," she said. A

narrow smile then turned broad.

Incredulity washed over him. Had she not just heard what he'd said? Yelled? "Are you serious? How could you trust someone like that? Did you not hear me?"

"I don't judge a book by its cover," Jane said.

The door lock beeped, and Corey entered the room.

Aaron could see everything, despite the small screen of his cell.

The man's hair was slicked back, beard trimmed slightly. He was wearing a Caltech hoodie and some blue jeans, finished with a nice pair of white sneakers.

Corey didn't seem to notice that Jane was on her cell, or that she couldn't see him. His brother-in-law laughed. "You were right, Jane, you wouldn't believe what people leave behind them in those changing rooms! It's like a homeless shelter in there, every mix and match of clothes one could want!"

Then he came closer, seeming to peer at Jane's screen and squinted. He stiffened, and his smile faded.

Pretty close to how Aaron was feeling about seeing him, too.

"Hi, Aaron. How are you?"

Aaron narrowed his eyes, clutching his cell so hard the case creaked in protest. "How many fucking years, Corey? Your sister, your fiancée, your friends, and all your family," he growled.

"Yes, I know, but I was suffering. I was in a bad place. I didn't see a way back. I'd just lost my sister."

"What about Ben? What about me? You didn't even come to the funeral." He forced a breath. Had trouble controlling the rage and sorrow rolling over him. In a million years, he'd never expected Corey to show up. Aaron didn't need the reminders of hurt and memories with the problem of the asteroid demanding his attention.

"Hey, I know it's been a long time. But it'll be an even shorter one if we don't figure out what the whole catastrophe thing is all about. The *six, six, six,*" Jane broke in.

"It's nothing, Jane, just rantings of a lunatic."

"No need to speak about her like that, Aaron," Corey barked.

He growled again, but wanted to laugh. "I wasn't talking about *her*. I was talking about *you*. I have to go. I actually have real work to sort out here." He ended the call and put his hand on his forehead.

When he looked over at the door to the US chamber, Eva was still standing there.

He headed to her with a sigh. Like he needed Corey to complicate what he already had on his plate.

The pretty French scientist's brows were drawn tight, and he could feel her concern. "Everything okay? Is there something I need to know?"

"Nothing right now, I'll chat to you in private, later." Aaron moved past her, and guilt churned his gut. He hadn't meant to brush her off, but he didn't want to think about the past right now.

It could wait until after they determined if they had a future.

19

WHITEBOARD

Dr. Carlton was at the whiteboard, seeming to be calculating some numbers on the board with his Prime Minister.

They were determining the length of time it would take to evacuate the entire population of the UK.

Aaron passed by them and sat in his seat, still flustered about Corey and Jane.

He felt various eyes on him, but ignored them.

President Jameson was closest to him. "Do you want to tell us what has you so hot and bothered?"

"No, thanks." Heat burned the back of his neck. No one was supposed to notice he was upset. So much for trying for a poker face.

"Nothing to do with what's going on here?" the president asked, as he was obviously trying to figure out the severity of a situation that wasn't really his business, but it wasn't like Aaron could tell him that in so many words. "No, nothing to do with what we're doing. Just family issues back home."

The president seemed happy enough with that answer, and turned his attention to the whiteboard. "So, Dr. Carlton. What's the situation with an evacuation?"

The man in question looked over at the president and seemed to need a second to gather his thoughts. "Yes, it's doable. We're basically trying to bring in sixty million people in less than three weeks. That's three million per day; the equivalent of an airport which could bring in over one billion passengers per year. Hartsfield-Jackson Atlanta International Airport can accommodate one hundred million passengers per year. O'Hare International in Chicago can take in eight million. LAX can take over eighty million."

"I appreciate that you're not from America, Tim, but surely LAX wouldn't be counted as an airport for this operation. It's in Los Angeles, and is further from New York than London is! It's too far west," President Jameson said.

"Yes, Sir, you are quite right. We won't use any non-direct transatlantic airports, or west coast airports, in our quest to reach the three million passengers per day," Dr. Carlton allowed. He wrote *Direct Only'* on the board in red and the remaining airport names in blue as he called them out. "So, if we add Atlanta, O'Hare, JFK, Newark, Dallas-Fort Worth, Charlotte, and George Bush Airport in Houston, we should get about four hundred and thirty million passengers per year."

The president opened his mouth but Dr. Carlton plowed on.

The Brit sped past the whiteboard and heightened himself on the plinth, overlooking everyone from a slightly higher vantage point. "I know what you're all going to say, that's not even half, what about Dulles, Orlando, et-cetera, but what we're factoring in is that some of these airports are in residential areas, so they don't operate twenty-four seven. We'll be able to add an extra one hundred and fifty million passengers per year if these airports were allowed operate twenty-four-seven. We can bring the staff from the likes of LAX, San Fran, McCarran in Vegas and other west coast airports to help with the efforts. We'll need this approved by the Federal Aviation Authority, FAA, at your command, President Jameson."

"What about Canada. Canada belongs to the Queen. Don't you know?" The lady indicated to Dr. Carlton.

"Keep them out of it for now," the president sighed as he sat higher in his leather seat. He looked around the boardroom, everyone paying attention as needed. "So that gets us around the halfway mark. How are we supposed to get the rest of the people in?" He obviously wasn't going to be deterred with his questions.

"Oh, right yeah. That's easy, we just cut the takeoff and landing time delays from every eight minutes to every four minutes. That'll double our capacity."

The major shook his head. "And, may I ask, have you actually calculated this with the FAA? Can it be done? Do they have the ability?"

Aaron butted in, "It can be done, but we'll need to run it by them and then have you, Mr. President, approve it, or order it. We can include military bases too."

Dr. Carlton was about to continue, before the leader of the free world raised his pen in his hand to pause the Englishman. He seemed to examine the numbers he'd written down in front of him and shook his head, too. "So, you're telling me all we have to do is run these seven airports for twenty days, twenty-four hours per day with a plane landing and taking off every four minutes."

Dr. Carlton's eyes jolted around the room "Amm. Yes."

Aaron followed his gaze, and read shock and disbelief on most expressions. He watched as the flustered number-crunchers all around the room were working to capacity.

The president shook his head again. "This just doesn't add up for me. There aren't enough planes."

"Oh, okay. Well, we've worked out that, for example, every plane that lands in Atlanta has about one hundred and twenty passengers, where we'd be running full flights at maximum capacity. This would increase the capacity of the airport by three-fold. We'd only need one third the number of planes."

He had to admire the guy. Timmy seemed confident. He was English after all, this could be their only shot of survival.

President Jameson laughed. "Okay, they add up now. So just triple the capacity, half the takeoff and landing time gap and run twenty-four seven. Easy peasy!"

Aaron frowned. The president's attitude wasn't going to help. He couldn't be rude, but he needed to speak his mind. "Can I just say, this feels like we're working on Plan B, when we haven't even exhausted Plan A. This is a really good math brain-teaser, but it's not going to save the world, and certainly isn't going to endear us to whatever is left of the planet in three weeks' time. Besides the fact, the UK doesn't have seven equivalent airports on the other side of the Atlantic! Even if you added up every airport in the UK, then tripled the capacity, then halved the takeoff and landing time and ran twenty-four-seven, you wouldn't even get close to the sixty million you're targeting. Maybe forty or fifty at the most. Save fifty million and see how the other ten million react to that. There'll be blood on the runways." His voice had slipped into 'rant' and people were staring, but he didn't care.

The truth was the truth.

He sat down to complete silence.

Aaron observed from his seat next to the president.

Everyone was still staring. Some looked shocked, others actually had their mouths agape.

"Sorry. Just got a little over excited there." He swallowed as embarrassment heated his cheeks and he fought the urge to shove his hand through his hair. He hoped his face wasn't red.

No one said anything for a few more long seconds.

Dr. Carlton did a few quick calculations on the board. "He's right. It could work up to the forty million mark, but we'll never get everyone out. We're looking at it from the wrong point of view."

President Jameson stood up. "Okay, we've let the

Germans and Russians sweat for long enough. We'll tell them it would be unethical for us to extract the UK citizens and leave the rest of them behind. We've decided to concentrate on the original plan, and we're willing to cooperate one hundred percent."

"This will look favorably on us. What was said in this room is to stay in this room. Do you agree, Mr. President?" the UK Prime Minister said.

"I absolutely agree, ma'am. Dr. Carlton, if you could erase all those numbers on the board, that'd be great. Now, let's get back to sorting this mess out."

"Hear, Hear," the Prime Minister said, and they all gathered their things and made their way to the main conference room.

Eva could tell there was definitely something on Aaron's mind. She sat beside him, commandeering the seat the US President had vacated.

The room was clearing out, but she wanted to make sure he was okay before they followed suit.

He smiled, but it was an exhausted smile. The stress cracks were starting to show.

Her heart went out to him, she was feeling it, too.

"Hi, Eva. How are you now? You okay?"

"Don't worry about me. What about you? Are *you* okay? You're the one who's always asking me if I'm okay. Telling me to calm down and to take a breath. When really it's *me* who should be asking you to take a breath and calm down."

"I know, I know. I'm just tired, and I have a lot on my plate. Other people aren't helping, either."

"We all have a lot on our plates. Everyone in this

room. Everyone in this world."

"Yeah. Eva, I know that. But it all seems to be coming back to me and you. Me especially, because I have my president constantly asking me about life and death situations." Aaron pinned her with his serious gaze.

Good god, please don't let this guy lose it!

"Now he's asking me about situations which will put whole populations of countries at risk. Your country, my country." He dropped his head into his hands as he sat there in silence.

Le temps de briller.

"Aaron, you're doing a great job so far. We got on top of this from the start. We've put the ideas forward and saved huge amounts of time. For all you know, if we weren't working on this, it could *already* have been too late. As it stands, we have a short window of opportunity before this whole thing gets taken out of our hands. Before the asteroid gets too close so no matter how much explosive power we have it will not be enough to deflect it off course and away from Earth." Eva put her hand on his neck. She rubbed his back, gently reassuring.

He put his hand on hers, caressing.

She stilled but didn't pull away. Her heart took off, running a race.

Aaron didn't look up, but he grasped her hand and interlocked their fingers. He finally glanced up, and she froze, her face flush. His eyes were so blue.

She scanned the room to make sure they were the only two people left.

The room was clear.

"Thanks, Eva. That means a lot. I appreciate it—"

She silenced him, pressing her finger to his lips. "Shush," she ordered. Gathering all her courage, she kissed him. "We may not get this opportunity again."

She was in heaven. All the thoughts of life-threatening decisions vanished. Just the feeling of his luscious mouth on hers was enough to set her free.

Aaron pushed into the kiss and went with it with all his gentle might. He slid his fingers through her long hair.

Eva moved closer, leaving the president's chair, easing herself onto his lap.

No need for two seats when one seat will do.

She jolted upright and looked into his shocked face. She heard a noise; searched under the large conference table and watched Dr. Carlton finish gathering his computer leads and audio-visual equipment from under the head table.

He stood and closed his AV case; oblivious to what was going on in the room. He picked up his case and made his way to the main conference room, but stopped in his tracks.

Eva and Aaron halfheartedly separated seats, pretending nothing was going on.

Admiring the roof structure.

Dr. Carlton smiled as he sauntered by. "Okay. I'll just leave that to you," he said, as he passed them by.

Aaron was obviously mortified; he stuck his face into her opened shirt. The curtains of cover, hiding his red face. "Yeah. we'll be with you in a moment, Tim. Thanks," he mumbled from her chest.

"Hurry up and finish. It's just the whole world waiting for ye." Dr. Carlton left the room, beaming from ear-to-ear. His voice sounded as if it'd included a nice dollop of passive sarcasm and a sort of accidental, nerdy, snort, of what appeared to be, laughter. Like he was just as embarrassed as they were.

Eva looked over at the main door closing a bit too slowly. She began to button up her shirt. "We'll finish this later," she said seriously.

"Is that a promise?" Aaron stared her down and her body bristled with anticipation all over again.

God, I want him so bad.

"You betcha," she said as she dismounted.

"I hope it's because you like me, and not because the world's ending."

"A bit of both." She laughed. "No, but honestly. Are you okay? Who were the other people who were landing things on your plate, as you said?"

He gathered his belongings. "Just a few people back home. My brother-in-law and a student of mine."

"What were they saying to you? Is there something wrong?"

"My brother-in-law has made a connection between RQ26 and the number six hundred and sixty-six."

"How is RQ26 connected to six hundred and sixty-six?" She cocked her head, studying him.

Despite their overheated little moment, there was a tremor to his broad shoulders that betrayed the calm in his voice.

Something was scaring him.

"The asteroid count. It's sixteen for q. So, it's sixteen plus twenty-five, times twenty-six."

She calculated the result in her head. "Half twenty-six is thirteen, half of thirteen is six point five, times one hundred is six hundred and fifty." The answer dawned on her. "Plus, sixteen."

Aaron nodded. "Six hundred and sixty-six."

Eva waved her hands, clearing away all rational of the number coincidence. "It's just silly. There's nothing between RQ26 and the number six hundred and sixty-six."

He shook his head this time. "You'd think that, but my brother-in-law thinks the world is going to end and it's all going to be my fault."

"*C'est stupide*," she said, trying, in vain, to bring him back to that rational place he'd just come from. Where he'd been all this time.

They needed to be on the same page to convince the heads of state to handle this problem for the benefit of the world, and not their individual countries.

"This guy hears voices; he thinks he can see the future." Aaron grinned, but it was off somehow.

"What did he see? How does the world end? How is it *your* fault?" Her questions became more *blasé*, trying to show him visions were merely the product of ridiculous thoughts.

"He just said he thinks I'll be the root-cause, and maybe I shouldn't be involved in all this work here with the other countries. I don't know. He's not very clear. He's a deranged man who thinks he's Nostradamus or something."

"Nostradamus, the French prophet and author of '*Les Propheties*'." Eva denounced her fellow countryman with her tone. "He was a self-medicating drug addict. The only book he ever wrote which was worthwhile reading was a cookbook back in the sixteenth century. Yeah, your brother-in-law is a deranged man. A man who has visions. A man who *you* shouldn't be listening too." The more she spoke, the more her tone hardened.

"You really are a feisty woman, aren't you?" he chuckled.

She laughed, too. "You only know the half of it."

He rushed to open the door for her.

Eva, in turn quickly stepped up to open it herself. "I'm well able to open the door myself, Mr. Man."

Aaron laughed again, and let her open the door of her own accord.

She then held it open for him, with a smile. "*Rapide, rapide* your ass," she said as she playfully ushered him out of the room. "*Le président va avoir des idées sur vous et moi.*"

He smiled. "No one will be getting ideas about us."

20

ZERO PERCENT

Jane and Corey sat side-by-side in the observatory. She felt very comfortable with him after the call with Dr. Jacobs. It confirmed he was a genuine good person and she could trust him.

He reclined in his chair, as if he was the captain of a plane, talking to his co-pilot. "So, show me the asteroid in detail?"

The large high definition screen in front of them showed a mass of brownish, red, surface moving from top to bottom on the screen.

Corey panned his hand across the area. "Just give me a perspective of what's going on. Maybe we can work through what Aaron was working on, and see if we can find a mistake. Maybe we can help him, or just do something, anything, to make sure this whole thing doesn't end in disaster."

He's the smartest guy I've ever meet.

However, she wasn't too pleased with his lack of belief in her favorite professor. "You really think he's that stupid? That he'd really miss something."

"No. I think he's one of the finest minds I've ever had the privilege of getting to converse with. I think he's an absolute gentleman." His voice was earnest, showing his sincerity. He looked her in the eye and nodded. "He's a good man. He cared for my sister while she was ill. She loved him so much. I respect him for that."

"Well, why do you distrust him so much? The way you're going on, you'd think he was Mr. Perfect. How can you be so nice in one breath and so demonically dismissive in the next breath?" Jane's tone was flippant to her own ears, but she couldn't help it. She was a little jealous of a dead woman.

She had to admit it, at least to herself.

"I don't know. Maybe he comes across like he's perfect. And actually, he's as close to perfect as anyone is ever going to get. But perfect is the enemy of good. If he's ninety-nine percent right. That means we just have to be the other one percent." He pointed at the screen. "Easy, right?"

"I just think you're being hard on him," she said, trying to ease the small bit of tension that'd built up between them.

"It's because I care about him. I care about the earth, the world." Corey stuck her with a hard stare, as if to garner more attention. "I'm sure he's been hard on you before."

"Yes. He has! It's his job, he's a great teacher."

"Yes! Because he's a great teacher. A great professor. He cares about his students. He cares about you"

Jane looked into Corey's eyes for a split-second.

He was right. His beady blue eyes, accentuated by his exaggerated tan confirmed it.

"One percent. That shouldn't be too hard," she said with a smile.

"Easy," he agreed.

She took control of the joystick and zoomed out as far as it could go. "Let's start from out here, and see what's going on. We'll work our way inward and see if there is anything we notice."

Corey watched; his breathing calm and demeanor patient.

Jane zoomed out until the asteroid was just a pixel on the screen. She typed in a few commands and clicked, then drew a square over the asteroid pixel.

The telescope started to zoom in slowly as it tracked toward the square.

He pointed to the monitor. "It's definitely slowly spinning on an axis. Can we figure out what that axis is, in relation to the earth?"

"Yeah, but not on the live telescope. We'll have to model it." She used the mouse and opened one of the modeling programs. "This is open source. Anyone can access it on campus. It says Aaron was using this a few days ago."

He sat up in his chair. "We don't want to go disturbing him now. He's busy at the meeting."

You don't want him to know you're double checking his work!

"Let's start here. Let's see whatever he was using and maybe we can discover the direction he was thinking."

Jane played along and clicked open a few programs on the computer. "He has remote access to this. He used two other programs here, one being a calculus program, where he worked out a couple of different timing derivatives."

"Can we load the original simulation he put together?" Corey asked

She was feeling the same vibe; detective work. She opened the last saved simulation.

The PC made a few clicking buzzing noises and opened a three-dimensional virtual model of Earth and the asteroid.

"Press play."

Jane frowned. "Okay, bossy boots. What the hell do you think I was going to do? Just sit here and imagine what the virtual simulator was going to do? God, hold your horses!"

Corey laughed.

She pressed '*play*' on the simulation. It moved forward at a rate of about one day every few seconds. The whole simulation lasted less than a minute. It showed the asteroid and the planet's tracked collision course, as well as the date and impact of the collision, all of which were accurate to the reports that had been forwarded to the authorities.

Jane looked at Corey and shook her head. "We're not learning anything new here."

Why's he being so nosey and overbearing? He still believes Aaron's going to destroy the Earth.

"Can we use some new information to try and see if there's a more accurate date, or maybe a different area of collision? Surely we can find an improvement here."

She held her hands up. "I'll try. I can update the 2D to 3D scans of the asteroid from the telescope."

"What's that? How does it work?"

Jane gave him an inquisitive stare.

Corey shrugged his shoulders. "It has been a while. Things have moved no."

"Okay, the computer scans hundreds of 2D images and trics to convert that to a 3D replica. It'd be like, if I took photos of you from all different angles, I'd be able, well, the computer program, would be able to generate a very accurate 3D image of you. It's pretty standard stuff these days. I think my cell has something like this on it."

"Wow. That's pretty cool. Can we update it?"

Jane clicked on a few drop-down menus on the simulator. She got to the part where she could choose to update the 3D mesh or not. "No point, he's already clicked the checkbox for constant update. He's been updating this for a few days now. It's as accurate as can be expected without having the asteroid laser scanned."

"So, what've learned now, that he may not have seen a few days ago? We need to think outside the box here, Jane."

"Yeah. The only real difference—he would've seen the asteroid's own movement. Its trajectory wouldn't have changed."

Corey reclined in his chair. "Its mass wouldn't have an effect on the trajectory."

"Just on the impact zone. The kill zone."

"Yeah, well that's insignificant, really. The asteroid likely has a density of anywhere between, I don't know, light sandstone or hard heavy iron, for example."

"It would mean the destruction of most of Europe, as opposed to the destruction of *all* of Europe. Either way, it's a catastrophe!" She clicked on a program's icon, and a spreadsheet opened. "He has a few calculations here. He put in a density of 7.874 grams per cubic centimeter."

Corey stood up. "Yeah. He put in the density of iron. Okay, so the trajectory won't change, the speed won't either. So, what *has* changed?" He perched his hands on his hips. "Again, just the mass of the asteroid, which will make things better if it's lower."

Jane pointed at the asteroid and made a repeating circle with her index finger. "All I can see is; it's spinning, as you've said already. We can find the axis to the earth. Aaron wouldn't have known this until now."

"Great, let's find the axis relative to the earth."

She clicked on a little motion camera symbol, then clicked on the center of gravity of the asteroid. "The center of gravity's the only point on the spinning asteroid that will be spinning the least."

"It'll be rotating, but on its own point," he confirmed.

"Exactly. So, we'll mount our virtual reality camera to this point and direct the camera toward Earth, and we'll get a very good idea of the axis line." Jane finished her work and looked at her new friend. She paused, her hand on the mouse with the icon hovering above the *'play'* button. She smiled. "Will I press play?"

Corey scowled. "Hurry the fuck up." He smiled. She laughed.

The 3D simulator revealed a view of the earth from inside the asteroid. In turn, the asteroid was shown to be semitransparent in the video.

At the start of the simulation, the planet was directly in line with the asteroid. As the simulation began to play, the rotating axis of the asteroid in relation to the earth could be seen quite clearly.

The earth moved away from the path of the asteroid and slowly moved back into its path, finishing beside Bern, Switzerland.

Jane looked up at Corey. She was a little bit queasy. "It's spinning at ninety degrees, to how the planet is rotating."

He nodded. "It's rotating north to south, while the earth is spinning east to west."

"Yeah, that's what I see too."

He shook his head. "I'm not too sure how relevant this is to the grand scheme of things, and I'm sure the NASA guys and Europe, Russia, etcetera, will all have this information by now; but how is this relevant to Aaron?"

She shook her head, too. "I don't know. But maybe it's that zero point zero, zero one percent of the puzzle, and we need to get it to him."

Corey nodded again. "Listen, we'll just park that there and keep searching. Maybe we'll find something more significant. But at least it's a start."

21

UNDER PRESSURE

All of the delegates were in the main conference room. Each country took their allocated seats.

A loud murmur had taken over the room, as if a show or musical was just about to begin; all that was missing was an *'A'* from an oboe and the sound of the orchestra tuning up to follow.

Aaron exhaled as he watched the Japanese Prime Minister stand up and tap his water glass with a small spoon.

Here we go again.

The dinging noise penetrated the room and a hush descended.

"The evening grows late. We have some progress already, but we have a long way to go. One thing we all agree on is, time is the most important commodity that we possess. I ask the United States President to outline where they are, in relation to the evacuation of the

United Kingdom, and if we should end talks here and start the evacuation of Europe in general."

President Jameson cleared his throat and stood. "Thank you, Mr. Chairman. May I compliment you again on the excellent role you've played today."

The Prime Minister of Japan bowed before taking his seat.

"We have discussed long and hard about the pros and cons of taking people into the United States. The United Kingdom is our greatest ally, going back over one hundred years."

The German Chancellor shifted in his seat, as if uncomfortable with the speech.

"We've fought side-by-side on too many occasions." President Jameson took a sip of water. His pause was palpable. "We've come to the conclusion, that it would be unethical for us to take all the UK's citizens into the US and leave the other countries to fend for themselves. It would cause a mass exodus from Europe, and would have a knock-on effect in Russia and beyond. There would be mass hysteria, looting, and all-round chaos. This would put innocent lives at risk, and would be a recipe for disaster. I've instructed Major Russell," he gestured to the military man. "To cancel said evacuation and, to ready all of our space rockets to assist the Russians in the logistics and transportation of their nuclear devices to the United States. We entered this room as individual nations; we'll leave this room as a single one world entity."

The room exploded into spontaneous applause.

The president acknowledged the delegates' reaction with a slight nod, smile, and sat down.

The Italian president stood up and spoke with an accent of passion and body language to match. "This is excellent news, President Jameson. Our deepest thanks and gratitude must be extended to you."

The Russian president didn't stand up, but he waved his hand. "Yes. Mr. President. It's great you had the decency to turn your decision around. I hope it had nothing to do with the logistics of moving sixty-plus million people three thousand miles by air." The sarcastic comment from Russia didn't break Aaron's president's smile.

The UK Prime Minister raised a hand. "So, what's our next plan of action? I think we need to get back on track and focus on the remaining options. As far as I can see, from our discussions, blowing up the asteroid is out of the question. Do we know now what the properties of the asteroid are?"

The entire room looked at Aaron.

"Yes. We've just got word back from NASA and ESA that the infrared probe picked up signs of iron and a sandstone type rock. Basically, it's very dense, in the region of about six or seven grams per cubic centimeter."

"What is that in old money?" The UK dignitary asked. The shake of his saggy under-chin revealing his age.

"Old money! What do you mean?" Eva popped up immediately.

"Yes, what is grams per cubic centimeter in imperial form, please?" he demanded.

She laughed. "Don't you get it by now? In international physics, we use the metric system as the common language, we don't use the Imperial System anymore."

The belligerent old man was flabbergasted; he looked over at his colleague, Dr. Carlton, who in turn nodded agreement. "You've let the French take over the standards of our scientific institution?" the old bulldog asked his countryman.

"It's a much better system. It's decimalized, as opposed to your fractional system. Much easier to deal with." Aaron backed Eva's comments. He tried to keep his voice even, so the older man wouldn't be insulted.

The room came to a natural hush as he continued.

"The asteroid seems to be reasonably stable. Structurally, that is." He looked around to gauge how many delegates he'd lost at this early stage. "By structurally, I mean, if the asteroid's made of iron girders, for example, you'd join all those iron girders together with nuts and bolts, you definitely wouldn't use concrete. It is held together but could break apart very easily."

"Just wondering there, Dr. Jacobs, would it be a bit like reinforced concrete then?" Dr. Carlton asked leadingly.

"Yeah, I suppose it would, but reinforced concrete uses rebar, which is tied together in a very strategic manner. It would be strong, but not as strong as a solid block of iron. So, it's a good thing really." Aaron had some notes he'd been working on with NASA; they were a good segue to the next solution on how to tackle the asteroid. "We have some good news from NASA, regarding the deflection of the asteroid. There's a theory; not deflecting it, but slowing the asteroid down or speeding it up. Either could allow our planet to get out of the way, or not to get in front of it in the first place."

"How would we accomplish such a feat?" the UK Prime Minister asked.

Aaron's cell beeped. "Yes. Great question." He spared a tiny glance to his screen. An email from Jane.

He needed to stall the conversation, despite his very important audience. He leaned in to see the subject line. *The asteroid is spinning perpendicular to the rotation of the earth.'*

The room was hushed, waiting for his reply.

"Well, Dr. Jacobs, can you explain, to our colleagues just what that means and how we can accomplish it?" The PM's impatience was evident in her brusqueness.

"Umm, yes." He'd considered a hypothesis that the asteroid could be slowed by detonating a device in front of it. But he'd never measured that it was elongated and spinning. "I'm going to have to take a call here about this very topic."

"Who from?" President Jameson arched an eyebrow. His tone suggested Aaron shouldn't even consider leaving them, unless the person calling was important, like Top-Secret-Clearance-*important.*

He cleared his throat and his neck scorched. He was about to lie to his president—sort of. "It's from a colleague of mine who's working on this very thing." He was too embarrassed to admit one of his students might be more up to date on the asteroid than he was. "I really need to take this. It's crucial," he insisted. He shot a look to Dr. Carlton. "Tim, can you go through the deflection theory and math behind it?"

The Brit stood and whispered, "Maths. It's maths,

not math!" Emphasizing the 's' on the end of the word.

Aaron had his cell to his ear, calling Jane, even before he left the main conference room, and it was ringing.

"Hi, Dr. Jacobs. How are you?"

"Please tell me you are *not* still there with that guy?"

"Your brother-in-law? Yes. I'm still here with him."

"He's not my brother-in-law anymore. I'm a widower; that means I'm not a member of his family, by law anymore," he said as he paced the deserted marble lobby of the hotel.

She scoffed. "That's not true. Once a brother-in-law, always a brother-in-law."

He sighed. "Okay. I'm not getting into this with you right now. What're you still doing in the observatory?"

There was a shuffling noise, or something like muffled movement.

"Hi, Aaron, we're just working on your *'how to perform a controlled slowing down of a spinning elongated asteroid'* hypothesis."

"How did you know I was working on that?"

"We just checked on the last few files that were opened."

"Checked on them?" Aaron bit his lip in annoyance.

"No, we're just going over the numbers. That's all. We've come to a logical conclusion, that you can't. Not in a controlled way, that is." Corey's voice was now in his ear.

"Ha ha, very funny, Corey. Always the one for the joke. Pity you didn't invest more time in them, instead of wasting time on actual physics. At least the jokes would have been funny."

"Yeah, Aaron. It was a joke, not a dick. Don't take it so hard." He barked, his irritation as obvious as his insult.

Jane started laughing in the background.

"Can you put Jane back on please?" he demanded.

"The asteroid is spinning," she said. "We feel it'd be a bit like throwing a stick into the front wheel of someone's bicycle. It would be too uncontrollable and could make things worse by increasing the impact zone."

He went silent.

She's right, dammit.

"You still there?" she asked, jarring him.

"Yeah. I'm still here." Aaron took a breath and bit his bottom lip again. "Who figured this out? You or Corey?"

"We checked your computer, to be honest, you did. We just noticed it."

"What d'you mean? Me? How did I—?" he frowned.

"Yes. I don't mean to piss you off, but we looked at your simulation and went over the figures again. They were all correct. We couldn't find anything wrong with them."

Irritation, and a little bit of anger rolled over him. "You mean the two of you have been checking my numbers, going over my simulations?"

"Yeah. We're just trying to help. We don't mean anything bad by it." Jane's voice held the edge of a plea. Like she was begging him not to be mad at her.

He wasn't…exactly. He was aggravated that someone—not an expert by any means—felt the need to check *his* figures.

He didn't trust Corey, either.

"Okay. Thanks, Jane. I really appreciate you two geniuses checking over my work. That's really encouraging." Aaron couldn't help his sarcasm.

"No, no. We trust your calculations; we're just trying to find out if you missed anything. That's all. You would've seen it if you'd been here. It was because the telescope was tracking the asteroid, it made a more accurate 3D mesh of it, which meant the simulator realized it was spinning, north over south relative to earth."

"I know, Jane. It's because I'm going to miss something, and the world is going to end. Fucking great. That's all I need. More pressure." He ended the call.

She'd said she didn't want to piss him off; well, screw that.

He *was* pissed off, but at least he hadn't wasted fifteen minutes going through the calculations of how to slow or speed up the asteroid, with the president and all the delegates watching him.

Aaron went back to the conference room.

Checking my numbers, no one trusts me; they think I'm going to screw this up. Maybe I am going to screw this up, maybe they are all right.

Dr. Carlton was explaining the degree deflection needed to cause the asteroid to miss the earth, and how the degree would have to increase the closer it got to the planet. He paused when he noticed Aaron.

Aaron shook his head, and grabbed his previous chair. "No, you're okay. Keep going."

The German Chancellor shot a hand up. "No, wait. Can you explain the speeding up or slowing down of the asteroid? That's a brilliant theory." His accent reminded Aaron of a brilliant professor he'd once had, he always encouraged him and told him he was special. That he'd accomplish something amazing one day.

Did he speak to me as I spoke to her? No.

"We've just had new information. The asteroid is spinning, so that would make it unsafe or uncontrollable to slow the asteroid down, if even possible. We've also received information the asteroid is rotating perpendicular to the rotation of the earth," Aaron cut in, but kept it short, and he had no intention of revealing where the information had come from.

The UK Prime Minister looked confused.

Dr. Carlton stepped in with the aid of the whiteboard. "It's like this, ma'am." He drew an image of the planet and an image of the asteroid beside it. "The earth, as we know, rotates along the line of the equator." He drew an oval to indicate the equator. "The asteroid's rotating perpendicular to this." He drew an oval over the top and bottom of the asteroid.

The Prime Minister shook her head. "They're rotating at ninety degrees to each other." She put her hands together in the shape of a cross to demonstrate.

Dr. Carlton paused for a split-second, as if calculating his answer before he spoke. "Exactly, ma'am. I couldn't have said it better myself."

"This limits our options. We can't blow it up, we can't deflect it north, we can't deflect it south, we can

182

only really deflect it east or west. We had three dimensions and obliteration to work with previously, but now we're down to one dimension. Positive or negative x," Louis said from his seat beside Eva. The older man hadn't said much all day, but it was good to hear his comforting French accent now.

"Who are you? Do you mind telling us? What's your role here?" President Jameson gestured.

"Yes, of course, President. I'm with the French delegation, obviously, as I am sitting in the area of the French delegation."

This caused a ripple of laughter around the room.

"I am a professor of astrophysics, as well as the curator of the *Côte d'Azur* Observatory in Nice, where the asteroid was first discovered. Professor Louis Marchonie, at your service."

"I thought *we* discovered it." He waggled his eyebrows and shot a look toward Aaron and the major.

No one laughed.

"I'm here as a confidante and mentor to the French Prime Minister, and my esteemed colleague, Dr. Eva Monnier, respectfully."

She smiled; her pride, visible to all. Even across the room, Aaron could feel it shining from her beautiful face.

"So how come you haven't said anything all day? You're the professor, yet you haven't professed. The quiet man, seems to be the brightest man, seems kind of strange, don't you think?" President Jameson said.

"I'm no John Wayne," Louis replied. Obviously, he'd caught the president's reference to the old fifty's movie.

The president smiled.

"I've sat here in silence, mainly because I'm in awe at these amazing people in this room. They come out with answer after answer in relation to every question anyone has put to them. Aaron, Tim, and Eva are by far the youngest people in the room; half our age, Mr. President, yet they have knowledge beyond us. I sit here quietly, confidently, because I can see they're systematically going through all the options and eliminating them, one by one. So much so, we're now left with two clear options. One is basically symmetrical to the other."

Aaron could see why Eva idolized her mentor. Such an astute man. His English was perfect, but so was his French accent. A short jolly type man, who Aaron would only love to have many a drink with after this emergency has passed them all.

The stories that man could tell!

The US president started clapping as soon as Louis finished his monologue. "I completely agree."

The rest of the room followed suit. A rapturous round of applause came from all sides.

Eva's face turned puce-red as she buried her face in her notebook. She was adorable and Aaron couldn't help but smile at her and the praise.

He let the moment settle in for a few seconds. A sense of something *happening* or accomplishment had come over him. The best feeling that he'd had all week.

We got this, we're nearly there.

Dr. Carlton snorted his nervous laughter, and his Prime Minister smiled, as if she liked it.

The room quietened down of its own accord.

The Japanese Prime Minister tapped his glass

once. "Can we have a quick preview of the actions we need to address? We'll have a short recess for five minutes. Just so we're all clear in our heads where we are going from here. Maybe, Louis, you could direct us here."

"Thank you, Mr. Chairman." The older man stood as he read from his notes. He fixed his gray tweed waistcoat. "My understanding is; we basically have two options. Deflection to the west or deflection to the east. They're practically the same. Symmetrically. We need to figure out what explosive power we have, what we can send up, how fast we can do it. We need to know when that deflection will be too little to work, and still hit the planet."

"Is everyone clear on our actions going forward?" the Japanese Prime Minister addressed the room.

A muted *'yes'* was the collective answer.

Some delegates took the five-minute break as a chance to use the facilities, others decided to grab a coffee.

Eva went to Aaron and sat beside him, in the same seat the US president had formerly occupied. She was still very pleased with the round of applause and Louis' vote of confidence. "Well, hello, Mr. Hot Shot," she said flirtatiously.

"Well hello, teacher's pet," he retorted with a snigger.

She spied her mentor for a second.

He was smiling, looking at them, as if oblivious to the seriousness of what was going on. He seemed blinded by love. She felt confidence was growing again inside him. He'd found his voice, and the nerves had settled.

There were people mulling around the room, but her focus was back on Aaron. "Are you going to tell them about the six, six, six thing?"

He ducked his head down. "Please don't bring that up. They'll think we're crazy," he whispered.

"I don't think so. These countries represent hundreds of millions of people whom each have a religion. Maybe the RQ26 and the six, six, six will be seen as a positive, as a way to beat Satan himself."

He squirmed and his cheeks went red. "I'm a scientist, Eva; so are you. We shouldn't be letting a coincidence dictate *any* decisions we're making." He took her hand. "Please don't bring this up again."

"Don't bring what up?" Major Russell asked. Obviously, his proximity had allowed him to eavesdrop.

"Nothing," they said at the same time.

"What has the asteroid's name got to do with the number six, six, six?"

"It doesn't have anything to do with the asteroid. We were just joking around with some numbers. That number came up in one of our simulations. It's nothing really," she insisted. She was proud of herself for sounding completely confident as she'd played it off.

"Timmy, come over here for a second," the major called.

"Yes, sir?"

"Stop that," Major Russell said.

"Stop what?" Dr. Carlton asked.

"Saluting me. I'm not one of your countrymen."

"Oh, okay. What can I do for you, sir?"

"What do the numbers six, six, six and RQ26 have in common with each other?" The major stared at Eva and Aaron, and back at the Brit.

Oh, how Eva wished she could send him an appropriate answer so Aaron wouldn't be mad at her. The stupid man had eagle ears!

She stared Dr. Carlton down, but the stupid man didn't seem to even want to look at her.

Aaron sat beside her, his shoulders hunched and his brows drawn tight. He was angry.

"Maybe it has to do with the number of that asteroid in relation to when it was found," Dr. Carlton said as he peered at her and Aaron, then back at Major Russell.

The stupid guy was clueless, but his answer was…actually not too bad!

"Okay, thanks," the major said.

Eva sucked back a sigh, and Aaron looked relieved, too.

He'd at least relaxed a bit in his chair.

The US President returned, so she went back to the French table, as all the delegates started to return.

"We're going to start with the two deflections," the Japanese Prime Minister said, garnering everyone's attention.

"Excuse me, Mr. Chairman." Major Russell stood. "I have a question for Drs. Jacobs and Monnier."

Aaron sighed, and Eva shot him a look.

"Could Dr. Jacobs explain where the asteroid's name, RQ26 comes from?"

Her American nodded, before she could, and stood. At least the answer was an easy one. "Yes, of course, sir. Originally, it appeared on the screen when Eva clicked on the asteroid, when she discovered it. It automatically came up, as in, it was computer generated."

The major gestured for him to continue. "And what's the significance of the name? Where does it come from?"

"Well. It references what number asteroid that asteroid was, when it was discovered."

"Can you tell us what that number was, Aaron?" Major Russell prompted. His expression was open, eyes wide, as if he was processing it all. As if he was completely innocent and not on a fishing expedition.

"Yes. Six hundred and sixty-six."

There was a sudden audible inhale of shock around the room.

The Italian Prime Minister was the first to voice his concern. "*Santa Maria madre di Dio.*"

"No need for translation there, *padre*. May the Lord be good to us all," Major Russell said.

"Okay. Okay. Can we all calm down? This seems to be merely a coincidence." The UK Prime Minister held her palms flat, motioning down, toward the table.

The major didn't seem happy. "Well. Our guy here and Frenchy over there shouldn't have kept this from us. The people have a right to know."

President Jameson nodded. "Yes. People believe deeply in a lot of our countries. This is an Armageddon scenario. We should've been informed. What have you got to say for yourself, Dr. Jacobs?"

"Well, Mr. President. We—sorry, I—I just felt it didn't need to be put into the public domain so soon. The asteroid's name is public knowledge, someone would've retraced the number from it and come up with six, six, six eventually. I just thought it would cause too much mayhem if it went public too soon. Especially since we don't have a Plan 'A', Plan 'B', Plan 'C' or any plan whatsoever locked down. The religious extremes would latch onto it and make it a free for all. Declaring *'the end is nigh'*, and so on. It was a decision I made because I felt it would protect the integrity of the summit, for the time being."

"What does everyone else think about this? Should we release it? Is it of concern to us? I don't know." President Jameson cupped his chin and cocked his head to one side.

"I think the gentleman was doing the honorable thing. I think he was correct. We are scientists, not religious fanatics," Louis, who was seated beside Eva, said.

She shot her boss a look and nodded. She tended to agree. The room was warm now. Eva could feel the heat. Could feel the tension building, too. She gazed around the once comfortable clean conference room that she'd walked into a few days ago; it was looking more like a stockbroker's floor.

Paper strewn across ever table. Ties off, shirts open, sleeves rolled up, everyone working as hard as they could under extreme pressure.

"*Excusez-moi*," the Italian Prime Minister said in a mock French accent. "We are not religious fanatics, and some of us are actually *not* scientists."

"*Sei scusato*," Louis replied in an Italian accent. "You are excused. The only thing that's going to deflect that asteroid is *science*." His voice grew louder. "There's no amount of prayer, that you, or anyone in the world can say that will get that asteroid to deflect from its course. Not even a petit minuscule degree. Science. Mathematics. Calculus. Differentiation. Nuclear physics. E equals m, c, squared is the *only* thing that's going to get that asteroid away from us. A bunch of fanatics making people act crazy is going to make matters worse." He retook his seat, thumping his pen on his notes. "The young man was right to keep this to himself."

The room fell silent for a few moments. It seemed everyone needed to process.

"I respect our colleague, and his efforts to do the right thing. I think it's still the right thing to do. We need to come out with a solid plan first, then we can let the public know of the connection between the name and the number, if necessary." The Prime Minister of the United Kingdom made her feelings known.

"Can we have a show of hands for those who want to keep the number connection, an internal notion for now?" The Chairman asked.

The Italians and the Russians were the only two countries who voted to release the findings.

"So that's that. We're a group of countries who have come together as a democratic alliance. We vote democratically. Our outcomes are agreed on by the ballot, by the vote. I can only trust the alliance that we have, and hope all nations stick to the agreements that we develop today." The Japanese Prime Minister nodded as he sat down.

The Russian president stood up, knuckles pressed into the table in front of his. Seething. "Everything that happens in here is a free democratic vote. But we are not tied to anything. We are *not* pawns to the US, the UK, or any other coalition of countries who want to constantly outvote everyone else. On this occasion, we will, however, keep the information about the numeric coincidence silent." He was obviously affronted by what the Chairman had stated.

"*Sì,* we agree. We will not make these coincidences public," the Italian president stated with a definitive nod.

Major Russell glared at Aaron, his eyes promising vengeance and wrath.

Eva could see it clearly, even across the room. She cleared her throat and stood, tugging her skinny jeans down with her Converse shoes. Her palms were sweaty, and she reached for her inner confidence with both hands. Her next addition to the goings-on would be a key piece to the whole puzzle. One that would also contradict her mentor. "In relation to our only two real options at the moment, may I humbly correct my mentor and longtime friend Professor Marchonie? The two options are not symmetrical. The earth is turning, how would you say, right to left…" She tried to keep things non-technical, so the heads of state could keep up with her explanation. "If we deflect the asteroid to the right, and it doesn't clear the planet, it will make an impact into the rotation of the earth. If we deflect the asteroid to the left, it will make an impact *away* from the rotation of the earth."

"So, to reduce destruction, on the off chance that we do not successfully deflect fully, we should deflect to the left," the US President stated, but there was inquiry in his voice.

"But the earth is moving from right to left of the

asteroid, so shouldn't we deflect to the right, so that we give the planet as much time as possible to get out of the way?" Aaron asked.

Eva nodded. "Yes. These are two factors we need to calculate. It could come down to the lesser of two evils."

He smiled. "I'm glad I won't be the one who will have to make *that* decision."

She shot him a look. His words had been a tad shaky, nervous and out of place. Rather un-Aaron-like. He was having thoughts of this particular decision being the one that ended the earth. The Armageddon decision. She could easily empathize that not only did he *not* want to be the one making it, but he didn't even want to be involved in it.

The further he was from it, the less he could jinx it and cause the terrible outcome that his nearest and dearest were so politely notifying him of, constantly.

His slightly out-of-place humor was quashed with silence throughout the room.

Eva watched Aaron look around the room, as if he realized he'd just broadcast a lack of confidence.

He shook his head. "Okay. I really need to talk to my son. I'm going to need to take a break and just see what's going on back home. Excuse me."

"We're not finished here, Dr. Jacobs. We have a lot of work to do," President Jameson said, reaching for his arm.

Eva blinked. It was unlike him to be rude.
He must be really upset.

"Sorry, sir. I need a break." Aaron refused to make eye contact.

The president let him go, and Aaron left the

room.

She wanted to go after him, to see if he was alright.

Louis tapped her arm and shook his head. "No, leave him," he said.

She sat back down, but frowned.

Her mentor stood, and picked up his jacket. "We're all under a lot of stress here. Sometimes we just need a break to refocus and retrain our thoughts."

The room agreed with their standard murmur.

"Aaron has put a lot of work into coming up with good honest answers here. I'm sure he'd want us to work on logistics in his absence. This is something that the Russian and US presidents' delegates, will have to decide for themselves." Her mentor nodded as he returned to his seat.

22

OXFORD

Aaron went back to the pillars where he'd sat the last time he'd video called Ben and Katie. Perched between two pillars, he was almost hidden, alone, and grateful for it.

He looked out the window. It was late, so it was very dark.

The hotel lobby was practically empty, apart from a few delegates, most of whom were in the conference room.

The concierge staff were nowhere in sight, but off elsewhere, likely waiting to be called on at any moment.

He gazed at his screensaver, a photo of his son on the small screen. His heart broke at the thought of Ben not having a fruitful long life, not being able to enjoy it as much as he'd like to.

Emotions were running high, although it was by

no means Aaron alone. The whole world was at stake. Literally.

He opened his contacts and located Katie's information. The cell rang for a moment.

"Hi. How are you?" She answered quickly. Aaron's night time was her daytime.

"I'm good. How are you? Is Ben there?"

"He's watching cartoons. Why don't you video call us?"

A stream of tears ran down his face as the gravity of the situation ground him down. The fun and games were well and truly over. "Umm… No, it's the connection. Too many people on it at the moment. The quality would be terrible." He tried to hold back his sniffles.

"Are you okay?" she asked after a few seconds pause.

Aaron stood and composed himself. Pinched the bridge of his nose and took a deep breath as silently as he could. He really wanted to be strong, super strong for his boy, for his extended family. "I'm good, Katie, I'm good."

"Aaron, I know you're dealing with a lot over there. You're out of your comfort zone. They're piling everything on top of you. You're an amazing guy. An amazing father. You were an amazing husband. I'll never forget the look in Deb's eyes when she walked down that aisle to you. She seemed so happy and complete. You looked stunning too, by the way. I always had a little crush on you. A little bit jealous of my sis."

He laughed. One of those laughs one got after crying, where it was not so pretty, but still cute. "How the hell did you used to like *me*? We were always fighting. I thought you always thought I wasn't good enough for your sister." The sudden amusement had helped him get his bearings even more, and his voice had actually sounded normal.

"No, Aaron. I argued with you because I fancied you. I was jealous of my sister. She'd found the most handsome, smart, caring man in the world."

"That's not true." Discomfort made him dismiss her.

"Honestly. It's true. When you're a kid, you always throw snowballs at the other kid you like, not at the kid you *don't* like. It's like when Ben was going through his difficult times after Deb died, he was just looking for attention because he loves you so much."

"They were tough times," Aaron admitted, reminiscing at how much his son had lashed out.

"You handled that situation so well. I don't think I could've done it. You took care of Ben so well, and you kept your sanity after it all. It's not easy. I tried to help, but you were determined to do it yourself. You took each day, one day at a time. Look at you now. He's such a good kid."

"I know, Katie, but this is different, this isn't just Ben, this is him, you, everyone, the *whole* world. I still have memories of your sister, my wife, shouting at me, in my head, in my dreams, nightmares; she's still telling me I'm going to kill everyone."

"She was deranged. She'd lost her mind. There's nothing you or I could've done to help her more than we did. You gave her every bit of help you could find. You have *got* to stop blaming yourself. You saved Ben, and you have me here if you want me."

He squinted and shook his head.

What did she mean?

Aaron didn't dare decide if the emphasis was on the 'have me' or the 'here', as in, watching Ben if he needed.

She'd just admitted to having feelings for him, even if she'd referenced it in a way that seemed to have been years ago.

"Listen, Aaron. You know I'm here for you. But first, you need to get back in there and stop worrying about the end result. Take each day, one day at a time. One piece at a time. That's how you work best. I know you better than you think. I have faith in you. My mother once said dreams are often the opposite of what they seem. Like, death can actually mean new life. Sadness can mean something good's gonna happen. You're not going to destroy the world; you're going to *save* it. It's your destiny, I feel it."

He looked up at the ceiling of the corridor and sighed.

If you spend all this time being someone else, who's going to be you?

Somehow her pep talk felt like pressure from both sides of the spectrum. "Okay. I'll take that into consideration. Thanks, Katie."

"Do you want to talk to Ben?"

"No. I have work to do here." Despite his reservations, he was invigorated. He had to solve this.

For his son.

For the world.

"We're close to actually getting a timeline on our plan. Once I have that, it'll be out of our hands, I'll call you and make my way home," he said.

"Great, will that be soon?"

"I'm not leaving that room until we've finalized things. It'll be tomorrow when I call. Definitely."

"That's more like it. That's the Superman I know. Confident and ready. You go get'em."

"Thanks, Katie. I needed that. Nothing like a kick in the pants to get you moving."

"Okay. Chat tomorrow. Love you." She ended the call when Aaron was in mid-reply.

"I love you, too," he said to the dead air.

He heard footsteps and his gaze zoned in on a familiar female.

"Was that your son?" Eva's tone hinted at the fact she'd heard his parting words.

Aaron gazed at her. It never seemed to fade, how beautiful she was. Her dark tresses curled at the ends and swept past one of her shoulders. Her dark eyes were fathomless, so gorgeous it took his breath away. "Yes," he replied, and pocketed his cell.

"Great. The delegates are running through logistics. We'll need to liaise with them to work out the timeline so we can work out the minimum and maximum deflection degrees. They need us. Are you okay to rejoin?"

He sprung toward her.

She smiled.

"Yeah. I'm ready to roll. Let's get this done. This is really the last part for us. I can feel it."

They marched back to the large conference room together.

"We've done a lot. I think they appreciate that now. We're piecing it all together as a team," Eva agreed.

"Trust me. They wouldn't have been able to get this done so quickly without us. We're like astronomical translators."

Her smile widened. "Thank God mathematics is a universal language."

They burst through the doors like they meant business.

They did mean business.

Aaron's vigor was back since his talk with Katie. He—they—would conquer this problem.

They would save the world.

"Thank you, Drs. Jacobs and Monnier. We appreciate the work you've put in and how you have done it so efficiently," the Russian president said by way of welcome.

Aaron nodded in thanks and smiled.

"Now. We have the nuclear capabilities to deflect the asteroid and the United States has the rocket capabilities to get our part of the puzzle into space. With the help of the German high-gross aircraft, we can transport the nuclear devices to the US at the most convenient time, or fastest speed. Excuse my English," he continued in his commanding Russian accent.

"We have any amount of Saturn solid fuel rockets at hand. I know she's old, but the Saturn V is the right ship for the job. We'll utilize Kennedy Space Center, Cape Canaveral for now," President Jameson added.

Aaron covertly slid his cell from his pocket. He held it under the desk and without looking he typed,

Im going 2 call u, don't say anything just listen. Mute your cell.

He finished the message and took a glimpse to proof it, as well as to ensure he was sending it to the right contact. He flipped his cell to silent.

Aaron hit *send*, then waited a few moments before connecting a call.

When they answered, he placed the cell on his knee.

Major Russell stood, but before he opened his mouth, his gaze landed on him. "We've been working on a Planetary Defense Coordination with NASA and the UK, Oxford, and Cambridge; a joint venture for some time. It's one of the reasons Dr. Carlton's here. He was the lead liaison between the trifecta of NASA-OC. Dr. Carlton, could you run us through the joint findings from the unilateral coordination?"

The man in question addressed the crowd in his usual nerdish way. A slow start, plenty of fixing his notes and hair. He paused before speaking on a number of occasions, which screamed his discomfort. Dr. Carlton coughed. "So, as you know, everything we say in here is backed up by a team of engineers and scientists. When I write something clever on the screen, it has about ten people checking and double checking all the ins and outs of said calculation."

Jane and Corey looked at each other and smiled as the sound from the summit was broadcast from the speaker on her cellphone.

"What does this mean?" His excitement popped out a little too loud for the call.

She covered his mouth. "Shush." She pressed the *mute* button. "He sent me a text not to make any noise on our end. He must be trying to get us involved."

Corey was even more excited now. His eyes went

wide and he made a silent clap. "He must actually value our work!" he whispered.

"You can speak normally; it's on mute on our side. We can only hear him now, he can't hear us."

"It's like a bug in the G8 summit." He punched the air. "We're like spies. The name is Leonard, Corey Leonard."

"More like Corny Leonard." She smirked.

"Hey..." he said, but he smiled, too.

"Okay. Shush, Corey. We have work to do. We have to save the world."

"Do you always take things this serious?"

"Yes. Especially saving the world. Well. No. I actually take everything this serious. Even what cereal to eat in the morning. I know. I have issues."

He patted her back. "We all have issues, my dear. Saving the world isn't one of them. Trying to prevent your future husband from destroying the world is what our main goal is here."

She scowled. "Shut *up*. He's not my future husband. He's too old. And so are you, so don't get any ideas!"

Corey laughed. "You wish."

They ended their banter and listened to the 'bug', as he'd referred to it.

They heard a cough and a male English accent speak after one last pause. "So, we, or should I say 'us' so far, which will be a 'we' after it is voted on. I'll refer to 'us' as 'we' for the foreseeable future, because I know the Germans and Russians would've thought of this anyway. We will be detonating the nuclear devices approximately one kilometer from the surface of the asteroid. As you can see, the devices are relatively small in comparison to the asteroid."

Jane gawked up at their three-dimensional model on the large screen in their observatory. She could only imagine what the whole thing would look like from inside the confines of the summit meeting.

"The explosion would be massive, but the dissipating energy would be only a fraction of the resultant," the man explained.

She frowned and glanced at Corey. Confusion washed over her. "What does that even mean?"

He pulled a large shiny red apple from his hoody's front pocket. "Imagine if this was the explosion of the nuclear bomb."

She nodded as he took a massive bite out of the apple.

"Now, imagine that the bite is the piece which has an impact on the asteroid." He held his palm next to the apple bite mark. "The rest of the apple explosion would be going off into open space and would have no impact on the asteroid."

"Oh, okay. Well, why didn't that guy just say that? He sounds like a bad teacher."

Corey tilted his head and arched an eyebrow. "You shouldn't judge a book by its cover. You don't know if he *is* a teacher. I'd say he's a doctor or scientist. He wouldn't be standing up there in front of the heads of the most important countries in the world, trying to save the world, if he didn't have something to offer."

Jane scoffed. "He sounds nerdy and I bet he's confusing all the heads of state. He's definitely confusing *our* head of state."

"Oh, Jane, Oh, Jane, Oh, Jane. What will we do

with you?"

She glared in answer.

Aaron fixed the position of the cell phone on his knee as he watched Dr. Carlton pick up his glasses. The guy couldn't have looked any more cliché nerd.

He hoped Jane and Corey could hear clearly, but he didn't dare check his cell. The screen was dark and he couldn't hear anything on their end, but Jane was smart, so she'd likely put their end on mute so they wouldn't get caught.

With another cough, the Brit continued. "This is all well and good, but the real issue is getting there on time. The detonation will produce energetic neutrons. When these neutrons hit the surface of the asteroid, they'll be converted into thermal heat. They won't penetrate the surface, but just heat up the surface of the asteroid. It's made up of rock and metal. The thermal heat will cause the surface to produce ejecta, or kind of like," he used his hands to show an explosion. "Like, pressing the top of an aerosol can. This'll cause the asteroid to practically become a rocket engine itself. The ejecta will cause an equal and opposite effect, following Newton's Third Law of Motion."

"What's our timeline for getting the *Tsar II Bomba's* to the US?" Aaron asked. They needed to go over the logistics again, since they'd decided most of it when he'd been on his cell with Katie.

"Our colleague here from Germany, will transport seven *Tsar II Bomba's* to the US as of today. The chancellor has arranged for seven cargo vessels to transport each *Bomba* from each location, along with equipment and military men to the United States for us," the Russian president said, gesturing to Germany.

"Could you not transport them yourself?" The Japanese Prime Minister wanted to know.

"Yes, in an ideal world, we could. But we don't want any accidents or confusion when we try to enter American airspace. It just takes one trigger-happy gunner to make a mistake and we have an international crisis. A world crisis," Russia replied.

The US President nodded. "While it would be ideal, both our countries have an impressive working relationship with the Germans. It would be prudent to use them as our go-between, for this sensitive plan anyway."

"To answer your question, Aaron. Our planes have been preparing for the flight for the past hour. We'll need at least one days flying time. We'll need at least half a day to load and unload all the *Bomba's* safely and securely, along with the equipment and men."

"So, you need two days anyway?" Aaron asked.

"Yes," replied the chancellor.

The Russian President nodded.

Aaron made some notes. "So, we were at Time Minus Twenty Days to Impact." He looked at his watch. "Right now, that's practically Time Minus Nineteen Days. These next two days will bring us to T-17."

There was a collective nod, and murmurs of acknowledgment, and maybe some worry throughout the room.

"How long to get the Saturn V rockets to Cape Canaveral?" Aaron asked.

"It'll take five days from today, that'll bring us to T-15," the major said as he put his hand to his ear. He paused to catch something through his earpiece. "There'll be some modifications needed to each Saturn V ship, to accommodate the *Bomba's*." He pointed to Dr. Carlton.

The Brit stood again. "Oh, yeah. I was going to get to this part. Will I continue? Or do you want to keep going with the T-minus stuff?"

The UK Prime Minster cocked her head, her brows drawn tight. "No. Press on, Timothy."

"Will we take a short break? Please. It's all about velocity and slingshots and double slingshots. I honestly think we should all take a break," Dr. Carlton said.

President Jameson let out a puff of air. "Okay. I'm with Dr. Carlton on this one. Let's take a breath of fresh air. Can we get the a/c on in here? It's starting to get a bit musty." He sniffed the air like a mouse.

Eva moved to a spare seat on the outer edge of the large oval table in the summit room.

Aaron took his cell from his knee and put it into his top shirt pocket.

Dr. Carlton joined Eva, and Louis and Aaron soon followed suit.

She asked him what he was thinking about the whole process.

"I think everything is going to work out," Aaron said. Relief washed over him and he breathed a long sigh. "I reckon we have a day to spare. I'm just having all my calculations double-checked." He raised his voice so Jane and Corey wouldn't have any issue hearing him from his pocket.

Jane laughed. "I think he's starting to get us on his side."

The connection ended.

"God. The Russians still don't trust us."

"Even after all these years," Corey agreed. "What does he want us to concentrate on?"

"I'd say he wants us to concentrate on the number of days until impact."

"Sorry. No disrespect, but that was a rhetorical question." He held up two fingers. "Two things. One. He hasn't given us much to work with. Two. I'm starving. Let's go catch a few rats." He smiled at her immediate reaction.

"Oh. God. You're disgusting." She shook her head. "Are you serious?"

"No, you fool. Come on, we'll raid the cafeteria. We have half an hour. Bring the cell phone in case he calls again."

Jane pocketed her cell, and they made their way to the security door. Her cell beeped with a text and a contact number for Katie.

Give this contact to Corey. Tell him 2 call and say we have a good plan and Ill call her later. L8r

"A text for you. It's a contact for a 'Katie'."

He took the cell as they hit the stairs. "I'll give it back in a minute, Jane. Thanks."

Katie answered Corey's call when he hit the bottom of the staircase. Hearing her voice rocked him to his core, and he was overcome with emotion. Jane watched as he stood, motionless. her mouth hung open as she looked at him. What on earth was wrong with him? She held back as he put the cell phone on speaker.

He started crying and slumped to the floor, as if he couldn't help it. "Hi."

Jane heard an inaudible high pitch voice.

"No, Katie, it's me. Corey." He sobbed into the cell phone. He couldn't hold back the tears.

What must he be going through?

The years of pain. The loss of his sister came rushing back to him. The loss of Katie, by proxy, was almost as painful.

Jane was so confused at this stage. She set down the hallway, giving Corey a little bit of privacy and slid down the wall to take a seat. She heard crying at the other end of the cell phone.

Corey cried even harder when his sister started to cry, too. "I'm sorry, Katie. We lost one sister; I didn't mean to lose you, too. I was just struggling with it all."

She got off the floor and went into the stairwell to comfort Corey.

Jane silently slipped her arm around his waist, and he appreciated the comfort.

Corey smiled, but continued to talk to Katie. "I think Aaron's going to be instrumental in the deflection of the asteroid. He discovered it, you know?" She could hear the pride in his voice.

Jane reached over and pressed the video call button.

"Oh my God. Look at you!" Katie whaled.

"You haven't changed a bit sis."

"Aaron's doing great work. Ben and I are so proud of him. When you coming home, Corey? I miss you so much. I want to kick your ass so much too.

You're such a silly little man, but I love you."

He wiped some tears away. "We're helping Aaron with some of his calculations. He told us to tell you he thinks it's all going to be okay. They have a solid plan. He'll call you later."

"Oh, thanks, Corey. Thanks for letting me know. I'm worried sick here with Ben. Who is 'we,' by the way, who are you with?"

"A student of Aaron's. Jane." He flashed the camera to her. She offered a little wave and a smile. "She's a smart cookie. She helped me get my shit together today. We're going to grab a quick bite and get back to the numbers. Just really wanted to keep Aaron's mind at ease with the facts and figures; keep him focused. I'll see you tomorrow sometime maybe."

"Okay. I love you. I can't wait to see you."

"Thanks, Katie. I love you, too." Corey handed the cell back. He waited in the silence for her to say something.

Jane rubbed his shoulders for a second or two, a friendly jolt back into life. "Come on. We got stuff to do, and not a lot of time to do it."

He stared for a moment, but didn't really see her. He was still lost in his head, she felt.

"Come on, old man." She started jogging backward in the hallway, then jumped and gave a high kick. "Catch me if you can." Jane turned and dashed toward the cafeteria.

Corey smiled. She was just trying to get him to keep moving and not to dwell on the past. She was a smart girl, for sure. He sprang up and started running after her.

The university was extremely quiet; all she could

hear was the sound of their sneakers pounding down the halls along with the laughter and screams of freedom they expelled.

So often these corridors were the bane of her existence, the constant bullying, the nerd jokes, always feeling like an outsider. The release was real, as she bounded past the 'No Running' sign, then a 'No Distracted Walking' sign.

Corey passed that particular sign just as Jane turned around, and he wore a look of confusion. "What the hell is 'No Distracted Walking'?" He shook his head.

She stopped at the cafeteria. "It's when you walk while you text or you're looking down at your cell. You're not looking where you're going, so it's called 'distracted walking'."

He laughed. "We should be in the sign business. They have something for everything. Is this high school or University? For crying out loud. No wonder you guys are all *snowflakes*."

They'd reached their destination.

She twirled around with her arms outstretched. "I don't think there'll be too much need for another signage company right now. I'm just all about breaking rules at the moment. I don't give a damn anymore."

"Okay, *Fräulein*, let's get some food before we actually end up eating rats."

23

CAMBRIDGE

"You guys have all the answers, don't you?" Major Russell's voice was as patronizing as his tight, drawn expression.

Aaron scowled. Who did this guy think he was? Did he think he was addressing children? He didn't hold back his sarcasm. "Yeah. We're pretty clever."

Dr. Carlton started laughing nervously, as if he definitely wouldn't have had the nerve to say something so bold to the military man.

Remorse hit; he shouldn't be rude to someone the president valued so much. Aaron smiled, trying to show the major he wasn't serious. Or really offended. "I'm just pulling your leg, sir. It's not all about us. There are a hundred men and women behind all of our decision-making processes."

"Are there? Dr. Jacobs. Like who? The person on the other end of the phone? Don't forget, you're an

American citizen. There isn't much I can do about your cohort here, but there is a hell of a lot I can do about you sharing information that shouldn't be made public."

He swallowed. It looked like he'd landed on the bad side of the major. "Like what, Major?" He glanced over at their president. He was in the good books with the boss, so did it matter what Major Russell thought?

The man followed his gaze. "Oh. The president might like you now, but if you keep hiding stuff, your D-day will come faster than the asteroid."

Aaron wanted to laugh, but he managed to hold it back. "We'll all just work together to avoid a collision with the asteroid. That's my only goal here."

Major Russell frowned and uncharacteristically said not a word. He shook his head.

His head spun and his knees wobbled. He was aware of the major's anger, but his head went fuzzy. He couldn't focus.

Eva sucked back a gasp. Her eyes found Aaron's, but he wasn't looking at her.

He was pale and disoriented. He seemed like he was going to faint.

Louis must've had the same thought, because he quickly shifted behind Aaron so he wouldn't injure himself if he fell.

"What did you say to me, boy?" the major finally demanded.

She stuck her hand out between them. "Not now, sir. He's in trouble."

Aaron's eyes rolled into the back of his head.

"Medic," Dr. Carlton roared.

The whole room seemed to collectively look over at the commotion.

Aaron fell back into Louis' arms. Her mentor lowered them to the carpeted floor and Aaron looked demonic, pale. He sat behind him to keep his body upright.

The American had gone white and sweat dotted his brow, dampened his hair. "You'll be first, Major. You'll be first to die. We'll all die then." Slurred words drifted from his mouth in a voice that didn't sound like the man Eva had grown so fond of in such a short space of time.

She puzzled over the low statements as she stared at Aaron and Louis. She peered at the Major; a bulging vein protruding from his forehead could almost be seen beating.

"What did you say to me, boy? Are you threatening a commanding officer? Do you know who I am? I'll have you locked up!" The older man's face was red from exertion, and spittle gathered at the corners of his mouth. "You may think you've left the Marines, but once you're in the Marines, boy, you're always in the Marines. That means I *own* you. You little shit." Major Russell leaned over Aaron and put his finger in his face, continuing to rage.

Eva ignored the angry man and slid around him. She slapped Aaron's cheek as hard as she could.

Dr. Carlton wobbled, as if she'd hit him, instead.

She ignored him, too, and moved closer to her American and her boss.

Louis shook Aaron, trying to revive him.

They took turns calling his name, but the dazed expression never left his handsome face. He looked so peaceful; oddly it was the happiest Eva had ever seen him.

A number of medics arrived to help the struggling doctors of the incorrect field.

Aaron looked up at them, but his eyes were still hazy.

Her gut told her he couldn't see them, not yet. "Aaron," she said again.

"You're going to die. You're going to die!" he shouted, appearing to be addressing Major Russell again. He was pointed in the man's direction, as if he could see him, but the cloudiness was still in his eyes.

Something inside her told her he didn't know what he was saying.

She placed her hand over his mouth. She needed to shut him up, but Eva pulled her hand away from gnashing teeth.

Aaron was deranged.

The fear of him snapping one of her fingers off with his teeth was real.

He tilted his head away from her hand, and blinked twice. Then rolled his shoulders, and looked in the direction of Major Russell again. "A piece of pie. I need a piece of pie," Aaron muttered.

Eva hit her knees in front of him. She placed herself in between him and the major, hoping blocking the military man would help. She cupped his face and tugged. She needed him to look at her. "Are you okay, Aaron? What do you need? Talk to me."

"I just need a piece of pie. My sugars are low. I need some pie and a coffee with extra sugar," Aaron said as he tried to lie flat, but Louis was still holding him.

"Tea, Aaron?" Dr. Carlton asked. "With three sugars? That's what our school nurse used to give us back home."

"Sounds good, Timmy." He nodded and closed his eyes.

Dr. Carlton ran off to help the situation as best he could. "A nice cup of English tea is the solution to everything; three sugars in the tea is practically a pharmaceutical remedy for everything in the UK."

Aaron addressed the medics. "False alarm. I'm okay. Just low blood sugar."

The major stormed off. Without so much as an offer to help.

She shook her head. "What is up that guy's ass?"

"He's a major for a reason. They're born with something in their anus," Louis said.

"*Anus*," said Aaron with a smile, The French inflection propagated on the final word of her mentor's sentence.

"What the hell were you saying, Aaron? You were telling the major he was going to die and everyone's going to die. Do you want to get taken away? Get taken off the team?" Eva demanded, both hands planted on her hips. She searched his eyes, now that they were clear, like normal.

Louis stood and offered Aaron a hand.

She quickly stepped closer and offered him her hand, too.

"I'm sorry. I was having some sort of an episode. I don't know what came over me." He straightened from the floor.

They sat him on a chair just as Dr. Carlton arrived, holding treats.

He held out his wares for Aaron to inspect. "A nice warm cup of tea and a piece of apple crumble. It's basically pie, Aaron. I'm sure you'll enjoy. Three sugars of course. A mix of the best of British, the tea, and the best of America, the humble pie."

She smirked at the friendly dig between allies.

"Thanks, Tim, you're a true friend." He smiled.

Eva smiled, too and relief washed over her. He'd be okay now. She glanced at Louis, and her mentor looked as if he'd relaxed as well, and one corner of his mouth was up.

"Thank you, Aaron. I appreciate that," Dr. Carlton replied.

"I won't lie. I wasn't looking for some pie. It was the closest word to rhyme with die," Aaron said with a shrug.

The small group laughed.

"I wish I could fly, right up to the sky and I'd..." he continued, but trailed off, obviously stumped for another rhyming word.

"Make that asteroid pass right by," Dr. Carlton piped up.

Eva laughed, and her boss echoed it.

Aaron finished off the poem, "But alas, the end is nigh!"

Her smile slipped. "Nice one, Aaron. What're you trying to do, make us all cry?"

He glanced up at her. His eyes went wide as he gave her a once-over.

Did he just realize she was serious?

Aaron and her mentor exchanged a look, and

Louis smirked and shook his head.

Dr. Carlton gazed at her, then at Aaron, and started laughing.

Aaron and Louis laughed, too.

Eva gasped and frowned. "What's so bloody funny? *Petits garçons très stupides. Merde.*" She stalked off to the ladies' restroom.

No boys allowed in there, and she needed a break. They were stupid!

"We're only joking! Come back, Eva!" Aaron shouted after her.

She didn't pause her journey. She wasn't listening to the *'very stupid little boys'.*

Eva pushed the door open and glanced back as Aaron took a sip of tea.

He grimaced. An upside-down frown appeared on his face. "That's disgusting, Tim." But he took another drink.

Tim nodded and smiled, "Well, at least you're back and alive."

"For now, Tim. For now."

She closed the door behind her.

24

SWEET TOOTH

Jane and Corey rifled through all the foodstuffs that'd been left behind in the cafeteria. The vast eating area had over a thousand seats that lay empty.

The presses and cupboards, behind the large stainless steel and glass bain-marie's, were abandoned but fully stocked.

He pulled out a big bag. "Look what I found. I've got some real goodies here."

"Me too. I've found tons here," she said excitedly as she started throwing bags and bags of chips, crisps, snacks, bars of chocolate, Twinkies, gummy snakes. A candy store full of delights.

He reared back and shook his head, his eyes wide. "That's not food, you dope. That's cancer right there. That stuff will kill you."

She stopped gathering her treasure trove of goodies, he'd just drained the fun from it all. "What did *you* find then?"

He dragged the cloth bag over and showed her the contents.

"Fruit! You have a big bag of fruit. I thought you said we were here to get food."

"This *is* food," Corey said in the most patronizing voice Jane had ever heard.

She put her hands on her hips and glared. "No. If you were stuck in the wilderness in the middle of nowhere, at the height of winter, you'd want high energy, high-calorie bars of chocolate. Not apples and oranges. It's about survival." She nodded to convince him she spoke the truth. "*And* tasty," she added.

He laughed. "We're *not* stuck in the wilderness in the middle of winter. We're at a college. Anyway, your teeth would rot in a couple of weeks."

"Oh, right. You're the guy from the streets. You'd know. Coco!"

His demeanor shifted to something dark; all playfulness gone, and a glare marred his expression. "You know what, Jane?"

"What?"

"I'm beginning to figure out why you have no friends."

She stopped in her tracks, sorrow and hurt poured over her. Jane opened her mouth, but no words came out. She stalked back down the hall toward the observatory.

How could she be so destroyed by a guy she didn't know?

"Jane, you didn't get your food. Don't you want it?" Corey called. His voice betrayed a little remorse, but it didn't make her feel better.

218

"Suddenly, I'm not hungry anymore. Maybe I'm too fat as well." Jane winced at the defeat in her words. She didn't want to show him how he'd hurt her.

"Hmm. Hell, hath no fury like a woman scorned."

She ignored his last word and kept going. Until her cell rang. She heard Corey's shoes, and knew he'd followed. "Hello, Aaron," she said as she put her cell to her ear, grateful she'd sounded normal. But there was no answer.

She reached the stairs to the observatory and ascended, Corey quietly on her heels now. His stealth was the only thing to keep her wrath at bay; she wanted to lay into him.

Jane opened the doors with her keycard.

The same English-accented man could be heard on her speakerphone, even his usual cough, and a slight pause. "As we reverse-engineered our plan from the explosion to takeoff, to the logistics of it all, we realized one of the most difficult things to get right was our timing. A day late and we won't get the angle of deflection correct." He stopped again, and she imagined him looking around a room at all the attendees Aaron had mentioned. "The logistics must be firm dates. If you say it'll be here on day ten or twelve, then it simply must be here on day ten or twelve, or whatever day you firm-up."

"You're right. He's a bit much, isn't he? He does go on." Corey said, as if trying to appease her. He smiled and handed Jane a peace offering, a chocolate bar.

She frowned but snatched the bar.

I'm not finished with you.

Jane gestured to the cell phone and placed her

index finger over her lips. She hadn't muted the call, but she wanted him to listen, and she wasn't really ready to talk to him.

"If the takeoff is on time, and we're a day late to the asteroid, it can only be that we didn't travel fast enough. This area falls under the astrophysics department."

"NASA-Oxford-Cambridge to be precise."

She heard Aaron's voice and it had a jovial tone, as if he was laughing or smiling. She smiled too, remembering his handsome face.

"Okay, we get it. Now tell us about the slingshot," the familiar voice of the US President said.

The room broke into laughter, the president's impatience with the Englishman was starting to show.

Jane quickly pressed the mute button to cover her and Corey's bursts of laughter.

She offered him a smile. "You're right; he does go-on a bit."

"Yes, sir," the Brit said, assumingly answering President Jameson. "The slingshot maneuver has been in operation for about half a century. It's nothing new. In order to get to the asteroid fast enough, we'll need to speed up our ship. We can use the moon to help us. Technically, this is called a gravitational slingshot or a gravity assist maneuver. The Saturn V rockets will get up to approximately ten kilometers per second, or about six miles per second. It's like this, if you were on an overpass and a truck was close to passing under the overpass, and if you threw a tennis ball at the front of the truck with a speed of... I'll keep the numbers easy for us. If you threw the ball at fifty miles per hour, and the truck was traveling at one hundred miles per hour.

Effectively, from the driver's point of view, the ball would bounce back off the truck and would be moving away from the driver at one hundred and fifty miles per hour, but it would be traveling away, relative to the overpass, at two hundred and fifty miles per hour. This has a doubling effect of the speed of the truck on the ball."

"So, the speed will increase to twenty kilometers per second. Is that enough? Will we get there on time?" Another English accent, but this one was female.

This voice was a tad familiar, too. Like Jane had heard it on TV or something. Maybe the UK Prime Minister?

"No. We won't, but we can now perform a double slingshot," the first English accent answered with obvious excitement.

"What on earth is a double slingshot? If it was a drink, I'd order one now," President Jameson said, and it sounded like a quip.

Over the following silence, a murmur could be heard in the background of the air coming over the call, as if a lot of people were whispering at once.

She looked at Corey, and he shrugged.

"Maybe we'll invent one, if it hasn't been invented already. The double slingshot means we go around the moon completely. This'll get our speed up to about fifty thousand meters per second. It's a bit risky, because we are getting very close to the surface of the moon. But it'll get us up to the required speed," the same Englishman said.

Corey frowned and tapped her arm. "How will they break away from the moon's gravity if they have orbited the moon fully?"

She didn't have an answer for that. She picked up the cell phone and texted Aaron.

Escape moon gravity?????

Aaron felt his phone vibrate, and pulled it out from under his desk for a glance at the new message.

Jane had sent a text.

He looked at Major Russell, who in turn was staring straight back at him. He ignored him and changed his view to Dr. Carlton. "Tim, how are we going to escape the moon's gravitational pull after we orbit it? If we're so close to the surface."

Dr. Carlton fixed his jacket and adjusted his skinny frame as he delivered, with a smile, what had to be his *pièce de résistance*. "Excellent question, Aaron. We've been working with NASA on this very project for a number of years. The Saturn V uses five F1 rockets—that's where the *five* or the *v* comes from in Saturn's name. We'll use one of these F1 rockets, which will fire at the correct time to tangentially peel away from the moon's gravity. As you know, the moon's gravity is one-sixth that of Earth's, so one Saturn rocket will be enough to push us away from the moon. Also, we have no air drag to contend with around the moon."

He nodded. "So, we have to retrofit a rocket to the nuclear head and put this on top of seven Saturn rockets."

"Exactly. Actually, we have to retrofit two rockets, one to slow the nuclear warhead and then to speed it back up again relative to the asteroid." Dr.

Carlton stood at the head of the leaders' table, nodding and looking around the room.

Heat and nerves flushed over Aaron, and his spine tingled. He fidgeted in his seat. The stress of the timeline was beginning to affect him. "So, we have to get the rockets to Cape Canaveral, get the *Bomba's* there, too. Rig the whole thing, and add two more rockets, is this all possible?" he asked.

Major Russell took out a piece of paper and slid it to him. "Yes, if you'd been paying attention, we have outlined the logistics."

He frowned, but didn't want to show the military leader he was agitated. "Sorry, Major, I must not have heard it."

"Because you were outside on a call. We can't wait for you every time you want to call home. We all have wives and kids at home, you're not the only one," the major barked.

The air was getting hot and concentrated with carbon dioxide.

"Hey, Aaron, I'll go through the complete plan now, so everyone will be on the same page. We're all on the same team here, let's work together," Dr. Carlton said.

"Dr. Carlton, that's a great idea," President Jameson said.

The Brit cleared his throat. "Yes, sir. So, we have seven *Tsar Senior Bomba's* weighing in at forty thousand tons each. That's a total nuclear power of six gigatons of explosives, equivalent, with four hundred megatons left to spare. The Germans have already dispatched large cargo planes to pick up these *Bomba's* from the various locations. They'll be in the US in a couple of days. In the meantime, there're seven Saturn V rockets making their way to Cape Canaveral. There'll also be an extra fourteen single rockets which need to be sent to the Cape, so they can be retrofitted to the ships, where the nuclear devices are going to be loaded. We only need six ships; one is on standby, just in case there're any issues with one of the others."

"We'll have our *Bomba's* on time, so what is the retrofit timeline looking like at the moment?" the Russian president asked.

"Yeah. So, Aaron and Eva spotted the asteroid on T-minus twenty-three. They reported it, and the UK and US delegation met the following day. Right now, we are on T-minus eighteen and a half. The *Bomba's* will be on US soil tomorrow, and transported to the Cape. The Saturn rockets are being shipped to the Cape now and will be there from today to T minus eighteen. Modifications will start today and will take half a day each. They'll be done and ready for launch on T-minus seventeen, taking the time zone into account. NASA has stated they can launch three rockets per day."

Louis raised his hand. "How come we can't use multiple sites? We could get the rockets off all at once."

"That's a great question also, NASA feels they want to keep a period of time between all the rockets because they'll all be taking the same trajectory, and the same double slingshot, we don't want any accidents. They can consolidate all their efforts into one location. All the rocket modifications will be made by the same team. Trust me, we've worked out the statistics, it's the best way to do it."

"You're putting all your eggs into one basket. This is crazy!" the Russian president barked, wearing a huge frown.

Dr. Carlton shook his head. "Sorry, sir, but we've done the calculations. Even down to the weather predictability. The stats say the Cape with all six rockets plus the extra one"

"Okay, *Tim-o-fey*, on your head may this lay," the Russian president shook his head.

The harsh comment made Aaron uneasy.

On Tim's head?

"Thank you." The Brit dipped his chin. "NASA actually conducted those stats, but, I take your point. On me, so it shall be," he uttered each word individually and low.

No one in the room seemed to be helping the English scientist out with the weight of the world on his shoulders; maybe they thought it was foolish to launch all the rockets from the same place, or maybe they agreed with NASA and Dr. Carlton.

Aaron would watch and learn before he offered his opinion.

The doctor continued, in a much more subdued tone. "The rockets will take four days to reach the moon. The double slingshot will be performed and the first will be fired to push the capsule away from the moon. Then another four days to reach the asteroid. At this point, the second rocket will be fired and the capsules will decelerate from about fifty thousand kilometers and accelerate up to twenty-five thousand kilometers the opposite way, relative to the asteroid. We'll be at T-minus seven days at this stage. T-minus six is our most important day. If we go past that, we're into destruction of the earth in some form or another,"

"Do we have any kind of idea how bad things will get if we miss one day or two days?" the Canadian Prime Minister asked.

Aaron watched as Eva stood confidently with her colleague. "Yes. If we detonate on T-minus seven, then great. But if we detonate on T-minus six, we're still good. The problem increases exponentially every hour we go past T-minus six. We have the seventh spare rocket, which we can detonate on T-minus five and a quarter, this will keep the asteroid clear. So, we have a few back checks, in case anything goes wrong."

The Italian Prime Minister waved a hand. "Do we have enough back checks, if everything goes wrong?"

Aaron shrugged. "No, sir. But it's all we have. Don't have any other option. We don't have any more rockets and *Bomba's*. This is our *only* option."

President Jameson tapped Major Russell's shoulder. "Get NASA on the phone now. Find out how sure they are that this will all work."

"I think it's abundantly clear, this is the only solution, and even if it was ten percent certain, we should at least try it," Louis gave his expertise on the matter while the major made the call.

"No, Mr. Professor," the Russian president said. "If you explode the nuclear *Bomba's* toward the east, and it only works ten percent, then France will be saved, and Russia will have a hole in it the size of the Atlantic Ocean."

The UK Prime Minister nodded. "He has a point, would it not be better to deflect it to the left, or west as we know it, so as to reduce casualty potential?"

President Jameson shook his head. "No. I'm not sending our rockets into space to deflect the asteroid into our path. We can't do that."

The Russian president stood and glowered. He made as if he was going to leave the room. His Russian accent grew thicker the more agitated he became. "Well, we won't be sending *Bomba's* into space to deflect the asteroid toward Russia." He turned to his staff. "Okay. Enough done now. Let's go." He commanded his people to leave the talks.

The whole thing was falling to pieces. Aaron looked at Eva and felt sorrow as he saw the hurt on her face.

Back to square one.

"Please. Let's have a talk about this. You know how precious time is. We really need to release a statement tonight or at least first thing in the morning," the UK Prime Minister pleaded.

Aaron was hoping her femininity would be the antidote to all the excessive testosterone which was suffocating the room.

The Russian president ignored her pleas and continued out the door.

Russian delegates muttered as they left. The door closed behind them with a resounding slam that rocked Aaron.

They needed to all agree here, and they needed Russia's cooperation. He'd assumed they were past this, as no doubt did most of the delegates.

The room fell silent for a few moments, before the Japanese Prime Minister stood and cleared his throat. "Did he give an order for the German planes not to collect the *Bomba's*?"

"Not to us, not to me. I'll keep going as asked. Until he tells me otherwise, I will collect those *Bomba's* and send them to the US," the German Chancellor replied.

"Thank you so much, Chancellor. Will you keep us informed if he tells you *not* to collect them? Will you let us when you know that the *Bomba's* are in the air?"

"Yes, President Jameson. They should be in the air very soon."

"We'll need every fighter jet available to protect those *Bomba's*. They're the key to the survival of hundreds of millions of people—well more likely, billions. Be on the right side of history!" the US president addressed the UK and France.

The leaders of both countries nodded without comment.

"We'll end this session now. If the Russians return to the table, we will reconvene. We'll continue on with the plan as normal unless something changes," the Japanese Prime Minister said. He sighed, and his dejection was felt across the room.

Eva shot a hand up. "The Russians will have those nuclear weapons encrypted, so they'll be useless."

"Don't you worry about the encryption, we have people for that. The finest people," Major Russell said, wearing a smug expression.

Louis gasped. "Are you going to steal the *Bomba's* and decrypt them? That's a bit much, isn't it?"

President Jameson frowned. "Not in our book it's not. Trying to save the world here, and all." The *country* coming out in the president now.

"We're not at that juncture, yet. We have a few

days. We'll talk him 'round. Anyway, do we have a press statement? Something to just keep them at bay," the UK Prime Minister said.

Aaron looked around the room, the double bank of tables and chairs, the flustered heads, the paper and pens strewn everywhere. Disposable coffee cups bulging over the top of the trash can.

Dr. Carlton put up his hand to attract the attention of his Prime Minister. "I'll do that if you want, ma'am."

"That would be great, Timothy, if everyone else is okay with that."

"Knock yourself out." President Jameson pushed his chair back and stood.

No one else in the room disagreed.

25

NUMBER CRUNCH

"Are you hungry?" Corey asked.

Jane started typing numbers into the computer. "Yeah, but let's just get this up and running, and we'll be able to track everything ourselves in real time. The sooner we get it going, the quicker we'll be able to see if there're any mistakes or anomalies we've missed." She had her head down, entering coordinates and velocities into Aaron's program.

He paced the room, turned back to her, and sat down beside her, looking straight at her. Remorse was high on his agenda. "Hey, I'm sorry about the friends comment earlier. I don't know you at all. I don't know what you've been through. I don't know anything about your journey."

She glanced up for a second and continued typing. "Yeah, Corey. You don't know me. I took a risk getting to know you and you insulted me to my core. I have enough *a-holes* around here making me feel like shit without you fucling the fire."

"I know. I was just making a joke, trying to lighten the air between us. I know you took a chance on a bum, a homeless person."

"A stinking, dried up old bum." Jane steadfastly typed away, not breaking stride.

"Ouch! Yeah. Okay. Fair enough," he conceded.

"A dog wouldn't have pissed on you, by the way." She stuck the knife in and twisted it.

"Ok again, ouch! but still fair. Not exactly accurate. Many a dog has pissed on me, actually. It's more frequent than you think."

"A smelly old man. A *silly* smelly old man." She glanced at him again.

Corey gave up. He shrugged. "All right, now *you* are taking the piss out of me. That's just mean. I'm not old. I'm in my forties. That's considered young these days." He stood and went to the tinted windows.

She swiveled around in her chair, looked up at him with a kind forgiving smile. Jane grabbed her long black hair and tied it up. "See. It's not so nice, is it?"

He glanced back at her, and noticed she was smiling. "No." He smiled, too. She'd gotten the better of him. A lesson learned. "It's not funny."

"Come over here and check these numbers," Jane commanded. "I'm sick of playing dumb just to get attention from my inferior peers!"

The air was cleared again as Corey approached the computer and checked the figures she'd just inputted. "So. You have the launch times of the projectiles, the velocities, the trajectories. That all looks good."

"Yeah, we'll get the simulation up and running

and if we need to change it tonight or tomorrow, it won't make a real difference to the actual outcome. We just really need to get it started as soon as possible." She pressed *play* on the simulator. The computer made a few clicking noises and started working.

He gazed around the observatory, watching all the computers going into overdrive. The visuals were performing on the flat screens, everything seemed to be handling itself. "Sounds good to me. So, can we get some food? I'm starving."

"Okay, let's go to the cafeteria and see what nice food they have down there." Her voice was a sarcastic reference to his healthy food versus her not so healthy snacks.

"No need," Corey said as he produced a bag of goodies.

Jane's cell phone rang. She quickly showed the cell to Corey to let him know who was calling before answering. "Hi, Aaron. How are you?"

"Tired, Jane. How are you holding up with Corey?"

Unknown to her professor, Corey was close enough to hear the conversation.

"Yeah. He's good. He's teaching me a few lessons in mathematics, and I'm just teaching him a few lessons in life," she smiled.

Corey shook his head.

"Hmm. Sounds interesting. Anyway, did you hear the info? Can you get a simulation set up, just to double check everything?"

She gave Corey a high-five. "We're already on top of it. We've set the simulator up and it's running, as we speak. It's not a hundred percent accurate; we'll need more information to make sure it's perfect."

"Excellent work. I knew I could trust you. You're a smart kid. A lot smarter than you give yourself credit for."

"Kid! I'll take that as a compliment," she retorted.

Corey snorted. It wasn't a secret the girl was crushing on his brother-in-law. He leaned closer so he could hear Aaron more clearly.

Jane arched an eyebrow, but didn't move away.

"Sorry, yeah, kid? I meant woman." There was a groveling in his voice. "Lady? I don't know. Person."

Corey spoke into the cell phone. "What about the Russians?"

"We don't know yet. We'll just have to see what they say. NASA has done the simulations with the explosion to the right side of the asteroid, sending the asteroid to the Russian side of the planet. They're getting back to us now about the opposite side of the equation."

Jane's eyes went wide and she rocked on her heels. "Maybe we'll run the simulator with the explosion on the right side, sending it toward the Atlantic, USA. Might even get it in before NASA."

Corey nodded as she excitedly made her way back to her swivel chair.

"Yeah, definitely. That's the best way to go. Knowing the Russians, you'd be sure they won't back down from this one," Aaron said. His voice wasn't so defeated, like he was feeding off Jane's excitement.

"Okay. So. Will we speak again later, or will I just text you?" Jane asked.

"Text me when you're done. I have to help Dr.

Carlton with the press release. Don't want to cause
mass hysteria or anything."

Aaron hung up and smiled. "That went well," he
said to himself, and glanced over at Louis and Eva,
who were struggling to help Timothy with his press
release. He joined them. "You should definitely call
Olivia Hargreaves about this. I don't know why they
didn't bring her here."

"Bloody good point, Aaron," Timothy said. "This
is harder than I thought. I'll call her now." He went
over to a corner of the room and took a pen and paper
with him along with his cell.

Eva scooted her chair closer to Aaron.

He smiled.

"I think I'll get a bit of shut-eye. There's nothing
we can do anyway for the next few days, as long as the
Russians don't scupper the whole plan. I bid you
farewell. Good night," Louis said, blocking a yawn
with one hand.

Aaron looked away to the blank space of the wall,
concerned at the waning confidence of the professor.
"Good night, Louis," he and Eva said at the same
time.

The older man nodded and made his way out of
the room.

Aaron exchanged a look with Eva.

Her grin was mischievous and it made his
stomach jump.

She stared sharply at the ceiling.

He shook his head and frowned with confusion.

Again, she looked to the ceiling sharply and

gestured her head in an upward movement.

Was she flirting? What the heck?

Aaron shook his head again and rolled his eyes up to heaven, his hands now outstretched with palms open. Had no idea what Eva was trying to say.

She looked up at the ceiling and started gesturing, with her hands, then shook her head in defeat, clasping her hands together like she was about to say her prayers. Eva placed her two hands to one side of her cheek, indicating that she was tired.

He perked up. Could he have been more stupid?

He shoved his chair back and scrambled to his feet. "*Voulez-vous coucher avec moi?*" he whispered as he flicked his head to one side.

She smiled, jumped up and whispered. "What about Dr. Carlton? Should we stay and help him?"

He shook his head, a firm *hell no*, he had more important things on his mind now. "It's none of our business. He's in charge of the press release; we're here to deal with the asteroid."

"*D'accord. C'est bon. Allons mon ami,*" Eva said in her sexy French accent.

Aaron waved to get Tim's attention. "We're off. We'll be back as soon as we're called. Try and get a little bit of sleep."

The man appeared to be searching his cell phone, probably looking through his contacts. "Okay. I'll see you guys in a little bit. I shouldn't be too long here. Where's Olivia's number when I need it..."

They left the conference room and Aaron was itching to take her hand as they walked to the elevators. His heart kicked up speed, as if the goings-on in the G8 Summit weren't enough.

He reached for the elevator button just as she did, their hands brushed.

How could two mature adults be so nervous?

Maybe he was falling for her a little?

Maybe she was for him, too?

Maybe it really was the end of the world as they knew it.

Whatever happened tonight or in the next few weeks, none of their lives would be the same.

Things would change for everyone.

Eva didn't flinch from his touch, she grabbed his hand.

He felt the strength of her grasp. Stronger than he'd expected for such a slight woman. Like the powerful handshake someone unexpectedly gave, when they're trying to come across as the *alpha* in the relationship.

Aaron didn't dislike it. Strong powerful women were the kind he liked, not submissive tame cats.

The hallway was quiet, with no one to be seen. A subtle *ding* broke the silence as the elevator door opened slowly.

She stepped in quickly, too quickly for him to catch up until she pulled him in.

The doors swooshed closed.

Eva grabbed Aaron close to her breasts.

He swept his hands from her hips to her bra, like she was being frisked by a cop or TSA, but less intrusively.

He dipped down to cover her mouth with his, and she kissed him back with her full lips.

A light faintness of exuberance came over him, making his head spin.

It'd been so long.

Aaron noticed the reflection of the elevator walls as she reached back, searching for the elevator floor buttons on the cold stainless-steel panel, tapping vigorously on the highest number she could find.

The elevator jerked as it took off at speed.

He bashed the stop button with the side of his fist.

The car jarred to a stop, causing them to lift from the floor together, shifting them into an even more perfect position.

He didn't struggle to remove her bra with one hand, the index finger and thumb to be precise, a click of the fingers. Aaron cupped her full pert breasts in his hands, her blouse still on, but gaping open.

He'd longed for this, for some time. This was the first time since well before his wife had passed.

He'd had no time to 'play the field' when there was such grief in the family he'd been trying to hold it together.

Thoughts—good and bad—dissipated as Eva reached inside his pants.

He took a deep breath as he held his stomach in, giving her an extra inch or two of room to reach down further.

Aaron kissed her neck then found her mouth again, biting down gently on her lower lip.

Her pants buttons were given the same treatment her bra had been afforded, opened in one second, off in two.

They embraced each other beyond closeness, togetherness.

She dragged her nails across his back.

Punishment for being so good.

Aaron groaned.

No need for foreplay, no need for second dates, no need for anything, only each other at that amazing point.

He reveled in her, and her eager response to him and his touch.

The electric elongating buzz of the stop button went off.

He couldn't hear anything but her. Her small mewls, and moans that spurred him on.

The stress, the release, the tingle in his toes, the warm feeling in his heart.

The raw honesty of what their bodies were doing.

Not an asteroid in sight.

The ground moved, it seemed.

Climax was too soon to arrive; the spell of the day had brought them so close.

They stared at each other for a few moments after it was over, and neither spoke.

Maybe they didn't need to.

The elevator jerked to life. It was descending.

Eva quickly started pulling her skinny jeans up.

Aaron started to laugh as he struggled with his pants and belt. "Shit, shit, shit. Quick," he urged, as he tucked his shirt in.

The door opened, and two Chinese engineers in blue overalls stood peering at them.

It didn't escape him that Eva hadn't had enough time to close her bra; she was trying to hold it on with her elbows, tightly, at the side of her chest.

The two engineers looked at him then centered on her hair; a mess, a bird's nest.

She smiled. *"Oh, pardon. J'ai touché le bouton d'arrêt avec mon cul sans faire exprès."* Her voice was polite as she pointed to the stop button.

One of the men blinked, and looked at his coworker.

They obviously didn't know what she'd said.

They both bowed and went on their way.

She quickly pressed the button for her floor. The doors swooshed closed again.

Aaron looked at her beautiful just-ravished face.

Then they burst into the loudest laughter he'd ever heard.

He shot his arm forward to press the button for his floor, but jokingly went to press the *stop* button again.

"No! You'll get us in trouble," she bantered. She gave a small punch to his arm, followed by a sweet caress of his wrinkled blue shirt.

Aaron pressed the floor for his room. "What did you say to them, anyway?"

Eva grinned pure mischief and his heart skipped. "I said, *'Oh, sorry, my ass just accidentally hit the stop button.'* I doubt they understood."

He chuckled and shook his head. *What a fine ass it was, indeed.*

The elevator came to a stop on her floor. "I'll get off here; I really need to freshen up. That was very sexy and fun, but very sweaty and hot, also."

He smiled and kissed her goodbye, for the time being.

The doors of the elevator shut as they looked at each other.

Aaron glanced at the reflection of his beaming

smile, returned to him from the inside of the elevator.

26

THE BULLY

Corey and Jane made their way to the deserted cafeteria to stretch their legs. They'd left the observatory computers to themselves. The whirling and buzzing were enough for them to quit the room.

The large empty food hall was quiet, as before. Chairs knocked over, food trays with half-eaten meals left on the tables.

He looked around and sniffed the air. "It's not rotten yet, but this place is going to be full of rats and flies soon."

"Yeah. It's going to be some fun cleaning it up." She crunched into a nice juicy green apple. "I think we should take some provisions back to the observatory; we'll be there for a while. As long as they don't cut off the power, we'll be in good shape."

Corey slouched back into one of the plastic chairs, a hand of bananas in front of him. "I'm pretty sure the university has backup generators. It's close to the hospital and on the same grid as the hospital generators. I used to live close by; our apartment was on the same grid. We never used to lose our electricity during storms or any sort of power cuts."

Jane took another bite of the apple and continued talking. An apple was probably the only food one could eat and appropriately talk with one's mouth full. "Where are you going to stay tonight? On the street? At home? Here?"

He picked up a banana. "I'm gonna stay here tonight, in the observatory. I want to keep an eye on the simulator. Maybe double check the numbers again and get it as accurate as possible. Really don't want any screw-ups. If we just keep doing what we're doing it'll keep Aaron's mind at ease and in turn allow him to concentrate more on what he needs to be doing."

She got up and threw her apple core into a trash can, then picked up a brown cardboard box from behind one of the self-service food stalls and started packing apples, bananas, oranges, and other fruits into it. She lifted it up onto the countertop.

He smiled and started adding some treats to her provisions box. "We might need some energy over the days; we'll pack a few bars."

Jane smiled back.

"Where are you going to stay? You got any family locally?" he asked.

"No, I'm a country girl. Well, I'm a city girl who was born in the country."

Corey sat on the edge of the food counter and crossed his arms in a relaxed non-confrontational way. "The country's too quiet for you. You're a city girl at heart."

She stopped packing fruit into the box. It was as good a time as any to have a proper chat with her new-found friend. "Damn straight. I love my family, and the place I was born, but it was just way too small for me. Too many people in my business. I told mom I was working on the asteroid project. She's very proud of me. I'll visit her soon."

"I bet she is. Still, it must be hard coming out here. New people. New situation. New everything." He tilted his head. "Boys, or girls, or actually, indeed, both. Things have changed since I was in college."

Why was he being so awkward? Was he blushing?

Jane grinned. "What? You didn't have guys and girls or both back in your day?"

"Um! Yea, of course."

She considered him before she spoke. "I don't like boys, or girls, or both. I like men." She nodded, perching her hands on her hips. "I don't have time for juveniles."

"What about living arrangements? You're not staying here as well, are you?"

"I'm in a dorm close by. My room is about the size of a prison cell, but doesn't have the amenities of a prison cell. Not to mention the cost." She picked up the full box.

Corey pushed off the counter and motioned to take it from her.

"No thanks. I can manage. I'm a city girl from the country, don't forget. Grab the crate of water. That would be a great help." Jane smiled again.

They walked down the bland cream hallway of Caltech, past the sports' halls where she'd once advised him to get cleaned up.

He pursed his lips. "So, do you play any sports here?"

"Yeah, I love basketball. Not too keen on some of my teammates." Jane carried the cardboard box in front of her.

"Um. Wouldn't you say, part of being a team, is getting along with your teammates?"

She scoffed. "Not if your teammates are complete bitches and man-sized women." Her eloquent reference to her 'teammate' *Ronna*. "Fucking stupid cu…" she stopped and glanced at Corey. Neither the time nor place to be showing one's countryside to the city folk. "She's just stupid."

"Who's stupid?"

"Stupid Ronna Young. Which is ironic, because she looks about thirty-five." Jane stared at the contents of the box. She shook her head. "Breasts of a pregnant woman." She couldn't keep her contempt away.

He barked a laugh. "Why would you say that?" he asked as she regained control.

"She makes my life miserable. Constantly picking on me. She's about two feet taller than me." A slight exaggeration, but worthwhile, if only to make the point. "She always has two or three of her friends with her, she'd never say anything to anyone if she was by herself. And Christ, would she ever cover up her massive bajongos in the changing rooms. Like as if we all need to see them every day!"

Corey halted her with a hand on her shoulder. "No, but seriously, has she ever threatened you?"

She scowled. "All the time. Every day, Corey." She didn't mince words. They approached the observatory door. "No disrespect, but you're a guy. Guys will never understand the shit women have to go through. Boys will tell you to *f-off* and trash talk you, but girls are just complete bitches. A different level."

"Jesus. That's hard." His expression was concerned, brows drawn when she spared him a glance.

"You don't know the half of it. This place is worse than high school. And that was bad enough. I assumed everyone would be so much more mature here! That's why I have no friends. That's why I got so annoyed with you earlier."

"Why don't you just quit the basketball team?"

"I'm not going to let that bitch and her bitch cronies get the better of me. That'd be giving into them." Jane placed the box on the ground as she took out the keycard. "Besides, Aaron's our coach. I really get along with him. He's very good to me, and encourages me so much. Kind of like a mentor to me. I hope!"

Corey stood at the door, still holding the crate of water in his hands. "Hmmm. So, you like older men, you have a very interesting student-teacher relationship, and basically have no other friends besides, Aaron. Am I correct in that assessment?"

She opened the door. A low beep noise paused her answer as the door unlocked. She stared, and held the door open for him.

A couple of thuds from the starter capacitors sounded, as the automated fluorescent tubes illuminated the stairwell.

"If you're implying I have a crush on Aaron; you're wrong."

He approached the steps but stopped when she spoke again.

"And personally, I think my student-teacher relationship isn't as odd as my homeless-man and woman relationship."

The windows of the observatory were shaded with a brown tint to prevent excessive glare. The glass box room made twilight seem close to nighttime. The air-conditioning was on and the place felt very comfortable.

They placed their box and crate in the kitchenette area.

The main computer *binged* to show the simulator had finished.

The computer's dialog box, with a large green correct mark in it, made them both smile.

Jane took a seat at the workstation. "I hope nothing crazy happens here. I hope we didn't miss anything."

"It's just, kind of..." Corey tilted his head to the side. "A draft, if you will. We'll tweak it and get it right."

She smiled again; she agreed with him on something at last. "That's the good thing about this simulator. You don't have to re-run the whole thing every time you change a small number. It'll sort that out for you really easily."

He jumped and clapped his hands, wearing a grin. "Come on. Press *play*."

She clicked on the asteroid and commanded the computer to show a camera view from it.

They sat back and watched the screen come to life. The 4K HD rendered computer graphics of the earth, the moon, the asteroid, and rockets were unbelievable. It was as if they were in space.

The rockets took off from earth.

Jane increased the playback speed.

The moon passed by right before the rockets, as they double slingshot around it.

The sixth rocket fired, causing them all to escape the moon's gravity.

They continued at an increased speed toward the asteroid.

The secondary rockets fired, slowing the rockets to zero then speeding them up so they were right beside the asteroid.

T-minus seven days passed on the impact clock, the nuclear bombs exploded, as planned.

The asteroid deflected past the earth on the USA side—the left, or west, as some countries had called that specific side of the earth.

Jane bounced up, mirroring Corey's delight. "It made it."

He punched the air and let out a yell. "It did it! And that's not even one hundred percent accurate. We can improve this when we get some proper numbers. I've gotta give it to you, you really are handy at this stuff. I'd say you've returned the rocket simulation faster than NASA has."

Jane smiled yet again, but her tummy kicked up nerves. "I don't think so. They have much more sophisticated machinery. Not to mention, hundreds of people working on it. I'm just good at this particular program. I've been using it for a few years." She grabbed her long jacket and her bag. "I'm wrecked. It's getting late in Hong Kong. I'm going to head home now and get some rest. We'll need to get on Hong Kong time really."

"Okay. Can you save these details of the simulation? I want to fine tune it and double check everything."

She grabbed the mouse and clicked on the save icon. Jane pulled her cell from her bag, along with her keycard. "If Aaron calls, you'll need the cell. You'll need the keycard to get back in if you want to go out for some air."

"Do you want me to walk you home?" Corey asked.

"No. If I can survive the past few days, I can survive anything." Jane made her way out of the observatory. "Bye, Corey. I'm glad we ran into one another. You're a pretty neat guy. Well…" She looked at him up and down. "Not pretty; neat, literally."

Corey watched the door shut behind her. He listened to the sound of Jane's steps fade, followed by the clunk of the main observatory door. Then the latch locking behind that.

He swiveled back to the main computer and opened the simulation program. He read over information in front of him; seven columns were shown.

The takeoff coordinates, the accelerations, trajectories, and a number of other relevant inputs. A drop-down menu with the type of rocket was an option.

The Saturn V rocket details were a default on the program and had already been selected. Payloads had been input, again by default.

Weather forecast had been grabbed from the coordinate area and auto-populated from governmental agencies. The lunar orbit had been activated and included.

He clicked the *draft render* button. A low-resolution graphical user interface with a projected trajectory line appeared in video form.

Corey forwarded the play sequence until the first rocket passed by the moon. The predicted trajectory spun around the moon where the sixth single rocket ignited, pushing the trajectory faster and further out into space.

Another rocket fired to slow the rocket and speed it up in the opposite direction, in line with the asteroid. There was a box with one thousand, two hundred megaton equivalents in it, representing the nuclear explosion.

He changed this number and replayed on the simulator.

As before; the video showed the rockets taking off, passing around the moon and out toward the asteroid, where the simulated explosion occurred.

The trajectory of the asteroid changed.

"Oh, my fucking God!" His mouth dropped open as he read the screen. "Impact Force: One point five by ten to the power of twenty-three."

27

PRESS RELEASE

Timothy had been on his cell with the US Press Secretary, Olivia Hargreaves, for a while.

"Okay, read the end part back to me again," she said.

He cleared his throat. "'*The leaders of Japan, France...* Yadda, yadda. *From all around the globe...* yadda, yadda. *The Russian contingent is supplying a number of large nuclear devices, which will be used to deflect the asteroid. The German partners are transporting the said devices to the United States, where the Americans will launch the spacecraft and devices into space over the next couple of days...* Then I mention all the countries involved... *This truly is a joint effort and includes help and dedication from nearly every country in the world. This is a world-wide effort...*'"

"That sounds great. Go with it. Send it out," Olivia said. Her voice seemed heavy with fatigue, but he tried not to focus on that.

"Thank you so much, from the bottom of my heart."

"No problem, Tim. Keep up the good work."

He gathered his pens, notepads and any other paraphernalia he had. He stood, fixed his trousers and left the empty seminar room.

Hotel cleaners arrived to spruce up the room, just as he left.

Timothy looked back at the state that the place was in. Coffee cups, water bottles, paper strewn everywhere. Better them than him to clean up. He nodded a greeting and went into the lobby.

It was pitch-dark outside; no one to be seen. The paparazzi and reporters had all gone back to their trailers.

He felt like the last man on the planet. He walked past the bar, and spotted the graveyard-shift bartender cleaning the bar top.

The oak-paneled room had dark mahogany tables and chairs. It seemed like they had a very nice English-style effect going on.

"Hello. Can I trouble you for a whiskey? Just a single, no ice, please. Room two-one-one please." He took a seat at the bar.

The man nodded silently as he stretched for a bit of top-shelf. He grasped a short wide tumbler in his other hand, and poured the whiskey before handing it out.

Timothy raised the glass and toasted the barman, "T-minus eighteen days." He downed the drink in one go. He grimaced and then savored the heat in his throat. He looked behind him spotted a red leather chair near the fire.

That would be a lovely place to relax for a few moments.
He blinked for a long second and sat down for a bit.

Exhaustion weighed him down, making his limbs heavier. Such a long few hard-working days. Constantly on the go. Living on tea with three sugars. *God bless tea. God bless Irish whiskey.*

His body creaked into the stiff leather. It felt good on his back. He let the taste of whiskey linger in his mouth, concentrating only on the warmth flowing down to his belly.

Timothy was tired, falling asleep. He was drained, mentally and physically.

Something tapped against the window beside him. *A pebble?*

He sprung up and looked outside. He couldn't see anyone, at first. Then another pebble hit the window, one that would've hit him right between the eyes if the glass wasn't between him and the stone.

He peered to the right and spotted a very pretty woman.

Rebecca Crawford—Becky the reporter. She was wearing a long racing green trench coat, a royal navy-blue brim-hat, and a bright wooden handled umbrella. She looked really nice.

"What the hell is she doing? She's *waving* at me."

Becky was gesturing to him to let her in.

"'*Stay away from her*', that's what Olivia would say," Timothy whispered. He opened the fire exit door closest to him.

She quickly ducked under a barrier and made a break over no-man's-land toward him. The darkness of the night, cut only by the street lights reflecting up from the wet street.

A security guard spotted her.

Timothy came to the edge of the door and shouted, "She's with me. Thank you very much."

The guard didn't look all that sure, but he waved casually and went back to his post.

"What're you doing here?" he asked the reporter. "Come quick, before anyone else sees you."

"Oh, Timmy, you're a lifesaver. It's freezing out there. I'm staying in a little broadcasting trailer around the corner." Becky took her jacket and hat off. She smiled. "You said you'd call me at eight!"

"I know. They wouldn't allow phones into the conference room. Sorry." He was a bit worried she was on the premises of the G8 Summit.

"It's okay. I'm here now. What're you drinking, Timmy? I'll have one of the same. I won't stay long. Just want to get off the street; it's so miserable out there."

This was a bad idea, but he figured one drink wouldn't kill anyone. "Just the one. I have to go to bed very soon," he said, with a wince. Why had he said that? He was such a nerd, and she was so pretty!

Her full-bodied head of blond hair framed her pretty face and luscious red lips. Blue eyes and lengthy black eyelashes to top it all off.

His heart raced. She was going to think he was an idiot. He waved to the bartender and showed him two fingers.

The man duly provided two neat whiskeys for them which were downed as quickly as they were served.

Timothy sat on the red chair again, while Becky took a seat on the couch beside him.

"So, what you got for me, Timmy? Anything good? They're killing me back home. We've had nothing to give them for two days now." She stuck her lip out in a pout, pleading with him.

He smiled and winked, then took the press release from his notes. "You can have the official press release. I'm sending it out now before I go to bed."

She snatched it out of his hand and started reading it as fast as she could. Her eyes scanned the sentences like a printer printing lines.

How could she read that fast? No way she was comprehending it all.

Becky looked up, wearing a sneer that marred her beauty. "Is this it? The next time you wink at me, you better have something more than a press release. That could be misconstrued as a sexual advance. Hashtag, think before you wink."

Timothy reared back, cutting off a gasp. "Yes. It's the press release. We worked on it for a few hours, I think. Is it not any good?" He was still keen to impress, but really didn't want anything important to get into the public domain.

Her expression softened and she smiled, the act so opposite it was like a coin flipping. "No, Timothy, don't be silly. This is fantastic. I'll take this and release it." Becky snapped a picture of the press release with her cell and the little whoosh indicating an email sounded. "We'll get the scoop on this, and the other networks can report on our scoop." She smiled again, this time adoringly. "You're such a good guy, Timmy. Come in closer to me. Come off that seat and sit beside me." She patted the couch cushion.

He didn't get many offers from pretty women, or

actually any women in general. He was obliged to not let this one pass. With a swallow, Timothy stood from the red leather seat and obeyed.

She crossed her legs and made room to get up-close and personal with him. "You must be exhausted, Timmy." She rubbed the hair at the back of his neck.

"I'm completely exhausted, Becky. Been such a long few days. So many issues and problems to deal with." His voice sounded far away to his own ears, as if a trance had come over him from the feeling of her nails gently stroking his neck and hair.

"Have another drink for yourself. You must be stressed to the nines." She gestured to the bartender to bring over two more whiskeys. She continued stroking his hair on the back of his neck.

The tingling sensation flowed through his body. He crossed his legs to cover his exhilaration.

The loud noise pierced his ears, and his eyes shot open. The bartender dropped two drinks off, bashing the whiskey glasses off the glass table.

The reporter glared at the intrusion, ruining her moment.

The barman turned and left without saying anything.

"Did you tip the bartender?" Timothy asked, closing his eyes again.

"Tip him? The only thing I'll give him is a personality tip," Rebecca continued her scolding.

He reached for his new glass and took a sip of whiskey, savoring the taste once more and relishing in the sensations at the back of his throat.

"Do you have anything interesting to tell me, Timothy?" she egged him on some more.

"I can't really say much. Olivia would have my guts for garters."

"That one! Is she still suffering from diestrus?"

"What?" he asked. His eyelids weighed two stone each.

She continued to rub his head.

Melatonin was flowing freely as he drifted off from everything around him combined with pure exhaustion.

Rebecca held Dr. Timothy Carlton's head and gently rested it on the back of the leather couch. She waved her hand across his face, looking for a response.

He didn't flinch.

Out for the count.

She quickly rifled through his notes. His main binder had numerous scraps of paper in it.

Rebecca flicked through them frantically, in case he'd wake, glancing at the sleeping man every ten seconds or so, just to make sure his eyes didn't open.

The notes seemed like gibberish. There were large circles with smaller circles and dates with speeds and velocities. It was a mess. Organized chaos to him no doubt, but a complete mess to her impeccably organized nature.

"How can someone, presumably on the spectrum, be so disorganized?" she quipped. Of course, she could admit that was a rude, generalization, that bright, borderline autistic people should be obsessively neat also.

She halted on something. She didn't know what *'arc tan'* meant, and she couldn't contemplate how fast thirty kilometers per second was or how far away sixty million kilometers was, but she knew what six, six, six meant.

Rebecca looked at the number written into the notes, written in *red*. It looked like it'd been repeatedly written on top of itself a dozen or so times, making it stand out in bold.

What has six, six, six got to do with anything?

She turned to the next few notes where she'd seen the asteroid naming sheet. "RQ26?" she frowned. "What's this all about?"

She peered at the numbers circled and read the description on how asteroids were named.

A cold chill came over her as Timothy started to stir.

"The Russians are not playing ball, need those Bomba's"

Rebecca grabbed her cell and took a couple of photographs. Then picked up her bag and left the lounge area.

The bartender was nowhere to be seen, it was too late for any guests to be up.

She exited the hotel's front door and went straight passed security, thanking them politely and flashing her American passport.

The guards didn't stop her—they weren't interested in people leaving, just people entering.

She hurried as fast as she could in her high heels, passing the long line of broadcasting vans, back to her own.

She opened the door and started getting herself ready. Touching up hair and makeup, making herself look as presentable, as one could possibly be in the middle of the night.

She Googled some notes in relation to the RQ26 asteroid name and started making her comparison case.

Rebecca read the description of how the asteroids were named, and discovered how the number six hundred and sixty-six was linked. She read it again just to make sure.

She was jittery as she contemplated the scoop of her life or the biggest mistake made on air ever. Butterflies took flight in her stomach.

She might've been manipulative, conniving, deceptive, but she was one of the best reporters in the game. "This is the type of reporting the public will lap up. Sensationalize everything is the name of the game."

Fear sells, extremes sell, religious connections definitely sell. Rebecca repeated it to herself, justifying the ends.

She took the large step down from her van, her notes in hand. She was ready for the broadcast.

It was dark outside. Her camera and lighting rig had been set up by her colleague. She couldn't risk waking anyone, so she'd record herself.

Any commotion would set the twenty-plus other broadcasting vans off like fireworks, all grappling to find out what was going on.

Don't want to wake the rats.

She fixed her hair one last time and flipped on the lights, then the camera and pressed record. Rebecca stood in front of the bright LED lights, composing herself with a breath. "Good Evening, America, or should I say, Bad Evening, world. It's been a difficult few days as the countdown to Armageddon is on. Yes. I said Armageddon. With only eighteen days or so left until the Devil himself arrives in Switzerland. Destroying all of Europe, killing hundreds of millions of people in the process, and displacing a further half a billion people from the fallout." She spoke with sincerity! The most serious bit of reporting she'd ever done.

Rebecca nodded in agreement to her own statement. "The Devil, I hear you ask. Yes. The unequivocal connection between the number six hundred and sixty-six, and the name of the asteroid RQ26 is frightening. While RQ26 is an innocuous code name for the Asteroid of Doom, it is actually the six hundred and sixty-sixth asteroid to be identified during this period of the year."

She forced shock into her expression for the world to see. "Why did the governments not release this information? Maybe they don't believe in God, or Armageddon, but I for one, do." Rebecca ruffled through her print out, for effect, even though it didn't contain Timmy's notes. "It's a fact they've known about this for some time, but that's not all they haven't told us. In a press release obtained by me, they've indicated everything is going according to their plan." She shook her head, as if she was scolding a child. "But we know, that's not true. The Russians have refused to give the Americans the vital bombs." She let her mouth hang open, projecting more shock for her viewers to lap up. "So, what does this all mean for us?" She paused for dramatic effect. "Well, you only have to read the last part of their press release to sum it all up. *Please trust us, please stay where you are, there's no need to panic*. Never have three parts of a sentence been more untrue. God bless us all." She remained still, in frame, for the drama to set in. "I'm Rebecca Crawford, reporting from the G8 Summit, in Hong Kong for WDCTV."

She quickly ran to the lighting rig and turned it off.

There was some commotion from the broadcasting truck beside here.

Rebecca ejected the memory card from the camera, and powered it off. She climbed back into the van and emailed the video to her producer in Washington, with the subject line,

Breaking news!
Just trim top and tail, and send out immediately.

28

DUPED

Olivia arrived home to her D.C. apartment, sipping on her take-out coffee in one hand, as she dropped her coat and bag on the sofa with the other.

She picked up the remote and flicked on the television, checking her mail as the news came on in the background. Her daily ritual.

She didn't take much notice of the breaking news as she swiped through her mail. Olivia grabbed her laptop and sat on her couch in front of her coffee table and television.

The incessant chatter from the reporters wasn't enough to distract her from planning her forthcoming day.

"...*six, six, six...*" snagged her attention, and she snapped her head away from her laptop, staring the TV down.

"What the hell is this bitch on about?"

Rebecca Crawford was on her screen.

Olivia turned up the volume only to hear the 'apparent' press release she and Dr. Timothy Carlton had written only hours earlier.

"What is she going on about? Timothy, you stupid idiot. Typical man. Can't keep his mouth shut. Ruled by his dick!" She grabbed her cell phone.

Timothy's phone was dead; she tried Aaron.

"I was just about to call you, Secretary Hargreaves," he said after the first ring.

"Did you see the news?"

"We're watching it." The man's tone revealed dejection. "What in the name of God did you write?"

"That is *not* what our press release was. I sent it to you, and everyone else involved. Where's Timothy?"

"We don't know. Couldn't find him in his room or in the conference rooms. His cell is off."

There was a beep, indicating her call-waiting. One glance at the screen told her it was Major Russell. "Oh, Christ. I better go. It's the major. This is going to get ugly, very fast."

"Okay. I'll keep looking for Tim. Chat in a little bit."

"Keep me posted," Olivia said, switching calls. "Hi, sir."

"What happened to that God damned press release?" Major Russell barked. He was angrier than she'd heard him in a long time. Irate.

She could picture his red face and spittle at the corners of his mouth.

"Major, I didn't say anything about six, six, six, or any issues with the Russians. I'm here in D.C. Where I shouldn't be. I should be over there with you."

"Well. You'd better fix this. Get on the TV screens immediately and release the proper press release."

"Major, it's not a press release issue. I've released it already. We never discussed the six, six, six, issue or the Russian issue. This is either Timothy himself, or that bitch Rebecca Crawford manipulated him."

"Go get Rebecca Crawford!" Olivia heard Major Russell commanding someone she assumed was with him.

She'd known Timothy Carlton for a long time. He could be foolish, nerdish, yes. But had he betrayed her—them? "Any sign of Tim?" She needed to sit down.

"No." Another harsh bark from the major. "The Russians think we leaked this on purpose. Everyone's going ape-shit over here. It's fucking Armageddon, for real. We've done our best to keep this under wraps for the past few days. Now everything has escalated beyond our control."

Her heart skipped and her stomach inverted. She forced a breath. "Okay, let me get in front of the cameras. I'll try clear up the Russian thing; I can't do much about the number coincidence. I'll make that bitch look off her rocker; propagating complete bullshit."

"No."

"Why not?" she tried to keep the snap from her voice.

"Because, maybe she's not wrong. Maybe there's something in it. We can't lie. We'll just leave things as they are, and say we are still in discussion with the Russians, because technically, we are! Right now, this is a big deal. The Russians think we've all gone behind their backs. But it might actually be of benefit; if they start to play ball about the *Bomba's* again. If the public go against them, then they'll have to change their tune. This six, six, six thing will cause issues with the religious fanatics, but we'll just have to live with that."

"Right," Olivia said. Why was everyone telling her how to do her job? She muted the television; having already heard enough of what Rebecca had to say. "I'll call you later."

She grabbed her jacket and bag and made her way to the press briefing room at the White House, ready to give her rebuttal of the allegations from Rebecca freaking Crawford.

Aaron, Eva, and Louis met in the hotel lobby. The early sun shone in horizontal in the eastern windows. Each of the individual delegate rooms were full, and the main conference room was empty.

The din of heightened arguments and frantic to-ing and fro-ing was visible through each of the open doors. No one seemed to be afraid of letting anyone else hear their thoughts; they were actively encouraging it if the volume and openness of the arguments said anything.

Eva shook her head. *"C'est une tempête de merde."*

"Shit storm?" Aaron asked as she nodded to him. "We call it a cluster-fuck in the US."

"Ecouter, I've looked at the European news channels. Things are starting to get out of hand. People are afraid. Real fear in people's hearts and minds. People from all over the Alps are leaving their

homes already. Packing up and getting the hell out," Louis said.

The three of them seemed to glance at the television in the empty lounge bar at the same time.

There were muted images of people fleeing with all of their belonging attached to the roofs of their cars. People who had recreational vehicles were ditching everything, just stocking up on supplies.

Looting had begun in certain parts of France and Germany. The television camera cut to a man with a megaphone and a sandwich board around his neck that reads *The End Is Nigh*', but the *'nigh'* part was crossed out and the word *'here'* was crudely written in its place.

"'The end is here'." Aaron sighed.

Louis pointed to the individual rooms and the delegates residing in them. "We need to get these government leaders back in that main room. They need to agree. The Russians won't budge off a left-side deflection."

"But it's not the correct side Louis, you know that. We should deflect from the right side, across Russia," Aaron said.

"But we all know how stubborn the Russians are; they'd rather die than give in to the Americans."

He rubbed the back of his neck and wrung his hands. "I don't want to do this, but if NASA says it's okay, and we can double check the numbers, I'll be okay with a left-side deflection."

She nodded. "I'll work on getting the Russian delegates back in the office."

"I can try and talk to the major and the US delegates," Louis said.

Aaron gave a one-handed thumbs-up. "I'll get

onto my guys back at base and see what the amateurs think." He was about to head off on his business when he spotted, out of the corner of his eye, a sleepy-headed man waking from the leather sofa.

"Hi, guys," Timothy nonchalantly called from the couch in the lounge. He offered a large yawn. "Did I miss anything?"

They whirled toward him.

Aaron exchanged a look with Eva and Louis, and his own shock was displayed in their expressions.

What the hell?

"What the hell have you been up to?" he demanded.

"Nothing, why?" Timothy said.

Aaron pointed to the TV, and the British scientist followed his indication and turned his head.

It only took a few seconds for his jaw to drop.

"Your girlfriend just blew the whole story. Scoop of the year. No thanks to you," Aaron added, his voice dripping with sarcasm.

"What?" Timothy looked down at his notes. "My notes! They're all messed up. Bloody hell," he shouted. "I didn't know she was a *'business girl'*."

"You let her see your notes?" Eva gasped.

"I fell asleep," Timothy sputtered. "It's not like I did it on purpose. I haven't slept since I left the UK. What... Forty-eight hours ago, or more. Seventy-two. I don't even know what day it is." He was visibly upset now.

Aaron stepped in. It was obvious their colleague felt like a fool. Betrayed by someone whom he knew to be too good for him.

"I'm sorry, guys. I've let you down. This is all just

too much for me."

Eva shot to his side and gave him a hug.

Timothy didn't respond at all. He just stood there standing in her arms, looking like someone had kicked his puppy.

Aaron sighed. What was done was done. No need to make the guy feel like a pile of shit. He jokingly joined in on the hug.

A tiny smile appeared on Timothy's face.

Louis too joined the group hug.

Timothy laughed.

The air had been cleared.

Aaron broke the hug. "Okay let's go, we have work to do."

"What work?" Timothy asked.

He gestured. "Come with me, Tim. Will you get onto the NASA guys and find out the results of their simulations? I'll find Major Russell and tell him what happened. I'll tell him it wasn't your fault, and we need to move fast and get an agreement between the Russians and the US."

Aaron didn't wait for an answer; he made his way to the United States delegates' room. "Hi. Just some information on the leak. It didn't come from anyone's individual office. The information was stolen from one of our colleagues. I'm sure you can figure out who, but that doesn't matter right now."

"No, you need to name the person now," Major Russell demanded.

"Sorry, Major. What will naming him accomplish? We need to work as a team. Something I've been going on about for the past few days. One of our colleagues fell asleep from exhaustion; the information was stolen right from under his nose. I, for one, believe him, so that's the end of the matter as far as I'm concerned."

"Well. It's not the end of the matter as far as *'we'* are concerned." The older military man indicated himself, and the president. The major seemed to think he was still on base, always in attack mode.

Aaron directed his attention to President Jameson. "We need to talk to the Russians. We need to agree on a left-side deflection, and send the asteroid across the face of the United States. I'm sure it'll pass with no issues, as of right now."

"How do you mean, 'as of right now'?" Major Russell demanded.

"We're awaiting the results of the NASA simulators, and we have a backup set of results coming from Caltech now. We need to show a united front as soon as possible, before the whole world starts looting and killing each other!" he pleaded with the leader of the free world.

"Yes. The faster we move to quash this ridiculous press fiasco, the better." The president nodded, but his lips were pursed.

Eva came to the door of the US delegates' room. "Everyone's convening now. We need you guys in there as soon as possible."

Aaron smiled and thanked her before returning his attention back to President Jameson. "Trust me, Mr. President. If you go out there and shake hands with the Russian president, it'll install trust back into the world."

The man looked pensive, but nodded again.

Everyone got up from their seats, picking up their books, notes, and laptops along the way.

Aaron watched them trudge into the larger room. He grabbed his cell phone and dialed.

"Hello?" a male voice answered.

He paused for a second, a dark cloud came over him; he was suddenly weak and sweaty. He took a deep breath. "Hi, Corey. You okay?"

"I'm fine, you looking for the simulation results?"

"Is Jane not with you?"

"Nope. She's gone home to get some rest. She wanted to be awake for the 'night shift', if you will."

Aaron heard an eeriness in his voice for some reason. Something he wasn't too pleased to hear. Maybe he'd heard it all before?

The negative thoughts started creeping into his head, and he tried to banish them. Not something he needed right now.

"Do you want the results?"

Aaron heard a screeching female voice, flashing from one ear to the other and back again. He froze until the noises dissipated. "No, Deb. I'm okay."

"What did you say?" his brother-in-law demanded, his voice sharp.

"No, Corey. I'm okay. Will you ask Jane to call me when she gets in?"

"Oh, okay. I thought you said something else. Well, the computer said yes. The right-sided deflection is okay, if we keep to the target plan. So that's good. I'll get Jane to confirm the results for you as soon as she gets in."

"Yeah. Please do, Corey. Good talking to you."

"Likewise."

Aaron slid his cell back into his pocket and walked into the main meeting room.

Timothy was meekishly waiting on the other side of the door.

"Hey, Tim. You okay? What're you doing, just standing here?"

"I just didn't want to go in by myself. They all think I'm a traitor or worse, a stupid fool," the Brit admitted, as he walked around the outer set of tables toward Aaron's seat.

"Don't worry about it. It's not your fault. Did you get the update from NASA?"

He handed him a piece of paper. "Here you go." Timothy continued past his chair and sat.

"Are you sure about this?" President Jameson trapped Aaron with a serious look.

"I'm getting there. We'll go through it all now, if you want."

The double bank of tables and chairs were fully filled. The room was a lot cleaner than the day before.

The Russian president stood, commanding attention. "We have been told to come in here by our German comrades." His accent was thicker than usual. "They've told us you may have a solution to our stalemate. You have the *Bomba's*, but you don't have the codes. Yes, you may be able to crack them, but you won't do it in one or two days, before you have to launch. Even if you send the nuclear bombs to space, unarmed, and try to retrospectively unarm them, you'll have ten or eleven days." He gestured and his large chest rose and fell as if he'd taken a breath. "Maybe you could crack them in two weeks. Maybe." He leaned on the table, staring level at everyone around him. "Or you could just cooperate with us and detonate the asteroid with a deflection to the left, across the American side of Earth." The older man retook his seat, as Aaron tapped President Jameson's shoulder, waving a small piece of paper at him.

The president gestured him to read it.

"Thank you." He stood to address the delegates. He took his cell from his pocket and placed it on the table. "First of all, I'd like to ask Dr. Carlton to tell us the findings from the simulations performed by NASA last night and this morning. But, actually, before that, I'd quickly like to acknowledge that the 'leak' from these meetings were due to notes and documents stolen from his position."

The room murmured in distaste.

"Thank you, everyone." He tried to keep the room calm. "It was by no fault of his own, it was a corrupt act by a certain reporter. So, can we please move on from this? Thank you, again." He sat, and Timothy rose slowly.

"Thank you, Dr. Jacobs. I'd like to take this opportunity to apologize. It was a combination of exhaustion and stupidity, along with misplaced trust which caused the 'leak'." He looked around the room, as if for some sympathy.

None was given, unfortunately.

"We've received the simulation data back from NASA. The asteroid is a little bit closer to Earth, but that's not a huge issue. They decided to put it in a percentage of absolutes. For example, if the deflection to the right or east across Russia was one hundred percent successful, then the deflection to the left or West across the United States would be ninety-five percent successful. Basically, over the whole system, getting the rockets ready, launching them, the slingshot, the double slingshot, getting them to the asteroid and detonating them; then five percent would be a lot, but because both systems are the same, except for the final five percent, it's a relatively small thing, and does not have a multiplying effect."

"So, both scenarios will get to the asteroid; they're both nearly one hundred percent. The only difference is, the deflection east or west, and that's that particular five percent. Thank you, Dr. Carlton." President Jameson always seemed ready to impress, with his ability to grasp complicated situations.

Timothy smiled at the older, but rather fit, president as he sat.

"Well, that concludes it for us. If Dr. Jacobs is happy with the numbers, then I'm happy with them. I think we'll take the risk of the five percent, as opposed to the Russians zero percent." The president held his hands open in the direction of the Russians.

Someone has to play ball here.

Aaron watched Russia with barely contained nerves. His country had put forth the effort; how would they be received?

The Russian president smirked back at his American counterpart, an obviously coy acknowledgment of the 'zero percent' insult directed at them.

He hadn't missed either, but was hoping Russia had.

Oh well, we're the ones capitulating.

"We also have the same results from Caltech. Which is great," Timothy said.

Aaron closed his eyes for a moment; he couldn't believe the Brit had dragged the Caltech results into the equation. He wanted NASA to lead the findings alone. The Caltech numbers had been confirmed by Corey, not Jane.

He looked at his cell phone. His brother-in-law had said the Caltech asteroid simulator had successfully passed the planet. Aaron's doubts were riding him hard.

Why am I questioning Corey? Why do I have a bad feeling about this? I can't afford to make a mistake.

He looked back at everyone staring at him, waiting for some more information, some more certainty.

"I'm just waiting on my own simulation results to come back. Provisional thoughts are that they will also pass us with no issues," he said, trying not to give in to the urge to ram his hand through his hair or fidget at the edge of the table.

President Jameson raised his index finger. "Are you questioning NASA? NASA's results?"

Aaron shook his head. "No, sir. It's just statistics and probability. Like, hypothetically, if NASA had a five percent chance of failure on their system, and Caltech had a four percent chance of failure on a different system, then we'd have a combined chance of four and a half percent failure, theoretically. The average of the two. If we test the results twice, and they're both correct, then it reduces the chance of an incorrect outcome, that's all. I'm not questioning NASA. Sorry if it came across like that." Seconds ticked by but felt like forever as he waited for a response.

The room remained silent.

It looked like the seed of doubt had been planted,

not only in the president's head, but in all of the other delegates.

Louis stood, and Aaron sat. "Sir, what Aaron's trying to say, and no disrespect to you—Aaron…" The older man shot him a sympathetic look.

None was taken, as far as he was concerned, he was just glad to be sitting down without the focus on him.

"Trying to reduce the percentages for all the parts of the plan is prudent. If something's ninety-nine percent perfect, that's great, but when you start adding or more precisely, multiplying ninety-nine with another ninety-nine, and then maybe a ninety-eight, things start to get difficult. We have seven space rockets we're trying to send to an asteroid; each rocket represents around fourteen percent of the total rocket ships. All these, one or two percent lost suddenly start adding up and you end up reaching a fourteen percent failure rate, which means we could lose a rocket ship or worse; fail. Thankfully, we're nowhere near that, because of the due diligence being carried out by Aaron and his colleagues at Caltech, and NASA and others." The Frenchman sat with a steady set to his shoulders, and Aaron needed his confidence.

Louis' explanation was enough to get a murmur throughout the room; a number of heads nodded.

"Let's go with that. We'll deflect to the west, across the Atlantic, and past the US. If the Russian president is okay with that, could he please hand over the codes?" President Jameson said with a definitive nod. He looked pleased with himself.

The Russian president made his way over to the US leader.

President Jameson stood to receive him, but his expression shouted he didn't know what was about to happen.

Russia stuck a hand out, and they shook vigorously.

The rest of the room stood and applauded the two nations.

Major Russell moved to his Commander-in-Chief. "Sir, we should do the press conference this minute. We need to show a united front here as soon as possible. This agreement can get things back on track."

Aaron sat peering at his cell, waiting for a call. He had such a bad feeling about all this. He couldn't help but shake his head, and his anxiety threatened to swallow him whole.

The statistics were correct, but the horrible voices in his head were telling him something else.

The meeting was adjourned.

All relevant parties had agreed, and knew what each had to do.

The Russian and American presidents walked out of the hotel onto the closed main street together.

The dozens of cameras and camera lights switched on.

The reporters hardly had time to fix their hair, straighten their ties or fix their skirts.

Aaron's reservations steadily rose as he observed it all.

The rest of the world leaders followed the two, mostly, antagonists, as they decided to hold hands and lift them aloft as if in victory.

President Jameson took to the microphoned podium.

A spontaneous loud cheer erupted from everyone involved.

He told the media of the current plan, and how all the nations had rallied together to save Europe and civilization as they all knew it.

Aaron slipped away when he couldn't stand anymore, slipping back into the chair he'd vacated what felt like a lifetime ago.

Eva joined him shortly, taking the seat beside him. She put her hand at the back of his neck. "Are you okay? You seem distracted, or…upset."

His cell rang, and it was Jane. He sprang up from his chair, and Eva's hand dropped to the backrest. "Hi. Did the numbers come out okay?"

"Hi. Yeah, they did. Corey told you that. They were fine. Plenty of wiggle room."

"But did you see the numbers yourself?" His voice was frantic to his own ears, but he couldn't remain calm.

"Yes. Aaron. They are my numbers. I set the simulator up. I inputted the numbers, set the parameters, and everything else. I've seen the results. They're good. I'm telling you. *They are all good.*"

Aaron let out a big breath. "Okay, that's all I asked. All I needed to know."

"Corey told you the numbers. He told me he already did. Do you not trust him or something?" Jane's questions held insult and disbelief.

"No. No. That's not it. I was just double checking. That's all. Nothing else meant by it."

"It's fine. Leave it at that, I guess," Jane said.

"We have a breakthrough. Russia and the US are working together to get the bombs over. We're done here. I'll be home soon," he said.

"That's great, Aaron. So, you won't need me tonight?"

"No. We're done. Everything's in order. I'll see you in a day or two."

"Yeah. Okay. See you then," his student said. He could hear a smile in her words.

Aaron tried to plaster over the cracks of mistrust he had with his brother-in-law. "Well done, Jane. Can you tell Corey I said well-done also?"

"I will do. Bye."

"Who's that?" Eva asked.

He looked around, but didn't smile at her beauty, this time. He was taken aback by her stealth. "That's Jane over in Caltech. She's a smart kid. Very, very bright student. I'd be lost without her."

"Oh, right!"

"How are you, beautiful? Looks like we're nearly there. We'll have a few days off while they prepare the rocket ships. Maybe we could go to California, or even France?"

"Maybe," Eva said as she walked off.

Aaron watched her skinny jeans walking away. He shook his head at her reaction.

Strange!

29

HOME AT LAST

The next evening, Aaron touched down at LAX airport in Los Angeles. He made his way off the plane alone. Went through immigration, showed his passport and exited the secure zone. He passed by baggage claim, no need for him to wait, as he'd traveled light.

"Daddy, Daddy!" The small blond boy bounded toward him, wearing a big bright smile. Ben had never seemed so happy to see him.

He knelt on one knee and pulled his son tight into his arms. His familiar scent of detergent from the little boy hit his senses and he closed his eyes.

"I missed you, Daddy." Ben's voice wobbled, and Aaron's stomach mirrored it.

He loosened his embrace and looked down at his son.

The boy's eyes were glistening with tears. His lower lip was full and protruding, a semi-pout.

His own eyes welled up, he glanced away only to see Katie looking straight at him.

Her eyes too, were full of tears, and she held a tissue to her nose.

He hiked his son to one hip and outstretched a hand to Katie, pulling her into an embrace.

She deserved one. His sister-in-law had dropped everything for him and Ben.

"I missed you guys. What a week. And it's not even started." He smiled, but laughed ironically at the severity of it all. "Have you been a good boy?" he playfully asked Ben as they started walking.

"I have, I've been a very good boy. I ate all my dinner every day, so I can be big and strong like my daddy." The child threw his arms into the air.

"He's been the best little boy ever," Katie said with a smile.

"Thank you so much, for everything you've done." Aaron wanted her to feel his sincerity.

"No, no. You're the one doing all the work. You're the one saving the world," she replied.

"Well, I wouldn't go that far." Embarrassment kissed the back of his neck. "Ben, we'd better get you home to bed. We'll go visit Daddy's work tomorrow. We might even go on a little trip to see a space shuttle."

"You going already?" Katie asked. "So soon?"

"We'll talk about it when we get home." He lowered his voice, so as not to worry Ben.

"Oh okay, yeah, of course."

They made their way to the parking garage, and got into Aaron's black Suburban.

"Do you want to drive?" Katie asked.

"No. I'm pretty tired. I didn't sleep much on the plane."

Ben sat in his booster chair, playing with a couple of action figures, and was heavily engrossed in his made-up world.

Aaron pointed to the right-hand lane, which lead to Caltech.

"You want to go to the university?" she asked.

"Yeah. I need a clear head. I want to make sure we're all on the same page."

"Same page as what?" Her brow was drawn tight, and he could almost feel her confusion.

"There're important issues at hand, I just really want to check something for myself. I won't sleep unless I check the figures. You guys can come up with me. We won't be long."

She drove down the university road and pulled into Caltech.

He directed her to the building where the old observatory was, and she parked the big Chevy.

Aaron took Ben out of the SUV. "Let's go see where Daddy works. I was going to bring you tomorrow, but today's as good a day as any."

Katie got out of the driver's seat and grabbed her bag.

They made their way to the observatory computer room.

He swiped his keycard and continued up the stairs, with Ben in his arms, and Katie in tow.

When they got inside, the lights were on, all screens were active.

There was a scruffy–looking man dozing in a chair at one of the workstations. His clothes were ill-fitting, and he had a massive beard; albeit, his beard wasn't as bad as it was when Jane first met him.

Minus the different clothing, the man was as Aaron had last seen him.

He must've heard their entry, because he jolted awake.

"Corey, is that you?" Katie asked.

"Hi, Katie. How are you?" his brother-in-law asked as he rubbed his eyes.

She ran to hug her brother. "I missed you so much, Corey."

Sobbing sounds came from them both as Aaron waited and watched, still holding his son.

"I'm so sorry, Katie. I just lost the run of myself over the past few years. I didn't want to talk to people or go back to the normal status quo of life," Corey said as he glanced over at Aaron a couple of times.

Aaron nodded to acknowledge his sincerity. He made his way to the computer that Corey had just been sitting at. He clicked on the latest simulation file and had a quick look at the numbers for himself.

They look good to me.

"It's all right. I'm just glad you're back and safe. It was bad enough losing Debs, but losing you too, was just awful." She was holding back more tears, her voice thick and wobbly. "Look at little Ben."

"He's not so little anymore," Corey said.

"Hi," Ben said shyly.

"Aaron, you've done so well. You must be so proud of him."

"Thanks, Corey. I'm very proud of him. And thanks for all the help back here at 'control central'." He flashed a grin.

"No problem at all. That Jane girl is one smart cookie."

Katie frowned, her brow drawn tight. "Who's Jane, and what's 'control central'?"

"We'll explain all later." Aaron tried to hurry everyone out of the observatory. "Why don't we all go back to my place? We'll have a bite to eat and talk tonight. We have a big day tomorrow."

"But I want to see the videos on the screen," Ben whined, pointing to the largest screen.

"I'll show you from the computer at home. You can even control the telescope yourself remotely." He ruffled his son's fair locks, hoping it would excite him.

"Okay!" the little boy shouted as they collectively turned to leave.

They piled into the SUV. On the way back, Ben fell asleep.

Aaron lifted him out. Ben's skinny arms and legs flailed about as he carried him up the stairs and put him in bed. He took off the little boy's shoes and covered him with his duvet.

Katie stood in the doorframe, watching him tuck his son in. Her slender form was silhouetted by the bright light coming from the hallway behind her. "He's such a good boy," she said, wearing a tender smile.

He quietly closed the door and they both went down the hall. Emotion—and mixed feelings— clogged in his chest; forming a lump in his throat he had to work to talk past. "Ben has been through so much in his short life already. I don't know how he copes. Maybe it's thanks to you. He loves you so much."

Corey waited for them in the kitchen. "I have the

kettle on," he said.

Looking at the siblings made thoughts of his wife race through his mind.

"We're still family, you know," Corey said.

Katie put her hand on Aaron's shoulder. "We'll always be family, Aaron."

"You could have come to me, Corey. I would've helped you. I'm always there for you." He wiped a tear away. "If you needed anything back then, a place to stay, clothes, money anything. Or just to talk, whatever you needed. I was there for you. You should've asked."

"Can I use a razor?" his brother-in-law asked. "These student clothes are terrible, too. Do you have a shirt and pants I could borrow?"

They all laughed.

Aaron put a hand on each of their shoulders. "I really need you guys. I need a level head for the next few weeks. I'm hearing all these voices all the time. Telling me that I'm going to end the world."

Corey looked down suddenly, as if he had something to say but couldn't.

He stared his brother-in-law down, but the man wouldn't make eye contact. "I'm hearing things in Debora's voice. It's like she's trying to warn me, like she has been all the time." He looked away from Corey, to Katie. "Do you hear these voices?"

"I don't. Never in my life have I heard her speaking to me from the grave, or whatever you're trying to say." Confusion was stamped all over her pretty face.

"Has she ever spoken to you like this, Corey?"

"Nope. No. Nothing." The scruffy man

continued to study the kitchen floor, and his denial had sounded like a blurt that put instant disbelief in Aaron's head.

"Nothing at all?" he asked.

Corey shook his head in silence, still avoiding eye contact.

He let it go for now, even though a voice in the back of his mind called the man a liar. He took a breath. "Okay, so… I just need you guys on my side. I know you have been, Katie, with Ben, you have been Corey, with Jane and the simulators. I'll need you guys more than ever this week. We're launching tomorrow, and we have a lot of sleepless nights to get through until this God damn asteroid is put to bed."

"I'll do whatever I can," Katie said.

"Me, too." Corey finally looked at him, nodding.

His heart fluttered before he spoke. "I'm flying to Nice tomorrow evening. Are you able to watch Ben, Katie?"

"Yep, no problem. Whatever you need."

"You're okay to hold down the observatory and double check any calculations we might come up with?" he asked Corey.

"Yeah. One hundred percent. Is Jane coming in tomorrow? I could do with her help. She's good on the computers and stuff like that."

"I was going to call her now anyway. I'll ask her." Aaron dialed and turned away from them. He went to the front door of his apartment.

"Hey. How are you? Where are you? I just popped over to the observatory to check on Corey. He's not here."

"He's over at my place. I'm here, too."

"Oh, okay. What're you doing?"

"I'm going to get some sleep. I haven't slept much this week. I'm going to Nice tomorrow, to meet my colleague, Eva."

"Oh, okay. That should be nice."

"It's not exactly a holiday," Aaron replied.

"Oh yeah. Sorry. I didn't mean it like that." Her tone held remorse, as if he'd reprimanded her.

"It's okay. What time are you going into Caltech tomorrow at?"

"Do you need me to be here?" Her question was the opposite of before; she sounded peppy.

"Of course, I do. You're an integral part of the 'team', for want of a better word."

"I'll probably just crash here for the night."

"Okay. I'll call you tomorrow so. Big day. Rocket time."

"Yeah. Rocket time. Bye."

30

BRIGHT START

"Hello," Aaron said into his cell, as he kicked a soccer ball to Ben out in the common garden. The sun shone and the sky was blue. The calm before the storm.

"Good afternoon, I hope it's nice there in Cali, it's a beautiful day over here in Florida, on the Cape." Major Russell sounded delighted. Cheerful.

He'd never heard him sound like that.

Aaron frowned. "That's great. Why are you calling me so soon?"

"We need you here ASAP," the major demanded.

"No. I'm going to Nice."

"Nope. You're coming *here*. The president wants you here. He wants you to ensure everything's okay with the rockets. Quality Control."

"What the hell do I know about the Saturn V rocket? Why me? There are plenty of more qualified people than *me* to look at them," he growled.

"That's what *I* said. Those were the very points I put to him. But he seems to have some sort of a hard-on for you, so get your ass over here. He wants you to work with the NASA engineers and make sure they're working well with the engineering troops on the ground. You can stop at Atlanta or Orlando, we'll pick you up. But you need to be here as soon as possible or the boss man will come down hard on us all."

Aaron didn't say anything. He was in a daze; it didn't make sense. He was raging, not only would he not get to meet Eva in the next few days, but he'd have to cut his fun time with his son short. He shook his head in disbelief.

"Do I make myself clear?" Major Russell shouted. "Come out, or we'll pick you up ourselves. It's a direct order from Jesus himself. Go to the Army desk at the airport, they'll have everything arranged for you."

He hung up on him with no reply, then passed the ball back to his son.

"Come on, let's go inside," he said to Ben. He looked into the kitchen and watched Corey and Katie laughing and joking, just like old times.

"Aww, Dad, we just started."

He smiled at Ben and scooped him into his arms, tickling the little boy into giggles of distraction.

Aaron went to his room and put on some shorts, flip-flops, and a loose shirt. No point in showering; he was just going on a plane.

He grabbed a bag and filled it with a couple more beach shirts, shorts, and essentials.

Ben came into the bedroom. "Daddy."

Aaron ruffled his hair. "I have to go and make

sure the rockets are working."

"Can I come?"

"It's work, buddy. I can't bring anyone to work."
He had to leave his son again. Sorrow washed over
him. He wished this nightmare he was caught up in
would be over soon.

But it wasn't just his family in the nightmare, the
whole world was.

His little boy rubbed his eyes. He crawled into
Aaron's bed. His arms and head were the only things
protruding from the large duvet. "Are you going to
save the world? Like a superhero?"

He smoothed Ben's hair, smiled and gave him a
kiss on the cheek. "Yes, Ben. I'm going to save the
world, just like a superhero."

The child smiled and went back out to the
common area to play ball.

He couldn't help but look over his shoulder at his
son even before he'd reached the door. Tears were
close to falling as he picked up his bag.

Aaron was upset and didn't want to hang around
to explain his feelings to his extended family. "I've got
to go to Caltech, before the airport. I'll call you guys
soon." He quickly shut the door behind him and got in
his car, driving down the quiet streets. Every day his
neighborhood seemed to get quieter, more stores
closed down than the day before. Reality was finally
settling in for people.

Aaron pulled into Caltech and went up to the
observatory.

Jane was fast asleep on the couch.

He tapped her shoulder. "Hey," he whispered.

She woke slowly and smiled. "Hi," she said with

one eye open, a small blanket wrapped around her. She sat up. "Sorry, I'm still on Hong Kong time. Aren't you going to France or something?"

He sat on the edge of the couch. "I know how you feel. I'm only right now after a good sleep. I'm going to Orlando. I'm heading to the airport now. I'm wanted there, to look at the rockets or something. The major's picking me up from the airport."

"Sounds good. You not going meeting your French girl?"

Aaron nearly laughed, but figured he better keep things serious with Jane. "No, I'm not."

"She seems nice. Very smart." She lay back down into the cushions. "You won't need me for a while so, if you're on the plane?"

He tapped her shoulder again. "Jane, look at me for a second."

She obeyed.

"You've been absolutely awesome. I'm so proud of you. You're actually amazing."

Her cheeks went pink and she smiled a little. "Stop, will you? I'm just typing in a few numbers into a computer." She laughed. "It's not like it's rocket science or anything."

He smiled, the irony not lost on him. "No, it's not like it's rocket science."

"Thanks for stopping by before you left. You never know, this could be the last time that we see each other."

Aaron stared, not speaking.

Jane grabbed his hand. "Don't worry. I didn't mean anything promiscuous by that. Hell no. You've been really good to me. I really appreciate all you've taught me, and it's been fun hanging out with you. You're a pretty cool guy. For a professor."

He smiled again. "Oh, you're funny." He stood. "We're not done yet, Jane. I need you to be on the ball for the next couple of days. There's a reason we're working on this project. I don't know what it is, or why we've all been brought together, but there *is* some reason."

"Fate. Or maybe I'm actually good at this stuff."

"You're definitely good at all this astro stuff. But fate? That's what I was thinking, but I wasn't sure if it was a bit of a silly way to describe it."

"Why would it be silly? It's accurate," she said.

"Because it's not science. It's kind of make-believe. It's accidental, it's coincidental."

Jane sat up again. "The universe is just a coincidence followed by an accident, followed by a coincidence, and so on and so on for infinity. Never ending fate turned into fact."

Aaron smiled for the third time. "You're good. I'll give you that."

"I learned from the best." She winked.

31

THE CAPE

It was early morning the following day. Aaron hadn't contacted Eva since he'd left California.

He needed to call her at her observatory.

"*Bonjour.*"

"Hi, Eva. I'm in Orlando and I have to go down to the Cape. Major Russell wants me to look over something. I'm going to be delayed."

"Why is the line so bad? Every other word is crackling." She sounded on edge.

"I've just landed. The battery died on my cell. I couldn't plug it in last night; power outage. I'm using the airplane phone. I'll be driving down to the Cape soon. The major wants me to check over something. Something to do with the rockets."

"You're not backing out on me, are you? I'm kind of in the eye of the storm here. Everyone's leaving except me and Louis. Essential services are just about working."

He could sense that she was nervous. Their plan was good enough to work, and they trusted their calculations, so that was a little bit of comfort.

They'd gone through the calculations hundreds of times on the simulator; they knew that technically the safest place to be was directly under the asteroids initial impact zone, due to the deflection.

Even if it were to go wrong, it would deflect the asteroid to the Atlantic Ocean. They also figured they'd have enough time to abandon Nice and still have a few days to get to safety. That was the plan, anyway. Aaron knew this, but living it was another thing. The outcome and accuracy had yet to be seen.

"After the deflection, Nice will be the safest place in the world," Aaron said in a calm, even voice.

"I know, I'm just scared. You promise you'll come over to me soon?" Nerves made her voice tremble.

The phone crackled again. "I promise I'll be there. You have the best vantage point for keeping track of any changes in relation to the asteroid. We'll need to be there so we can get a calculation on the most accurate degree of deflection," Aaron added some technicalities that would make Eva's internal calculator start to work. It was a distraction.

"Okay, that sounds good then. Thanks so much. See you soon, and let me know what's going on."

"I will do. Thanks."

Aaron deplaned at Orlando International.

Dawn was glimmering over the horizon. A black SUV waited for him on the tarmac.

Two Secret Service agents in fancy suits greeted him, but it was terse orders to get in the car.

They sped down the runway to a waiting helicopter and boarded together.

The heavy downburst of the helicopter rotors pressed on him with a blast of air. The machine's engines reached their highest pitch as the aircraft lifted off.

Two pilots sat in the front seats, obviously concentrating on their job while the two agents sat behind with Aaron between them. All of them were wearing headphones and mics, but no one spoke.

Within fifteen minutes of flying due east, Aaron's jaw dropped. As they approached Cape Canaveral, from about three miles out, all seven Saturn V space vehicles were visible.

"One hundred and eleven-meter-long monsters," he whispered to himself. They were laid out parallel with the morning blue sky, which displayed them in all their splendor.

Hundreds of personnel were tending to the rockets. The work seemed frantic but coordinated.

The helicopter came in for landing.

Major Russell was dressed in full Marine combat uniform. He gripped his hat for dear life as he rushed over to greet Aaron. "I didn't think you'd come," he shouted over the sound of the helicopter's rotor blades. "Get in the jeep."

"I didn't think I had a choice." He watched the *Tsar II Bomba's* being readied at Cape Canaveral. Four more giant Saturn V rockets stood high against the perfect blue-sky backdrop.

The major didn't answer as they rushed from one hanger to another, as trucks and armed forces passed him by with crowded intent.

The noise of the dozens of powerful trucks filled the air. Men and women in uniform rallied around like ants; everyone with a task and a purpose.

The early morning sun began to cast a long shadow on the runway and fields of the cape, none longer than the quarter-mile shadows of the enormous Saturn V rockets.

They dismounted and entered one of the hangers on the air base. Aaron looked up at the cross-shaped window frame shadows, which landed on the opposite walls. A number of military personnel were busy welding, cutting and reimagining the original Saturn V while NASA engineers oversaw their work.

"Keep up the good work. You're doing a great job," Major Russell said as he sauntered along. He went back outside into the blue morning, and took out his cell.

"I thought you said my presence was an order from the president?" Aaron eventually said.

"It was, but I had my doubts." The major escorted him to a temporary cabin that took them away from the hustle and bustle outside. A makeshift prefabricated white cabin. As bland as one could imagine. "Okay, Aaron. I'm going to be straight and blunt with you. The president asked me to gauge your opinion, and see if you can back up NASA's numbers."

"But I *have* backed them up. The numbers are correct. They're not *my* numbers, they are NASA's numbers."

"No, Aaron. There are new numbers." Major Russell made a cutting gesture with one hand. "No time to waste."

"What new numbers?" A sickening sense came over his stomach. It, along with his entire gut, wobbled.

"We cannot, I repeat, *cannot,* get these Saturn Vs up in the air in three days."

"Well, you have an extra spaceship, and an extra day. That'll buy you, a day and a quarter, maybe."

"We need an extra *four* days. It's taking six days to outfit the rockets onto the Saturn Vs. We budgeted for three."

"So how is it taking four extra days? If it's six, minus three days?" Aaron asked.

"We need to add extra *Bomba's* to the rockets. Twice as many. We think." The major seemed unsure. This un-surety was unlike the strong, even hard-ass military man he'd come to know.

He frowned and his fears spiked. His heart shot into overdrive. "You think?" he demanded.

"Yes. We need to run the numbers again. The extra fourth day is to allow adding on the extra *Bomba.* That's why it's seven days now."

Aaron gasped, and swallowed. "This is going to put the deflection from day T-minus six to T-minus three."

The older man presented flat palms, and pushed them down in front of him. "It's all going to be all right. Just take a minute."

"You'll need to double the angle of deflection, if you're fifty percent closer than you should've been!" He'd tried not to yell, but Aaron's voice had still come out loud.

"I know that! That's why we're doubling the amount of *Bomba's* on the ships," Major Russell retorted.

His head was spinning. "But what about the payload? It's too much for the Saturn V. The two *Bomba's* are going to be too heavy."

"Well, we can get to orbit, albeit much slower. We don't need to go out as far as the asteroid anymore, because it'll be closer to us. So, our slower speed will be canceled out by the asteroid's having longer to get here."

"Fair enough. But you're cutting everything really tight."

"How tight, Aaron? Can you crunch your numbers with your team? You've got everything right so far. The president trusts you."

It was too much. He was overwhelmed. The whole situation was resting on *his* shoulders. "I don't want to submit my numbers as fact. I'll check the NASA numbers. That's all. But I'm not making any call on anything whatsoever."

"Listen. President Jameson trusts you, we *all* trust you. The other countries around the table, too. The fucking, Goddamned Russians trust you. To be honest, *I* actually trust you. You've no vested interest in this. You're practically independent." Major Russell's expression was pleading, something Aaron had never seen from the man.

"What do you mean; I have no vested interest in this? I have a son, I have a friend I sent back to Nice, because I was ninety-five percent sure we could pull this off. She's in the firing line in France, and you say *I* have no vested interest in this." He clutched his fists at his sides so he wouldn't hit the idiot.

Not vested? The whole *world* was literally at stake.

Screw this guy!

The major stood, gesturing as he had earlier. "Hey, hey. You have extremely vested interests in all of this. More of a reason now to get cracking on those numbers, and make sure we're not missing anything."

He stared. "I'll need some stuff. I'm not sure yet, and I'll need a day."

"You got it. Go grab a bite to eat, and I'll have everything set up for you in half an hour, whatever you want."

Aaron stormed from the major's prefab and called Jane.

"Hi. I didn't expect to hear from you so soon," she said.

"Yeah. Big change of plans. We'll need to redo all the simulations."

"What?" He heard her inhale. "Hold on. Putting you on speaker so Corey can hear. We need to re-run the simulators... Why? Did we make a mistake?" she sounded puzzled.

"No, not at all. The opposite, really. Our simulations were really good. That's why they want us to double check them, along with NASA and Oxford/Cambridge."

"What changed?" Corey asked. He too, sounded confused.

"For a start, there are now two *Bomba's* going into each Saturn V. So, you'll need to adjust the payload weight. I'll need to know when the minimum T-minus day is for this takeoff. It's going to take longer than expected to get the rockets ready. About four days later."

His brother-in-law's sigh was audible. "It's going

to be so tight. We're going to go from high ninety percent of certainty to seventy or less percent success rate. This is bad, Aaron."

"I know it's bad, but we don't have any other options. We just need to get this done in one shot. We need to find some way of helping our guys here. Some way of increasing the odds. If you find anything, let me know."

"Yup. That's all we can do. Just do our best," Jane said.

"That's all you can do. Run that simulation, and I'll come back with some small adjustments soon." Aaron hung up and went back into the major's prefab.

The busy sound of the trucks grew as the level of work increased through the morning.

He walked up the steps and opened the door without knocking. "Is there any way you could manage to get a half a day or something back on our launch day?"

"We can try. But we're already putting two *Bomba's* onto the first three Saturn Vs. We're still waiting for the Germans to come in with the other seven. That should get things done a bit quicker. Hopefully, the team of engineers will have it down to a fine art, so when we're working on the other four, we'll be able to get done faster. I'm sure we'll be able to pick up more time here and there."

Aaron shook his head. "What about more staff?"

Major Russell waved away the idea. "It's not about staff; it's about working correctly. Too many cooks spoil the broth." He looked out the window at the sea of engineers and technicians.

They were working on the rockets, putting

floodlights up so they could work at night.

Laying new roads so they could transport the rockets from different areas of the Cape to the launch pads. Building infrastructure, putting in communications, prefabs being heli-dropped. It was like they were building a city overnight.

"Fair enough."

"Are you going back to Caltech or staying here? You'll probably be wanted here. If I have any more information for you to add to the simulator, I'll let you know."

"I'm going to Nice," Aaron said. He crossed his arms over his chest and waited for the inevitable argument.

"For fuck's sake. Why the hell would you do that?"

"It's as safe there as anywhere now. This whole thing could turn into a game of Russian Roulette in the next few days. Besides. I want to be closer to the asteroid when it's passing, so we can track it better." He tried to justify going to France to himself, albeit a little far-fetched. The major didn't need to know that.

"Good luck with that!"

Aaron ignored his comment. "Can I get a lift back to the airport?"

"You sure can."

His mind spun with worry for Eva and Ben, and the world. A daze settled over him as his brain went on overdrive. How had everything gone from near certainty to seventy-thirty or worse, maybe fifty-fifty?

"Aaron! Are you ready to go?" Major Russell said.

"What? Yeah. I'm ready. Actually, can you take me to Disneyworld?"

"No, you idiot. The hell I'll take you to Disneyworld. I'll get you to the airport in the chopper. You can go to France then and try not to get hit by an asteroid."

"I would've loved to take my son there."

"There is one in Paris. No queues either. Bring him to that one," the Major said as he escorted Aaron to a jeep, ordering his driver to take him directly to the helipad.

"One last thing, Aaron. I want you to run this thrust instead of the final stage rocket." He handed him a piece of paper with an extremely large thrust value on it. "This is instead of the rocket we're using to catch up with the asteroid."

"This number is either wrong or made up. It's too large." He shook his head in disbelief.

"Just run the number. You're the chosen one. Don't tell anyone. Top fucking secret. Definitely, don't tell the Russians."

Aaron didn't know what to say. "I guess this is the rabbit in the hat?" he finally managed.

"You betcha," the major said as he tapped the top of the Jeep a few times.

Aaron looked back at the major as the vehicle sped off and saluted him.

The major stood firm and reciprocated.

32

SCHOOL'S OUT

Corey and Jane were busy in the observatory at Caltech, trying to look for answers and anomalies.

He noticed confusion on her face.

"I'm not convinced with what I'm seeing. I'm getting good results from the simulators, Corey. I don't know why they're so perfect! I have a bad feeling about them."

"No, actually. It's not that difficult. The angle of deflection is twice what's needed now, so twice the amount of power is needed to move it, twice as much. Everything should be kind of similar. Just doubled," he reassured her.

"Well, why didn't we adopt this approach in the first place? If everything works out the same?"

"Because if things didn't go right with the last plan, we had a few days to fix it, with this plan, we have no spare time to fix anything," he said.

"So, basically, this is our last chance, and we really need to get this right."

Corey nodded. "Exactly. It's not even all your eggs in one basket. It's one egg in one basket. This is the kind of stuff I was talking about. Real destruction."

Jane's cell *dinged* with a text, she gave it a glance before showing him.

Aaron's message stated there was a slight increase in weight, due to structural supports added to the rockets for securing the second *Bomba's*.

"More weight to be added. Do you want to input these to the computer? The changes aren't huge. They shouldn't make any difference, but it's best to be one hundred percent accurate," she said.

He took the cellphone and started entering the new data. "Check these numbers, Jane."

They now had a double standard check on themselves.

She looked over everything and nodded. Jane finished what she was doing and headed to the door of the observatory. "I'll be back in a few minutes. I'm gonna get a bit of fresh air."

"No problem. Take your time," he said, with his head sucked into the screen.

Corey heard the second door close downstairs. He got up and opened the door, then wedged a seat up against it to keep it open, making sure he could hear if someone was trying to enter the lower door.

He quickly saved his work and immediately started making a few changes to the settings. He delayed the explosion to T-minus two days and added the seventh standby ship's explosive bombs.

Corey ran the simulator and looked at the

resultant render, shaking his head. He put his hands on his head and rested his elbows on the desk in front of them.

He saved his own file and opened the last file Jane had been working on. He ran the simulation, as she'd asked. He expected nothing new, so he wanted to walk in the fresh air also.

Corey headed down the corridor she'd brought him to on the first day they met, down toward Aaron's office.

He sat there, looking at all the stacks of paper on his brother-in-law's desk. He opened a drawer and closed it.

Jane heard a drawer close. She was only a short distance from Corey and in the dead silence of the university, so she could also hear where the noise was coming from.

She tip-toed toward Aaron's office until she could see her friend's hair through two windows.

Jane was nervous. Not nervous of Corey, but nervous about getting caught spying on him. She understood it would undermine their trust for each other.

On the contrary, she felt she owed it to Aaron to keep an eye on him; after all, Corey was going through his desk and personal belongings.

She edged closer to the office; so close she could make out what he was saying, or whispering to himself.

"There it is. It's fate, sis. You always could see it, no matter how hard they try to change it," he whispered as he picked up a picture. He kissed the framed photo. He looked up to the ceiling and raised his right hand in a fist. "And so, the sixth seal was opened and the rapture began. The stars fell; which turned the moon blood red and the sun dark." He gazed at her again. "You're the one who told us it'd all end, and you were right. They all thought you were mad. All of them, except me."

Jane stood at the exit to the ladies changing room, listening intently and trying to catch a glimpse of what Corey was up to.

The janitor had left a mop and bucket out, not bothering to finish the cleanup job.

She stepped back and tipped the mop over. The handle slowly slid against the wall; she tried in vain to stop it falling to the ground.

Jane couldn't grab it in time, so instead ran away from the ladies changing room before the mop hit the floor.

Corey heard a clatter in the hallway. It jolted him to his feet, and he dashed back to the observatory as quickly as he could; as if he'd been caught doing something wrong.

"Hey, Corey. Where were you?" Jane was back at the computer, as if she'd never left.

"Just getting a breath of fresh air, like you," he answered. How long had she been back? He wouldn't ask. "Any results on the simulation?"

"Yeah. We've run them so many times; they won't change much from where we are now. Do you think they're accurate?"

Corey cocked his head to one side. They'd spent a number of days working on this project together, going through different scenarios and working out worst case, versus best case. "Yeah, why do you ask?"

"I'm just wondering if you're happy with them. Do you think everything will work out from the simulators?" Her expression was open, and her voice light, but there was something in her eyes he didn't know what to make of.

"Why? Do you think there might be a mistake, or that I've left something out?" He wanted to glare, but tried to keep his annoyance at bay.

Maybe they'd been cooped up in the observatory too long.

"I'm just asking your opinion, that's all." She took a breath, but that odd expression didn't fade. Jane shook her head. "Never mind, forget about it."

"You've been here with me every second of every day. If the rockets takeoff at the specified time, under the specified conditions, in the specified direction, they'll do everything the simulator specified. Exactly the same." Corey frowned, staring her down.

"That's all I wanted to know. I'm just a little worried. Just needed a bit of reassurance." She slumped on the couch.

"Fine. That's all you had to say."

"That's great. So, there is nothing we know about that's not in the simulator?" she asked, as if she had to have the last word.

Corey drew a large *N-O* in the air with his index finger.

"Let's take a break and get out of here. We should get some popcorn and cola from the movie theater down the road," Jane said.

"Is the theatre open? I heard everything's closed in the city. The mall, the toll booths, the ferries. Everything has ground to a halt for the launches."

"I don't know, but, sure maybe we could break in and fire-up the popcorn machine. It's just impossible to make popcorn the same at home. I don't know what they put in it or how they do it, but it's just so much yummier."

"You're right. But, how about we break into the theater and hook up a live feed to the digital projector? We can watch it on the silver screen," Corey said with a smile.

"That sounds like a lot of fun. Let's do it."

They grabbed their belongings and headed to the movie theater.

He asked her to wait while he went to get something.

"I'll be here. I'll just send Aaron the results," she said. Jane walked on slowly. She texted Aaron while Corey went back to the simulator one last time.

As much as I like ur BIL, hes acting strange again. Saying world will end. Some 6th seal or something. Data came back 100% fine, I just feel hes hiding somin.

Corey returned with an iron crowbar in hand.

Chills ran down her spine, and she froze in place, her cell still in hand. She swallowed a few times.

"We'll need this to break into the movie theater," he said.

She was speechless, but desperately tried to find a couple of words to string together. "Great. It's like a universal key." She was afraid her voice belied her nerves. "Sure, we might even get a new car on the way home, complete our day's looting."

He flashed a grin. "If you're up for it. Could be our last few days on the planet!"

The movie theatre was only a few blocks away.

Corey forced the side door open with the crowbar.

Jane jumped nervously when she heard the sound of the inner lock snapping.

He gestured for her to enter into the dark.

She led the way and he followed. They made their way through the lobby, turning on some lights along the way.

"You make the popcorn, and get the cola machine working. I'll go up and get the projector heated up. We'll get our live feed going." He found the staff stairwell, a laptop tucked under one arm, and crowbar in hand.

She switched everything on as she went. The popcorn machine came to life, along with all the lobby lights, advertisement boards, and televisions.

The theatre was in full swing when she grabbed a paper chef's hat and put in on her head.

She found some corn kernels and some magic powder they sprinkled on top. Jane smiled as she tried her hand at making movie-grade popcorn.

33

STRANGE THINGS

Aaron was one of the last people to leave the aircraft when he arrived in France. The government was running the last of the flights back to France. Most of the returning flights were empty, while the outgoing flights were full.

The flight attendant ushered him off, but, he was busy reading Jane's text.

He needed to call her.

"Jane, are you, all right? Did Corey do something to you?" he demanded as soon as she answered.

"I'm fine, Aaron. I'm not concerned about what Corey could do to me. It's more about what he might do to our simulator or our project. He wouldn't hurt me, I'm sure of that."

Relief washed over him, but he was struggling to hear her. "What's all that noise? Where are you?"

"I'm at the movies; there are lots of people here

now. We're having popcorn and cola."

"Why are you watching a movie? The launch is on now. I thought all nonessentials were closed across the states."

"They are. We broke in. Some random people followed us in. Corey has the launch up on the main movie screen. Free popcorn and cola for all. It's a lot of fun."

"You broke in? Great. Committing a crime. Two even. Fantastic." Aaron shook his head.

"It's okay. It's just a bit of fun. We're engaging with the community."

"So, what's with all the strange things Corey's saying?"

"I don't know. Has he given us any misinformation?"

"No. All the data is coming back from Caltech perfectly. It's actually slightly more accurate than the crosschecks from Oxford and Cambridge. He's definitely not misleading us."

"Then I guess the jury's out."

"It sure is. Let's keep going. First launch is on shortly."

"You betcha," Jane said. The words were muffled, as if she was munching on something.

He made his way through the airport, where he spotted Eva. "Jane, I'll chat very soon. Thanks." He put his cell in his pocket. "*Bonjour, mon cher.*" He smiled, proud he'd managed some French on French soil.

She smiled back and gave him a warm hug of welcome. "How are you? Good flight?"

Fondness—and maybe more—washed over him

when he studied Eva's pretty face.

It'd only been a few days, but he'd missed her long flowing hair, her deep-set beautiful dark eyes. Her lips almost always pursed and ready for a kiss.

He wanted to explore the chemistry they'd discovered, but they had a responsibility to their friends and family, not to mention, to the rest of the literal world.

Such a responsibility couldn't be shared by just one of them; it needed to be amongst the whole team.

When this was all over, maybe they could be together.

Aaron hadn't voiced what he wanted, but he had a feeling she'd be up for it. Maybe he could broach the subject on this trip, or maybe not. They had to fix Armageddon first.

They arrived back at the Nice Observatory just in time for the first launch. He was in awe of how beautiful the place was. The architecture, the metal work. The nostalgia and history weren't lost on him.

On the ride in, there'd been no one on the streets. Everyone was indoors, watching the launch. The most watched television event *ever.*

Aaron and Eva, along with the world, watched as the first Saturn V rocket prepared for blast off. Louis had told them he was running a personal errand.

The recognizable old voice coming from the television was, *'the voice of NASA'*, Hugh Harris, counting down from control in Houston.

"T-minus nine, ignition sequence start, six, five, four, three, two, one, zero, lift off! All engines running, lift off! We have a lift-off, at thirty-two minutes past the hour; we have lift off of the Saturn W. The W standing for 'Worldwide' rescue of the Earth."

They sat in front of the bright HDTV, which displayed the beauty of the bursting flames and clarity of the Saturn V rocket thrusting downwards.

He was almost speechless at the beauty of it all. Aaron cleared his throat. "It's been well over a quarter of a century since that rocket was last launched. Hard to believe it's still the best bit of rocketry in the world. They don't make them like they used to."

The rocket looked as if it was going to stay suspended just above the launch pad until the fuel ran out; it didn't. It picked up momentum and shot into the sky as it performed a roll-program. Rolling to the left, then veering off on an intersection with the moon, as fast as physics would allow.

"Let's get some telemetry on the screen and see how we're doing," Aaron said. He had a hold on Eva's slender fingers, and didn't want to release her, but did so when she tugged so she could do as he asked.

"Since the next launch isn't for a few hours, I'm going to grab a nap. Is that okay?" she asked after she'd pulled up the numbers they could both study.

"Sure, that's not a bad idea."

"You can join me," she said with a suggestive smile.

He acknowledged with a nod. "I need to make a call first." He dialed Katie and waited.

"Hi. Did you see the launch? Oh my God!" Her voice went up with each word.

"Yes. It was beautiful. Went off without a hitch," he said as the reality and relief washed over him.

One down, six to go.

"Ben wants to talk to you."

"Thanks, Katie. Hi, Ben."

"Hi, Daddy!"

"Did you watch the launch with Auntie Katie?"

"I did. It went whoosh into the air."

Aaron pictured his son gesturing his little arms up to imitate the rocket. He grinned. "It must be getting late there now. Are you going to stay up for the next launch?"

"I'm going to stay up for them all," his boy said, the excitement in his voice was palpable.

"To watch them all? You'll never be able to stay up and watch them all, there are seven of them."

"I'm watching all seven."

He chuckled. It wasn't worth an argument. "Are you being good for your auntie?"

"I am. Are you still saving the world like a superhero?"

Aaron looked around, slightly uncomfortable with the question, as innocent as it might be. "I am. I'm doing my best. So far so good."

"I love you, Dad, you're the best!"

A tear welled in his eye. "I love you too, so much, buddy." His voice started to break, he sucked in air and swallowed hard.

"Are you okay Daddy?"

Of course, his little son was so perceptive. He laughed, but it was really a nervous cover up to a child who could see right through him.

"I'm really good, Ben. You're such a good boy. You'll have a long life ahead of you. I promise."

A powerful chill passed into his mind and seemed to leave through his skin, and he started to shake. His teeth chattered, as if he was freezing, and he fought the shudder and shiver.

"Are you okay, Daddy? Daddy?" Ben's voice was coated with worry he should be too young for. "Auntie Katie, Auntie Katie! I can't hear Daddy anymore."

"Aaron, are you okay? Can you hear me?" His sister-in-law's voice was back in his ear.

He tried to speak, but nothing came out. It was like his jaw was locked from the frigidness surrounding him. "You're going to kill us all," floated from his trembling lips.

"What did you say? Aaron? I can't hear you. You sound far away."

His teeth were clasped by lockjaw, but the weirdest sound came from his mouth. "Hey, diddle diddle, the cat and the fiddle, you're gonna kill us all, very soooooon."

If Katie responded, he didn't hear it.

He dropped to the floor; his cell hit hard, pieces flying.

Aaron lay unmoving.

Eva couldn't sleep, so she paced the observatory. She couldn't see Aaron, and he'd never joined her. As disappointing as that was, she presumed he'd left to go get something or another. Maybe some food for them?

She went into the main computer room. It was adorned with the standard HDTV jumbo screens everywhere.

Three-dimensional models, simulators, real-time visuals, direct audio from Houston, everything that'd be needed to run mission control.

As well as a nice large couch for crashing on;

she'd insisted on that. She was a night owl, always working late.

Her pacing took her by the couch, and she spotted a pair of shoes. She crept around the corner to get a proper assessment.

Eva saw his legs, then his torso. She scanned over a broken cellphone on the floor just before looking at his face.

His skin was grayish, his cheeks sallow.

Aaron looked as pale as death.

She screamed and dread washed over her. She rushed to his side. "Aaron!" she roared. "*Jésus Sainte Marie Mère de Dieu.*" Eva leaned over him, almost straddling him. "Aaron, are you okay?" She slapped his cheek.

He didn't budge.

"Aaron." She slapped him again. A lot harder this time, the sound of the smack could've woken him quicker than the hit itself.

"What? What? What's going on?" His eyes flew open, and she blew out a breath of relief.

Aaron groaned and rubbed his eye, then the cheek she'd smacked. "Not that I'm complaining, but why are you on top of me?"

"You were passed out, I thought you were dead!" Eva fought tears as her heart thundered.

"I'm okay, I think. Christ, my head." He cupped the back of his neck. "I must've hit the floor hard. I passed out again." His voice was thick, weary, and she grabbed his hands, then helped him to the couch.

"I'll get you a glass of water." She rushed to the kitchenette.

The room lit up with an orange glow, as the

muted televisions revealed the radiance of all five of the Saturn's engines firing.

"Number two," Eva called as she looked for a cup. "Telemetry should be in soon."

"Is the last telemetry okay from the first one?" he asked, while he still had his head in his hands.

"Yeah. What happened to you?"

"I can't remember!"

"Your phone is in pieces," she said as she returned with the water. She handed it over and started picking up the segments of his cell.

Aaron sipped from the glass, rubbed his forehead and started to put the cell phone back together. He inserted the battery, attached the plastic case and clicked them into place. He switched it on.

"Wow, I can't believe it still works," Eva muttered.

The device began to 'bing' frantically.

"God, how long have I been out? I've missed so many calls and texts."

She sat beside him on the couch. "A few hours, I'd say. Since the last launch, anyway."

Aaron scrolled through the texts.

She watched him scan his messages, trying not to read anything on his screen.

"I better call Katie first; ten missed calls, ten texts too." He put the cell to his ear.

Eva was close enough to hear the exchange.

"Hey," a groggy-sounding female voice answered.

"Hi, were you looking for me?"

"Looking for you? I've been trying to call you for hours. I fell asleep. The last time I spoke to you, you were telling me the world was going to end."

What? But Eva didn't say it aloud; she just listened to Aaron's conversation.

"Oh, fuck. What exactly did I say?"

"You were just saying the world was going to end, and you were going to be the reason. Then you started singing, *'Hey diddle diddle the cat and the fiddle, the cow jumped over the moon'*, but instead of the last line you sang, *'you're gonna kill us all very soon'*," Katie said.

Eva frowned. *What the heck?*

His brow was taught, as if he was just as confused as she was. "Okay, thanks for that. Now I've officially gone crazy, just like my wife. Freaking contagious!"

"Aaron, just keep your shit together. You have a family, friends so many people around the world backing you, banking on you. You're doing the right thing. *No one* is going to blame you. What we have now is a plan; we didn't have that plan last week. You're doing great. All you can do is try your best. It's no one's fault."

She appreciated the words of courage and reassurance to the man she'd come to care about, but she didn't like where they were coming from.

Eva was a tad jealous. She looked at him, studying his strong profile. His chiseled looks were outlined with his strong black head of hair. He appeared ten years younger than he was.

"Thanks, Katie. I only get one shot at this. No second tries."

She reached for his free hand and squeezed. She couldn't help her need to touch him.

Aaron spared her a glance and a slight smile.

"Just stay strong. You *are* strong. You are," the female said.

"Thanks, Katie. I'll call you soon. Tell Ben I love him."

Eva put her arms around Aaron as soon as his call was disconnected. "She's right. You're doing great. Now let's stop all the whining and get the telemetries into the simulation. We have work to do." She smiled.

He smiled back. "Let's go. Let's blow this shit out of the water. Or space, or whatever."

She giggled and slapped Aaron's back, in a very tomboyish way. "That's my guy. Aaron's back. He's back with a bang. Excuse the pun."

"Jesus, Eva. No bang yet, please!"

34

T-MINUS FIVE

Corey and Jane received the trajectory of the spaceship as it left the moon's gravitational pull, heading on an intercept course with the asteroid.

They'd watched as the first Saturn capsule exited the moon's double slingshot, the velocity and trajectory had changed significantly.

The radar equipment in space and on the planet quickly picked up this information and relayed it to all the relevant authorities watching. NASA, Cambridge University, Caltech, Oxford University, all the observatories in the world, all the Universities with astrophysics departments and any public domain.

Jane sat in the observatory at the main computer. She typed the new coordinates into the computer and pressed *'play'* on the simulator.

The numbers didn't seem to correlate with expectations.

She assumed she'd typed in something wrong. "Corey, can you send me those trajectories again? They're not working right. We're missing the asteroid with these."

He placed his coffee cup on the desk and leaned over her shoulder to look at the numbers. He glanced at a printout and nodded, confirming what they were looking at. "Open your email. Copy and paste them into the computer, at least then we'll know for sure we're not looking at them wrong or writing them down incorrectly." He picked up his coffee cup, went to a computer and forwarded the email he'd received with the telemetry on it.

As soon as she clicked on the numbers, Jane's screen blinked for a split-second. She blinked. "What was that?" She gaped at Corey. "Did you see that? What the fuck was it?"

"I don't know. A power flicker?"

"Do we not have surge protectors on the computers? Where did you get this email from?"

"Roscosmos." Corey bit his lower lip.

"Did you just send me an email from the Russians?"

"Yeah. I've checked the telemetry. The numbers are all the same across all the different federations, NASA, Oxford, et cetera."

She glared because his tone had been defensive. "You didn't even virus check it? Great, Aaron's going to kill me now for this. Consider ourselves hacked." Jane shook her head. She got up and leaned over the kitchenette sink. She filled a glass with water.

What the fuck have I got myself into here?

She copy/pasted the trajectories into the program.

There was no change in the numbers; they were already correct.

She pressed *'play'* on the simulator again.

Corey hovered over her shoulder when the result came in. "We're way off. What's going on?"

Jane looked up at him. "Something's changed."

"Can we get a printout of the previous simulation, and this one? Compare, and see what's going on?"

She nodded, opening the second simulation.

The printer made a few noises as it warmed up and began to spit out two copies of the reports.

They gave all the relevant information, trajectories, velocities, power, time, force, mass, everything that was going on in the simulators.

Jane and Corey both scanned the pages. Nothing jumped out at her; practically all of the numbers were the same between the simulations. "Aha!" She pointed to one particular number that'd changed.

"The velocity of the asteroid is increasing by more than we calculated," they said simultaneously.

Corey's wide eyes reflected the shock washing over her.

The cell phone rang, making her jump as she reached for it.

It was Aaron.

"The asteroid's speeding up, Aaron. This is *not* good. We'll be at less than fifty-fifty soon," she blurted.

"Yeah, we just got word from NASA. The sun's heating the rock on the asteroid, high-pressure gasses are escaping from the back of it," her professor said. His voice was urgent and full of worry.

"Causing an equal and opposite reaction to the

asteroid's velocity," she said. "What does this mean? Are we in big trouble?" She was biting her fingernails; couldn't help it.

"No, we're still going ahead, but we need to recalibrate all the rockets, *and* have them fire earlier so they can catch the asteroid."

Corey was close enough to hear the call, and Jane slapped it on speaker.

"Aaron. Are we in trouble? Can we get back on course?" he asked again.

"I don't know, Corey. We can just do our best. If it is possible to deflect, then we will. If not, then we won't."

Jane shook her head. "What? But you're in line with the impact."

"Well." He paused. "Not, exactly. It's going to hit earlier, so it'll be toward Portugal or Spain. But it's going to be even more devastating, due to its increased velocity. There isn't even a point in calculating it at this stage. It's going to wipe out Europe, and half of Russia and Africa either way. We're running out of time. We have to deflect this now."

"So, you're going to get wiped out. That's the simple answer. Just simple answers from now on Aaron. Please." She shook her head uncontrollably as she felt the enormity of the situation lay across her shoulders. "Please, Aaron, start making your way out of there. We have a few days left. Can you not get a plane out of there or get to a US Embassy?" she asked.

"Jane," he said calmly. "I'll be okay. I still have faith in the plan. I'll wait here for a few days, and if things get any worse, I'll get out, somehow. I want to get home to Ben. I want to be safe. I'm not doing this to be some sort of hero. I'm just trying to get the best angle on the telemetry as the asteroid gets nearer."

Tears rolled down her cheeks, and she had to sniffle before she could talk. "Please, Aaron, just get out. Please."

Corey put his arm around her. "Aaron, you need to get home. Your son's here. He needs you. *We* need you back now. You've done your best. No one can possibly blame you for anything."

"Corey, I appreciate that. But I'm not done here. I'll leave in a few days, I promise. Either way. If things get worse or get back on track, I'll still leave after the final rockets fire. I'll still have 3 days to get home, no matter what. All right?"

Corey looked at the real-time simulator, and clicked on the moon, removing it from the simulation's view. "This will make it easier to see the flight paths of the spaceships."

Jane sobbed, another thing she couldn't help. "Aaron. This isn't your fight. You have nothing to prove to anyone."

"I'll call you tomorrow."

He was gone; he'd ended the call.

Aaron looked at Eva.

She was sitting on the couch, her hands cradling her face. She was weeping, just like his student had been; only Jane had been trying to hide her tears.

He sighed as he took a seat next to her, sliding his arm around her slender shoulders and pulling her into his side. "It'll all work out. We're not done yet. We can still get this whole thing back on track. We just need to make sure NASA gets their rocket firing right."

He didn't want to voice what they could both see. The timing was down to the last few minutes.

The fifty-fifty chance was now, maybe, a one-in-ten chance.

Right down to the wire.

"Can we really get to the United States?" Eva asked between sniffles.

"I don't know. That's the truth."

There was a heavier sound of traffic and people outside on the streets.

They wandered to a window.

Even the last few people seemed to be mobilizing.

She left his side, flipping on the television; she put on the English language version of France 24.

The headline was *Time is Running Out*.

People had given up hope and were leaving Europe in droves.

"Maybe it's time to go, Aaron."

Her whisper captured his full attention. She sounded and appeared so worried. Her eyes were large and had every light in the observatory glistening off them. Her lips were pursed but upside down.

He could still see the beauty, but it was enough to stab him right in the heart. His feelings for her were real. He could feel it, he could see it.

"We'll go soon. I just want to work out the changes in trajectories and rocket firing times. Once we have that done, we'll know if we're safe. We'll know if we have time. We'll know, how much time."

"We should leave. Please." Eva's expression was a mix of concern and irritation. She perched her hands on her hips.

Aaron ignored her. He sat at the computer desk and started working on the changes to the simulation.

She plopped down beside him. "Please, Aaron."

He paused to gather his thoughts; annoyance tickled, but he took a deep breath; because he didn't want to snap at her. "Eva, I should be home, in the US, but I came over here to be with you and to work this thing out. I've been physically and mentally plagued by this asteroid before it was even, literally, on the radar. My wife had foreseen an end of days event like this. She spoke about it for years. I ignored her. Now, I'm having visions about it. Hearing things, just like *she* did. Right now, I'm not at fault for ruining the world, so that must mean I can only do good, do right. It's like a bad dream about death. Sometimes that dream is good, and actually means life. My wife, my brother-in-law, me. We're all connected to this thing. My wife killed herself over this. My brother-in-law nearly ruined his life over it. Come hell or high water, I want to see this thing out."

"Great, tell that to your son when you're dead." She stormed out of the room.

"This is a worldwide event. If you think my son is untouchable in California, you're wrong. This will affect the whole world. Every single person. No one is free now, no one will escape the impact!" he raised his voice as he called after her, but she didn't return to him. With another sigh, Aaron reached for his cell.

"Hi, Aaron, how are you? Not such good news is it?" Timothy said by way of greeting, his voice thick with sorrow.

"No, it's not. But all's not lost yet," he said, wishing he could have more confidence than he felt.

"No, no it's not. All is *not* lost." The Englishman he had come to call a friend sounded a little uplifted, and maybe a bit more relieved than moments before.

Maybe Aaron could take strength from that. "We need to get cracking on these revised trajectories and rocket firing times."

"That's exactly what we should do, but... I mean, is there even a point at this stage?" the hesitancy and sadness were back, and he didn't need that.

"Of course, there's a point. We can get the rockets to fire earlier so they can catch up with the asteroid. We *can* get back on track."

"Do you think so? We'll give it a go. But I'm not seeing it, off the top of my head. I don't see how we can catch up with the accelerating asteroid. It's maxed out! Maybe it'll become clearer when we go through the numbers," Timothy said, but he sounded unconvinced. His stiff upper lip was lost to Aaron. His accented-English eloquence had turned into a borderline inaudible murmur.

"Xenon ion rockets."

"What?" the Brit asked.

Aaron smiled broadly. His friend's eloquent accent returned.

"Are you telling me you didn't put F1 rockets on the nuclear device, but instead put Ion thrusters on it?" Timothy demanded.

"Yes. That's what I had to see the major about a few days ago. He wanted me to keep it top secret. I couldn't tell you, even if I wanted to."

"Is it the same technology we know about, or is it better?"

"It's better. This xenon ion thruster can get up to

six-hundred-and-fifty-thousand miles per hour."

"I knew it. I knew ye crafty bloody bastards would have something up your sleeves."

"You better believe it," Aaron said.

They discussed the velocity increase of the asteroid and how it'd brought the impact a day forward.

There were approximately three days left before the asteroid was going to impact their planet.

Skipping forward almost two full days.

Aaron worked with Timothy all night, trying to get the correct backup data for the NASA engineers.

The first spaceship carrying the *Bomba's* was set on its new trajectory to the asteroid.

The next phase was to fire the xenon ion thrusters on the spacecraft, which would slow the rocket to zero and increase it to the same velocity of the asteroid, just as it was passing.

That needed to be repeated precisely, six times, seven in total, and needed to be done immediately.

35

LAST CHANCE

Aaron, Louis, and Eva were on a video call with all the other members of the Saturn W rescue team. They sat in Eva's office, where it'd all begun, watching the TV.

He smiled at Eva. A positive smile. This was the last stand at the O.K. Corral.

Aaron had Jane and Corey running the numbers that he and Timothy had sent them earlier.

He'd gotten word from the Brit that the man was now in Oxford with his colleagues, on standby for this conference link-up.

The TV displayed NASA setting up with their team of seventy engineers. Ten engineers for each rocket.

President Jameson was in his Situation Room with Major Russell, and a number of important colleagues. Everyone was connected to the audio feed from

Houston.

Timothy came online, along with a number of other teammates.

"Last radio check. Testing, one, two," an engineer from Houston sounded off.

Aaron looked up at the TVs broadcasting the news. Every channel covered the last episode of the earths changing sequence of events.

Houston's silence came to an end. "Saturn V-A in position to fire in…ten, nine, eight, seven, six, five, four, three, two, ignition, zero."

The whole world watched through the Hubble Telescope, some three hundred and forty miles away in the sky.

Aaron was glued to the screens. He looked at Eva and Louis. She was in awe; he seemed overwhelmed.

The ion thruster fired.

The video feed had the velocity of the Saturn V-A revealed in the top right-hand corner of the screen.

The velocity dramatically decreased with respect to the structural capabilities of the rocket. It was in a vacuum with no air resistance, and didn't have the same gravitational pull of the earth that it would've had on the ground, so one hundred percent of the thruster function could gradually be put into slowing the spacecraft down.

He watched as the rocket stopped. "Zero," Aaron whispered. He couldn't help it. The words had come out automatically.

Eva smiled at him. He smiled back.

This was the first sign that something might be happening; something might actually be working.

For once.

The velocity of the rocket increased again as it continued to fire.

A while later, Houston fired thruster two. "Saturn V-B in position to fire…in ten, nine, eight, seven, six, five, four, three, two, ignition, zero."

The television screen changed to a shot of the second spacecraft, its thrusters visible, and the decreasing velocity of the ship revealed.

Aaron watched as Jane and Corey's feed came live, albeit a little late, they exchanged a smile.

He called them on speakerphone. "Hey."

"Hey," his brother-in-law said. "I'm adding the deceleration figure for the rocket in real-time and inputted it into the simulator."

"Great."

The live feed from Corey's computer showed him running render with the real data.

A few moments later, the simulator showed the rocket ship slowing down to zero before speeding back up until it was exactly right beside the asteroid.

Aaron nudged Eva; she viewed the simulation and clenched her fist.

"Tell them it looks really good. Everything's working so far," Corey whispered to Jane over the speakerphone.

His student shook her head. "Too many people are listening."

"NASA can't hear you, just the rest of the world, basically," Aaron assured her.

She coughed nervously just before she spoke across the live feed. "Hi, we've run the simulation for the second rocket, it looks really good. It'll get there on time."

Timothy was smiling, he looked excited.

Aaron thanked Jane for the feedback, and Eva smiled from his side. She placed her hand on his arm and squeezed it tight.

Eva's touch caused sweat to automatically protrude from the top of his back. It was a sign of his nerves.

Please God, let this work. Please.

Louis stood up in the observatory and decided to stretch his legs. He clapped his hands; he seemed to be delighted to see everything was working out.

Things were going well. He'd praised them both.

He's up and down. He's nervous too.

The process continued as planned for the next Saturn Vs—C, D, E, F & G over the period of the morning.

Saturn V-A reached the asteroid and was ready to slow down and berth beside the top spinning asteroid.

"We've reached the asteroid and are maneuvering to the center point as we speak," Houston said.

A camera on TV focused on two pilots sitting in a military drone cockpit. The cockpit was equipped with video feed from the Saturn V-A. It also had sonar information to indicate how close the ship was to the asteroid.

There were hundreds of information points coming into the skilled pilots' vision via heads-up displays, and through their ears via commands from their co-pilot. One used a joystick to position the payload.

The world was riveted as the pilot gently nudged the joystick forward and to the left. With each tap, a small blast of gas came from the back and right of the spacecraft.

The little bursts looked like something out of an aerosol can.

As the pilots carefully positioned the *Bomba's* as close as possible to the asteroid, Houston provided more information.

"That's a lock," the pilot said as the active locking system was activated, making sure the *Bomba* didn't move from the fixed location with respect to the asteroid.

Time had flown; no one dared miss a second of this real-life mechanical, physical, human work of genius. The last strategic ship was on its countdown; the sixth rocket to fire.

"Saturn V-F in position to fire... in ten, nine, eight, seven, six, five, four, three, two, ignition, zero."

The pilots waited the required time for the rocket to fire, then continued to position the explosives.

"We're very close to time over. How long do we have until we detonate these bombs?" President Jameson's voice sounded over the video conference call.

Aaron glanced at Eva, as another familiar voice answered.

"It's getting very tight now, sir," Major Russell said.

The seventh 'spare' rocket, V-G, fired and started to decelerate.

The sixth rocket hadn't made it to the asteroid yet.

The pilots had all the other bombs in position, neatly beside the asteroid.

"Why do we have to wait for the spare rocket? Can we just explode them as soon as the sixth one is in position?" the president asked. He sounded nervous, and his words shook.

The President is only talking now to fill the silence.

Aaron looked at Eva again, and she squeezed his hand.

They'd been holding hands since the whole thing had started.

He hadn't been able to not touch her.

"Sir, that seventh rocket is no longer a spare. We actually need it. We've gone past our six-rocket deadline needed to deflect past the earth," the major said with an audible gulp over the soundwaves of the conference call.

Everyone watched as the sixth rocket struggled to catch up with the asteroid as it increased in velocity due to the earth and moon's gravitational pull.

A cold sweat settled over Aaron. His back was damp, but the rest of him wasn't. It was a strange feeling. Like the last feeling, but cold instead of hot. He took a deep breath. He felt weak. "The asteroid's now going faster than the rockets can speed up."

"It's going to be worse for the seventh rocket," Louis added.

Eva put her hands to her mouth. "We're in trouble."

"Sir, we have a warning alarm here. It's saying we will not reach deflection deadline at this rate," Houston said.

"We can still fire six. It'll deflect the asteroid. Albeit, to a degree, but it's better to have the asteroid skim off the earth as opposed to hitting it directly." Timothy's voice sounded over the open call.

Louis shook his head. "I wouldn't be so sure

about that."

Aaron watched as the situation room went into meltdown. He sat back into his seat and closed his eyes.

The Hubble Telescope showed the seventh rocket and the asteroid in one shot.

On the other side of the asteroid, the sixth *Bomba* capsule was being positioned by the drone pilots.

The seventh was moving too slowly, in comparison to the accelerating asteroid. It was taking too long to catch up.

It was excruciatingly painful to watch.

Aaron opened his eyes for a second. He was torn between watching it and closing his eyes.

No one had control; it was just physics outnumbering physics.

"How do we look, Jane?" He shouted down the speakerphone as he watched his student frantically typing numbers to see what would the resultant outcome be if they exploded all the *Bomba's* at the earliest opportunity.

The video link showed Corey hovering over Jane's shoulder, watching her with an intensity that made Aaron squirm. He felt the same way his brother-in-law looked.

The simulator showed the deflection of the *Bomba's* wouldn't be enough to push the asteroid past the planet. It would, in fact, hit the east coast of the United States.

"Fuck. It's coming straight for the US."

Aaron watched Jane on the screen.

She viewed the result and then looked toward Corey. "Well. That's that. They'll never blow them up now. They'll let them hit you guys in Europe."

He took control of Corey's computer. He quickly entered the velocity and acceleration of the seventh ship, trying to calculate how long it would take to get to the asteroid, and what the result would be if all seven ships were detonated at that time. "It's so close, but it'll make it," he said. Aaron unmuted himself to the president and the situation room. "Mr. President. Just give it another couple of minutes. The seventh ship will get there."

He watched as President Jameson looked to Major Russell. "How long more will we give it?"

The major put his finger to his ear and acknowledged some information that he had received. "It'll be too close. Besides, the asteroid will have a lot of smaller pieces of rock which could break off. Any one of those could wipe out D.C. or New York or anywhere."

"Okay, that's it for me. If there's a threat to us, I can't allow it. Abort the mission," the president ordered.

"Please, sir, listen to me. The numbers add up. Give it a minute or two. We're nearly there. I'm begging you, sir."

The passion in his voice made Eva cry.

"This isn't just about us, this is about the world, this is about mankind. Please, sir. Trust me."

"I'm sorry, Aaron. We need to abort."

Aaron grabbed his live video camera and put his face in it. "No! Please. It'll work. I know it'll work. Do *not* abort. You've trusted me from day one. We've had all our numbers correct from the beginning. We haven't let you down yet."

There was a silence across the live link for five deafening seconds.

"Please. We won't let you down," he said as tears ran down his eyes.

President Jameson grimaced and looked away to the ground. "I'm sorry, Aaron."

"This mission now, is a national danger to the United States. We're aborting," Major Russell commanded the control room in Houston. "You heard the president. Abort this mission."

The room fell silent. The engineers were all stunned. Aborting the mission signed a death warrant for all of Europe, half of Russia and the northern half of Africa.

Everyone knew that.

Aaron blanched. His stomach inverted and his limbs shook.

Eva sobbed beside him, but he couldn't comfort her.

He sat down in his seat.

Motionless.

He stared at the screen. Looked at Jane back at Caltech as Corey comforted her.

All their hard work. All the planning.

All the hours given and tears shed, all over one person's command.

How can one man dictate the death of so many so that he can save his few?

Aaron watched the cowards leave the situation room.

The president stopped at the exit door and turned to the main camera feed. "I'm sorry, that's just the way it is. We told the Russians to deflect to the east, not to the west. It's their fault. Not our fault," he repeated, as if it'd make a difference. "We've done everything we could. Left no stone unturned. We did our best." He raised his hands. "Everyone, can I have your attention?"

The room hushed again.

Before he opened his mouth again, the room turned yellow like the sun.

Every television screen, every laptop, every computer lit up with an explosive yellow-orange color.

It was as though the roof had been removed from the room, and nuclear-brightness had lit it up.

The *Bomba's* had been exploded prematurely.

President Jameson ducked, along with the major and a number of other people with him.

It seemed like an explosion had gone off in the room.

Everyone watched as the biggest, manmade, nuclear explosion ever witnessed was broadcast live across the world.

Shock reverberated over Mission Control, the Situation Room, the observatory in Nice, Caltech, Oxford, Cambridge, London, New York; the World.

Aaron didn't know what had happened.

Eva and Louis spoke at the same time in rapid-fire French.

He didn't catch much, other than they obviously were trying to come up with some reason.

Timothy was the last person still looking into his live camera feed. He was the only one on any TV. He just sat there in shock, shaking his head.

Aaron checked his computer screen.

What the hell just happened? Did I do that?

Searching for some explanation. The screen blinked for a second.

What was that?

"The fucking Russians," Jane spat.

"The fucking Russians," Major Russell shouted. "Those absolute pieces of shit. They're the only ones with detonation codes, they did it on purpose."

Aaron, Eva, and Louis looked at the screen as the Marine went berserk.

"This is a declaration of war. Convene the war council. Get the Russian president on the phone," President Jameson said as he rushed back to his seat.

Aaron brought Jane and Corey's live feed up on the main screen. He looked at Eva and gave her a slight nod.

Everything is going to be okay.

He dared not say that out loud.

"I'm running the simulator now, Aaron. Give me a minute." Jane must've started tracking the asteroid immediately, trying to get a fix on the new impact zone.

Corey watched in silence, his hand on his chin, rubbing the newly formed stubble. An old habit dies hard. He had shaved for the occasion.

A few moments later, the impact trajectory popped up on the screen.

"Hey, Aaron. You're probably going to want to stay in Europe. In fact, Ben and the rest of us are going to be the ones who need to get out of here as soon as possible. The simulator is showing it's going to come in at a really low angle, but the outcome is still going to be catastrophic to West Coast US and the Pacific region. If the Russians did this, they saved their own skin, by sacrificing *us*."

Corey reached over her, grabbed the mouse and clicked on something. "You might need to run that again," he said, pointing to the moon.

Jane threw him a glare. "You knew that was off? Why didn't you tell me before I gave out information? Why did you turn it off in the first place?"

"Because it wasn't relevant. I wanted to get a clearer look at the asteroid. It was in the way."

"For fuck's sake. Give me another minute." She re-ran the simulation. This time with the moon included in the outcome. "The asteroid's going to slingshot past the moon and miss the planet," she gasped, gaping at her friend. "Did you know that?"

His expression was hesitant. "I didn't know, exactly. It was a hypothesis I came up with. Kind of a plan 'small b', since we didn't have a plan 'big B'."

"Why did you remove it? Are you hiding something?" She arched an eyebrow, staring him down.

"No. I've nothing to hide. Honestly." Corey shook his head and shot his palms up.

Aaron was listening intently.

Are we good? Did it work?

He looked at the news feeds. He couldn't quite believe it. He didn't know what to do. Shock rolled over him. He was too afraid to be relieved. Yet.

Eva comforted him. "We did it."

Louis was a blubbering mess.

She tended to him next.

Information from NASA regarding the asteroid, its slingshot around the moon and missing Earth went live over their connection.

"It seems as though the asteroid has been deflected into the path of the US. But the moon will be extremely close to the asteroid's path, which in turn will cause it to deviate even more and hence pass by the Earth without impact," President Jameson said.

Major Russell pointed to one of the screens in the Situation Room.

They could all see the Russian president on it.

"Before you start talking about war. We don't want it, but we are ready for anything. We did what was best for the world, not what was best for our country," the Russian shouted angrily, trying to get his words in first.

President Jameson bashed the table in disgust. "No, no, no, you deflected the asteroid toward us, which is the same as firing a couple of fucking million nuclear bombs at us. This is an act of aggression, an act of war. A declaration of war!"

"You will be going to war with the world. Because you don't make the rules for us or Europe or Africa. Three hundred and twenty-five million people do not supersede the rights of one-quarter of the world's population. If you want to go to war, fire the first shots. Until then, we'll be waiting for the asteroid to slingshot around the moon. If you want help, we can come in from Alaska and help," the Russian president disconnected the feed on President Jameson.

36

LOCKDOWN

Aaron sat with Eva on the couch at the observatory in Nice. Cuddled up in a blanket.

Louis had gone to his mother's grave. Tending to the flowers in the twilight, while everyone and anyone were watching NASA's television feed as the asteroid made its way across the universe.

"The asteroid is unpredictable. The safest place is where the original target had been forecast to hit; central Europe," he said.

"I hope you're correct. How are you going to get home? The whole world seems to be on lockdown."

The news had stated that the US had started evacuation proceedings on the west coast as a precautionary measure.

"The world's waiting for the asteroid and its final days; maybe even the final days of existence. I just hope the entire asteroid avoids Earth." He looked at

Eva.

She was staring at the ground. She whimpered and put her hand to her mouth. Covering her feelings.

She's not convinced. I don't think I am either.

Aaron had contacted the major, trying to see if he could get him back to California.

Major Russell couldn't, since there were no available planes, military or commercial. They were too busy getting people out of Western United States.

A lot of things could go wrong in the sky, so the president wasn't taking any chances.

The major had immediately decided for Corey, Jane, Katie and Ben to be escorted out of California and settled in a 'displaced persons camp' in central Pennsylvania.

Aaron shook his head. "That's where they are taking Ben," he said as he pointed to the news feed.

The camp housed tens of thousands of evacuees. FEMA had worked hard to erect it in less than a day.

There were countless white tents in rows and columns. The conditions were relatively good. Clean water, food, washing facilities, and excellent sanitary circumstances.

The grounds were large open lush green fields. Playgrounds were set up by the parents. Army patrols kept the peace.

"It doesn't look too bad. It's only for a short while. Just until the asteroid passes," Eva said in an upbeat manner. As if trying to cheer him up. "I can't wait to get to meet the little man."

Aaron smiled.

Countless west coast residents left to visit relatives and friends on the east coast, all in preparation for the slingshot to end all slingshots.

The Pennsylvanian camp was there for people who didn't have any other place to go.

He called Katie's cell, and his son answered.

"Hello," Ben said.

"Hi, buddy. How's the move?"

"It's really big. Lots of people here."

Aaron heard the hustle and bustle of the camp while he reassured his son everything was going to be all right. "It's a bit like that time we went camping. Isn't it?"

"I love it here, Daddy. You'll really like it. When you coming home?"

"Very soon. Probably tomorrow, if this pesky asteroid leaves us alone," Aaron said.

"That will be great, Daddy. I can't wait to see you. I miss you so much."

"I miss you too, buddy. You're my life and soul, kiddo." He closed his eyes and shook his head at the thought of what could happen sooner than he'd like. "Put Katie on, please."

"Hi," his sister-in-law said a moment later.

"Hi, Katie. How's everything there?"

"We like it. We wouldn't be into doing this every day for the rest of our lives, but for a week, it shouldn't be too bad. Ben loves it anyway. Jane's here too. She's so good with him. She's staying with me, and Ben's in with Corey. He loves it with his uncle. They are catching up on lost time. He's really good, too. How are you?"

"I'm okay. It's been stressful not being able to see you guys. I'm starting to think now maybe we should've just taken our chances and got out of

Europe."

"No." Her voice was hard. "It was the right thing to do. It would've been an absolute catastrophe if it hit head-on, into Europe. You played your part and saved the earth."

"I suppose, I'm just worried about Ben and the rest of you guys. Okay, I'll let you go; the asteroid's going to be visible very soon. It'll be like a really bright star in the sky. The brightest one you can see."

"We'll be fine. Talk to you after," Katie said as she hung up.

Aaron looked at the cell phone as the light dimmed. He looked up at an American news feed Eva had switched passed.

"Put that one back on. That's the bitch who took the information from Timothy."

She flicked back to Rebecca Crawford, broadcasting live from the tented village in Pennsylvania.

A large group had gathered outside one of the white tents. The tent had a small television hanging outside it.

It was bright outside, a warm evening. The sky was clear and the moon was visible from their vantage point.

"The world holds its breath again. These past few weeks have been a roller coaster. We worked together as best we could, but was it good enough? The Russians, took matters into their own hands, and we could be on the cusp of starting world war three if this slingshot doesn't go as planned." Rebecca Crawford made her closing statements before going live to the asteroid images.

Aaron was still wrapped up with Eva. A final embrace before their world was about to be changed forever.

Ben was safe, but he struggled with how much danger his son—hell, Katie, Corey, and Jane, too—could be in.

The speed of the asteroid was the first thing to strike fear into the world's heart. The planet's gravity pulling it into oblivion.

He looked up at the velocity on the tracking screen. It was accelerating again.

It started to resemble a comet at this stage, with a long gaseous tail trailing behind it.

Eva pushed against him until he released her.

He watched her long legs walk to a nearby window and she gazed up at the sky.

Aaron followed her, and he could see the bright-looking object and its tail following.

She held herself around the waist, as if she couldn't watch.

"Are you, all right?" he asked.

"I felt weak with the thought of what was about to happen."

A sense of calm came over him as the asteroid made a beeline for the moon.

The slingshot was now or never.

Aaron sat back down on the couch, and pulled Eva with him. He quickly found his cell and called Katie again.

She answered but he said, "Don't say anything. Just tell Ben I love him. Leave us on speakerphone."

It was the final moments before the asteroid reached the moon.

He wanted to be there, on his cell in case anything happened.

They all watched in anticipation, praying the moon had enough gravitational pull to get the trajectory away from the planet, and its new impact zone, the US.

It would save millions of people's lives, those same people who'd risked everything for Europe's freedom on more than one occasion.

Billions of people would be watching as the asteroid made its final approach.

Its size became clear from the video cameras tracking it.

"Just tuck in nicely between the earth and the moon, and we'll all be happy. Anything else and we're dead!" Aaron said.

The asteroid had no intentions of going quietly.

At just one second from the moon, the planet shook; a worldwide earthquake that lasted what felt like forever.

Aaron and Eva nearly fell off the couch. Arms and legs flailing in a tangle as they held onto each other.

He didn't take his eyes off the TVs.

"It struck the moon," he breathed. "It struck the goddamn moon! Oh, Lord, we're fucked."

The moon went from a sea of tranquility to a cloudy ball of dust in the sky.

Was that a shockwave or some kind of earthquake?

Eva's phone rang. "It's Louis. Hello."

"A gravitational wave. More like a gravitational tsunami. Oh my God. What have we done?" the older man said as the phone cut off.

Aaron stared at the news feed. Pleaded for some information.

Rebecca was live, and standing at her outside-broadcasting-unit. She was at peak enthusiasm, with the moon as her backdrop. "Reports have come in of an earthquake which has hit the earth simultaneously. We have confirmation of injuries, but nothing too serious. We can see from behind us; fragments of the asteroid are making their way into the atmosphere. These fragments seem to be burning upon entry and are predicted to land in the Pacific Ocean. The theory at the moment is that the moon has been struck by the asteroid. That's right. The moon has saved the earth from the predicted devastation. The moon is the hero here. People are out celebrating behind me. The world has been saved! The asteroid has been deflected by the Russians. The asteroid has been defeated. We don't know the complete outcome of the earthquakes, but the major impact the asteroid would've caused won't be one that the planet has to bear."

37

EIGHT DOTS

Jane stood outside her tent, pouring herself a small glass of celebratory wine. She was taken aback by the whole situation. She was behind a makeshift table while everyone danced and hugged in celebration.

A jovial passer-by accidentally hit her table and spilled a tiny bit of her wine.

Jane looked at her drink. It'd stopped spilling, but the more she looked at it, the more she could see her wine—the liquid—was tilted in the glass. As if the table was uneven.

She put the pint glass on the structural frame beside her. Surely the frame would be leveled properly. *What the hell was going on?*

Jane looked over at Ben. She tilted her head to the side as she tried to figure out what was going on. "Stand up straight."

"I am standing up straight," he said, obviously

puzzled.

Jane dashed inside the tent, grabbing her cell and laptop. She logged into the Caltech computers via her cell data.

She opened the simulation program and searched through the recent files.

An additional file had been opened. It had the same file name as hers but with a '1' added to the end.

She opened it and ran a simulation.

The asteroid deflected toward the moon. Then it hit the moon at about halfway across its radius.

The impact resulted in a massive crater on the moon's surface, with resultant debris scattered into its thin atmosphere.

The simulation continued to play. The giant crater started to revolve.

"The moon's rotating! What the fuck?" she whispered.

Corey glanced in at her, and she quickly closed the simulation down.

"You coming out of there, Jane? Everyone's celebrating. We can go home soon!"

"Yeah. I'm just calling Aaron to tell him we're all okay after the mini-earthquake."

"Okay, see you in a minute." Her friend went back to the celebrations in the camp.

Words tumbled out with preamble as soon as her professor picked up. Panic was a live thing, threatening to eat her up. "Aaron, Corey has a simulation on the computer he made himself. It shows the asteroid hitting the moon, about a quarter of the way across the diameter. It caused the moon to start spinning."

"Slow down, Jane. Catch your breath. Is everyone

okay there?"

"Yes. Yes. Everyone is fine. I think Corey has something to do with this. He's freaking me out now. It's like he can predict the future. He knew the asteroid would hit the moon." She was growing hysterical, even to her own ears.

"Jane. How could he have known that? Maybe he just ran a hypothetical outcome. He could've run ten different outcomes, and the one hitting the moon was one of them. How could he have done this? He couldn't." Aaron's voice was even, calm.

She took a breath. "Fair enough. It's just too much of a coincidence. You're always saying you were going to end the earth. But what if it wasn't *you*? It was him all along. You were just the vessel!"

"This is bad, that was a gravitational wave. It's really not good!"

Jane heard a man with a thick French accent yelling in the background.

"Jane, I'll call you back soon. I'll look at the simulation myself now. Thanks so much. Just hold on for a few minutes." Aaron ended the call and focused on Louis and Eva. "What's going on now?"

The older man was at his most hyper, he'd never seen him so animated. "Aaron. This is really bad. That wasn't an earthquake. That was a gravitational wave."

He shook his head and dashed to his simulation on the Caltech computer. He opened up Jane's last file and pressed *'play'*.

Eva and Louis gathered around him, and they watched the simulation of the asteroid hitting the moon.

She gasped beside him, a hand covering her mouth, and Louis gaped, then swore in French.

Aaron swallowed, as the asteroid's impact caused the moon to start rotating.

Louis pointed to the screen. "We only see one side of the moon, because it rotates on its axis at the exact same frequency that it orbits the earth."

"Synchronous rotation," Eva added.

"The asteroid has caused the moon to spin faster. The gravity of the moon is effecting our planet's rotation," the older man continued after taking a deep breath to compose himself.

"The moon's now rotating *against* the earth's rotation," Aaron said and shook his head.

The simulation continued to play. The moon increased in rotational frequency, relative to the earth, while the planet appeared to slow down.

He shook his head again and put his hands through his hair. "So, the Earth is slowing down and the moon is speeding up. Oh my God. What the hell have we done?"

They watched in silence as the simulation finished with the planet's rotation to the sun completely stationary, and the moon spinning so fast the naked eye could see it.

"What does this mean?" Eva asked, as if for the sake of reassurance. Perhaps she was too afraid to speak the unspeakable.

"You already said it. Synchronous rotation. But between the Earth and the Sun, instead of the Earth and Moon." Aaron sure as hell wasn't afraid to speak the unspeakable.

"The Earth is gradually, ever so slightly slowing down, and will stop rotating on its axis. There will no night and day, once it reaches synchronous. There will be one part of the Earth facing the sun all day every day and the back of the Earth will be plunged into darkness." Louis was the one to answer, and his voice was heavy, his expression somber.

Aaron shut his eyes. "I've destroyed the earth after all."

"You haven't destroyed the earth. We all have." The older man clamped a big hand on his shoulder.

Eva replayed the simulation after increasing its time laps to one year.

"What are you looking for? It's not going to change," her mentor said abruptly.

Aaron quelled Louis with his hand on his arm. It wasn't a shocker what she sought. She was looking for the point at which the planet would be closest to the Sun.

They studied the simulator again. The earth stopped rotating, just like it had before.

"Ninety days. It'll stop," he concluded aloud.

The center point of the earth stopped right at the tip of India. The simulator went on to show scorched earth and extreme temperatures as far as mid-Africa to the west, Kazakhstan in the north, and all of China to the east.

The only habitable areas were at the tepid points between fire at the front of the earth and the ice and dark at the back.

A ring around the edge of the world. Russia, Europe, West Africa, Australia, and adjacent countries.

"The rest of the world would be plunged into

darkness and freezing cold temperatures forever." Eva shook her head. "After ninety days, it's going to freeze solid on the dark side. The US, Canada, South America, hundreds of countries. Millions and millions of people."

Aaron's eyes rolled up into his head.

He was visited by that angelic figure again. The Godly one which sounded like his wife.

He collapsed to the floor, and the world went black.

The soft gentle voice spoke.

"It wasn't your fault, Aaron. It wasn't you. You're not the one who ruined the earth. But it is ruined. You were just a pawn in the whole thing." That sweet voice entered his heart and his ears like before.

This time he could see her face vividly.

"But why am I involved? What do I have to do?" he pleaded.

"There's nothing you can do. The world as you know is over. I tried to tell you. I'm still trying to tell you. You must get to your son and protect him."

"Our son, you mean."

"I'm gone, Aaron. He's your son now. Protect him. Love him, like I couldn't. You must fight for everything. The world is no more. It's anyone's now. Rightfully rebalanced. This is what man has made, so shall you all live by your product."

The angelic creature came close to his face.

Her eyes were hollow, and she had light in her mouth.

It petrified him, froze him to his core. He feared the earsplitting scream.

Slowly, the vision of her blended into the

beautiful wife who'd once been his.

Her eyes were blue and sparkled; her lips were red and full. Her smile infectious. Her white wedding dress looked stunning, the veil set it off.

A shudder of extreme pleasure whacked him, like he'd just taken an opiate.

"I love you, Aaron," Debora said as she faded to black.

Tears rolled from his eyes.

She disappeared from his mind.

He reached for her one last time, but was left there in the darkness.

All alone.

He looked around the nothingness. Just enough light to be able to see his hands in front of him.

Eight little black dots, like tattoos, appeared on the knuckles of his fingers.

"You must fight for everything."

JUSTIN CONBOY

ABOUT THE AUTHOR

Justin Conboy hails from Salthill, Galway. Ireland. Born in 1977, he graduated in 2015 as an Engineer from NUI Galway, where computers and mathematics were his first love. Justin soon extended his love to writing and combined these interests when he wrote this first novel, *Code Thief* in 2016.

He has fourteen years' experience in the military and has had a major interest in astrophysics from a young age.

Justin is currently working on a the second *RQ26* novel which will be released in November 2020.

Code Thief is available on Kindle.

If you find any errors in the calculations or book in general, please contact Justin on Facebook, directly.

31767595R00204

Printed in Poland
by Amazon Fulfillment
Poland Sp. z o.o., Wrocław